# The Finger of Saturn

# The Finger of Saturn

VICTOR CANNING

WILLIAM MORROW & COMPANY, INC.,
NEW YORK · 1974

Canning

# The Finger of Saturn

# PART ONE

*The last age, heralded in Cumean song, is come, and the great march of the centuries begins anew. Now the Virgin returns: now Saturn is king again, and a new and better race descends from on high.*

Virgil. *Eclogues.*

## CHAPTER ONE

FROM THE FRONT of the house and its big sweep of gravelled forecourt the land sloped away gently to the distant sea. Above the fringe of oaks that hid the drive entrance could be seen a ragged triangle of water-glitter, bright and metallic under the June sun. One of the farm dogs moved on to the drive far down by the oaks, stopped in mid-track and looked sharply towards the trees. Then it trotted away into the cover of a great patch of pampas grass that marked the lawn with a feathery, pale explosion. As the dog disappeared I heard the sound of the coming car through the open study window. Watching the car crawl up the long slope, I knew that this was the day of her return.

She wouldn't physically be in the car, but the car was bringing her. This I sensed with a certainty that denied logic, the certainty that springs from some instinct which, operating only a few times in any one life, finally rekindles the dead embers of hope.

It was a red, very dusty, Austin Mini-Traveller. The dust was leopard-splotched with the fat rain-marks of one of the month's rare showers. Drawing back a little into the study I watched a man get out. He was in his thirties, I guessed; a tall, leggy type, wearing a lightweight sky-blue linen suit with a white shirt and a red tie. He was bare-headed, his black hair close-cut and curly, and when he walked towards the steps there was about his movements the lazy, easy control of an athlete. He stood and looked along the length of the house façade. He gave a little nod as though of approval and then

3

disappeared up the steps, a thin oblong of black briefcase under his arm.

He was expected and the housekeeper, Mrs. Cordell, brought him to my study. His name was Charles Vickers. This I knew from a telephone call I had received the previous day. His face was long, humorous, and he had a very prominent chin which was covered with a three or four days' growth of blue-black stubble.

As though I had asked him about it he fingered his chin and said apologetically, "Forgive this, Mr. Rolt. I'm growing a beard." He offered no further explanation but set his briefcase on the round rent table and accepted a glass of sherry.

I said, "What can I do for you, Mr. Vickers?"

"General Sir Maxwell Campbell phoned you. What did he say?"

Just for a moment I resented the approach, but the feeling of hope was strong in me so I let it go.

"He said you were a Foreign Office archivist and wanted to go through some of my father's old papers."

"And what did you make of that?" He saw at once that I didn't like his manner—one of the bad points of most male Rolts was a quick temper—and added diffidently, "Give me a little breathing space. When a thing's tricky I'm always a little jumpy . . . abrupt." His eyelids flickered nervously.

I smiled. "I didn't make much of it. Five years before my father died he handed all his papers over to the Foreign Office."

"Good. The General is a very sound man."

"And an old family friend."

"Of course. The discretion had to be all on our side, not his. There is, of course, a Foreign Office archivist, but it's not me." He fished out a wallet and passed me a card sheathed in perspex. It was a Foreign Office identity card. I had once briefly owned one—but not one which carried the four blue stars on the corner above the head-and-shoulders photograph.

I handed the card back and said, "Perhaps I should check it."

"If you wish, please do so. The extension number is still

4

the same as it was in your day. Some things never change."

I shook my head. "For the moment I'll reserve that option."

He smiled. "One of the characteristics of Sir Henry Rolt was a remarkable intuition."

"It got him out of a few nasty situations, yes."

"Inherited?"

I said, "If you're casting about for the right scent, I don't mind. But don't make it too long before you decide your line. I'm a patient man when I see it is necessary."

He finished his sherry, put the glass down and rubbed his rough chin. His eyelids flickered rapidly and I had the feeling that he was under some permanent strain, some personal pressure that had nothing to do with his business here. I reached out for the decanter and refilled his glass.

He grinned. "Dutch courage. Not in my line normally. But then neither is this business. I don't like getting tangled up in other people's emotions. Far less taking advantage of them. Nice people that is." He raised the glass, sipped, and then, looking past me to the wall over the stone fireplace, asked, "Who did it?"

Without turning I knew what he meant. Nothing at that moment could have made me turn because I was poised on the brink of certainty, reining back, superstitiously wondering if to give longing its head might not change some seemingly absolute destiny. Nor could I yet ask the direct question. The ache of love had to be contained.

I said, "It was done by an Italian called Bordino. He's dead now. He was an old man full of youth." I could see her posed against the red-washed villa, dark cypresses and the vine-terraced hills in the background; see the slight lift of the ash-blonde hair as the breeze from the sea took it, the beauty of her face and the purple-blue depths of her eyes which Bordino had magically fixed. She was wearing a blue dress which had been one of her favourites and I remembered how Bordino had posed her so that a splash of red wine marring the skirt had been hidden . . . Sun-brown arms and legs . . . a goddess dressed as a peasant girl.

5

Suddenly, harshly, I said, "Have you found Sarah?"

He stood up. "Yes. We think so."

"Think so?"

"Only you can make it absolutely sure. She's alive and well and in this country."

I went past him to the window. The gravel stretched like a golden path to the dark green of the oaks and the sea was silver-fired above them. I wasn't letting myself unguard the impatience and passion that coiled inside me. Just over two years before she had driven down the drive in her car and out of my life. No reason, no warning, no hint passing . . . driven down the drive to go shopping in Shaftesbury. Her car had been found that night, parked neatly in a layby on the Shaftes-bury–Dorchester road, unmarked, giving no clue to her going. No note left, nothing. Since then only the months of numbness in the heart because she had been the only one ever to have lodged there.

Behind me Vickers said, "Just be patient with me. I've got things to arrange . . . here, I mean. It'll take a little while. They wanted to do it differently, but I couldn't see it. Quite frankly they said you might be bloody difficult. . . . Well, if you have to be, then be so. But just for now try to bear with me . . . be patient."

Without turning I said, illogical anger in my voice, "For God's sake do what you have to do. . . ."

I heard him go out of the room. Then I saw him go down to his car. From the back he pulled out two large, black cases and a long metal tube affair. The tube under one arm and a case in each hand, he laboured back up the steps.

I should have gone to help him, but I didn't. I knew that he wanted no help from me. The less he took from me now the more, perhaps, he could demand later. Even in these trivial exchanges I knew the principle held good. Instinct, perhaps some of the intuition which he had applauded in my father, told me that the demands would come. If there were to be none, no payment or pain to be extracted, then he would not have

6

been here with his worn, blue-starred identity card and his nervously blinking eyes. The police would simply have telephoned or called. It was their case, their job. But Charles Vickers was here, and I knew something of his world. Not much, but enough to recognise the approach and the awkward apologetics which masked a policy already firmly settled in the counsels of the world he inhabited. If my older brother had not died while I was in my late twenties I might still have been in that world, but in the Rolt family the eldest son had only one duty, the management of the estates and enterprises that had grown from a modest yeoman holding that had belonged originally to a Thomas Rolt of Rolthead in the County of Dorset in the thirteenth century. My father had escaped it until late in life when his elder, bachelor brother had died, and that had been the end of my father's ambassadorial career.

Vickers unfolded a small, portable cinema screen on a tripod and put it against the far, book-lined wall. On the round table he set up a cine projector, pulling the table farther away from the screen so that he could adjust the focal length, and then finding the wall plug near the door for his power supply.

As he worked, action smoothed away his nervousness, and he said: "There are three films. They're all in colour—but there is no sound. They were all taken secretly. A matter of routine. All within the last year. She appears in all of them. At least you can confirm that. Only one other person appears in all—though in the last one the term 'appears' is not strictly accurate. However, you'll see what I mean, Mr. Rolt. The first was in September last year." He moved past me and pulled the heavy study curtains. From the gloom, he went on, "The next was in December of the same year. The last one was in May of this year. Last month."

He went back to the projector and with the aid of a small pilot light began to fit the film.

I said, "The police know nothing of this as yet?"

"No. But they will, of course—when the right moment comes. You will choose that. There won't be any trouble. But

7

we'll keep the press off your neck. Even the local papers. However, don't let us anticipate for the moment. I'll run them straight through first of all. No comment. You just watch. The quality of the first length of film isn't very good. All right, then. Here we go."

He switched on and a small light from some grilled part of the projector zebra-striped his lowered face.

The film began to run. There was little feeling in me now. I just watched. There was going to be time and enough for feelings, for a hundred renewals of emotion and memories, and I wanted to be alone with them.

The first strip of film showed the lounge bar of a small restaurant. The shot was taken from fairly high up, near or in the ceiling. A man sat by himself on a red banquette, drinking. Above the banquette was a long brass horizontal pole across which ran a curtain, half pulled so that there was a glimpse of the restaurant beyond and people dining. The lights were all on and it seemed to be evening. The man was stout, grey-haired, dark-blue-suited and looked like a business type. He seemed tired and once or twice braced himself against the back of the banquette, his eyes closing momentarily as though he were fighting the fatigue from a busy day. People passed through the lounge. Hands on the table in front of him he would look up, obviously expecting someone. After a few seconds she came into the picture. She was hatless, wore a high-collared black coat over a red dress and there was a small string of pearls about her neck. I had seen neither the clothes nor the pearls before. I watched, removing myself from all emotion, feeling the self-imposed detachment harden my muscles.

The man rose, greeted her with a light touch on her right arm, and she sat down beside him, putting a big black leather handbag on the table. There was a cut in the film. Little time could have passed. They sat together, talking, and there were drinks in front of them. There was nothing exceptional in the manner of their talking. They could have been friends but

8

there was no sign of any deeper attachment. Then the man reached down to the seat at his far side and put a small, conical, paper-wrapped parcel on the table. She smiled and from the paper unwrapped a small bunch of white roses, their stems silver-sheathed in foil. At the sight of the roses, memory kicked in me like a wild nerve.

She took the roses and raised them to her face. The film went blank, a white, mote-scrawled slide, and then the next section started to run.

The next sequence was brilliantly lit, and again had been taken from some high vantage point. It showed an aisle between two long rows of bookshelves. It was clearly in some bookshop and not a public library because all the books carried their dustjackets and the nearer set of shelves held rows of paperbacks. The man from the first film stood in front of the bookshelves in profile. He took down a couple of books in turn, leafed through them and put them back. He wore a bowler hat, and a heavy topcoat. He took down a third book, began to leaf through it and then, quite clearly, as he held it with one hand, he put the other into his coat pocket, brought out a small envelope and slipped it into the book. He closed the book slowly and stood for a moment before replacing it. In these few moments I saw his shoulders droop, a slow collapsing of all spirit from his body, tiredness draping him like a mantle. Then he straightened, put the book back and walked away. There was a break in the film filled with a dance of black-speckled white squares and then the row of bookshelves came on the screen again. Sarah was walking idly down the row. She took out an odd book or two and then drifted to where the man had last stood and reached up casually and pulled down the book which the man had replaced last. At least, I presumed it was. She put it under her arm and walked back up the row. For a moment before going out of the frame, she stopped and looked back down the row, her eyes lifting, almost as though she were sensing the hidden camera. For a second or two she stood there, full face. She was wearing a belted white raincoat, a black beret from

9

under which her hair hung loose, and black, knee-high leather boots. With a little shrug of her shoulders, she turned and moved out of the frame.

The third sequence was taken from a much lower angle, almost it seemed from ground level. It showed a stretch of tarmacadam drive before a wide, pillared doorway. On the stucco of the entablature above the doorway was a thin black stone cross. From the doorway the camera panned away down the drive a little and I saw rose bushes with the odd early flower, a forsythia bush and an overhanging laburnum tree with long chains of yellow bloom. The camera picked up a hearse moving along the drive. Behind it came a single black limousine. The vehicles were followed up the drive and then held as they halted before the doorway. The people from the limousine got out and hung around in an awkward hesitant way while the men from the hearse unloaded a coffin, its top quilted with wreaths. She was not with the people from the limousine. There was a tall young man in a grey suit with a black armband, an elderly woman dressed in a black, awkward hat, and a tight-fitting black coat. Then there was a much older man in a black suit and bowler who walked awkwardly with the help of a stick. A few moments after the coffin had been carried through the portico the hearse drew away. The driver of the limousine said something to the young man with the black armband and the party moved slowly out of sight through the doorway. The limousine driver watched them go and then drove off after the hearse. As he went the camera panned a few yards down the drive and then stopped. She was standing back from the driveway, on the grass, and in the shadow of the laburnum tree. She was bare-headed and wore a dark grey coat of some heavy material. Tweed it could have been. In her right hand she carried a brown silk scarf and there was a black handbag—the same one that she had had in the restaurant—under her left arm. She took a few steps out from under the tree and stood on the edge of the drive and was clearly undecided about something. Then she put the handbag on the ground at her feet and adjusted the scarf over her hair. She moved up the drive towards the portico and the camera went with her, holding her until she disappeared into the shadows of the interior.

Vickers said softly, "That's the lot." He bent over the projector and began to fiddle around preparatory to rewinding the film.

I said, "Who was in the coffin? The man?"

"Yes."

"How did he die?"

"A road accident."

"Genuine?"

"Yes. An act of God. A lorry skidded, mounted the pavement. It took him, the street vendor he was buying an evening paper from, and severely injured a young office girl. The next time just tell me when you want me to stop and I'll hold it for as long as you like. It is her, isn't it?"

"Yes, it's my wife. You needn't rerun the film."

I went to the windows and pulled aside the curtains. The June morning was ablaze outside. There was a scarlet and pink fire from the massed rhododendrons beyond the sloping lawn. A kestrel hovered close to the tops of the pines and the swifts hawked and screeched low above the burning gravel of the balustraded sweep of turning space before the house. Inside me there was a coldness which for sanity's sake I had to cherish until I could learn the way to live with the hostile element which Vickers had brought into the house. It was there, spelled out unmistakably for me. No happy return could ever have this beginning.

I went back, nodding to him to help himself from the sherry decanter.

"Unless you prefer whisky," I said and went to the side table by the fire where the other drinks were always set.

"Neither," he said. He stood, blinking, and scratched at his growing stubble.

I helped myself to a whisky. I said, "Who was the man?"

He sat down on a hardbacked chair by the table and after a gesture for permission lit himself a cigarette. "His name doesn't matter. He was a Principal Examiner—Board of Trade—in the Patent Office and Industrial and Copyright Department."

"In trouble?"

"He merited watching. A lot of stuff goes through the Patent Office, not all of it immediately available to the public. He was monitored for over four years. We only have these three records of any meeting with your wife."

"The restaurant?"

"A place in Liverpool. Did you recognise any of the clothes your wife wore?"

"No. Her drink, yes. She always took Campari and soda. What about the roses?"

"There could have been something inside the silver foil sheath. We weren't really interested, in a sense. It was just a case of monitoring contacts." Now he was getting down to business, to facts, his manner was suddenly confident and assured.

"And the bookshop?"

"That was Glasgow. He went there at times officially."

"The Patent Office doesn't sound like a Foreign Office concern."

"Many things interlock these days. I'm sorry I can't explain more."

"What about the funeral?"

"A crematorium, not far from Manchester. It was thought some interesting types might find their discretion overridden by their sentiment. Your wife was the only one. Forgive me for putting it that way."

"Just let us keep this very straight and formal."

"The others were family. His wife, his father, and his son. All ordinary people. He made around five thousand a year at the Patent Office. He left very little."

"How did you pick up the fact that it was my wife?"

"The films were shown around to various people. Had to be because there was a lot of co-ordinating to be done. Someone in the Ministry of Defence who knew both of you—I don't want to give his name—recognised her quite recently when the last clip—the funeral—was shown. Or was almost certain it was her. It was hard to believe."

"For God's sake," I said quietly. "It's her without doubt. Anyone who'd been an hour with her would always recognise her again."

"Maybe, but you know how the official mind works. We had to check. First from our end and then... well, down here. There was a highly presumptive reason to think that she was engaged in activities which were . . . well, illegal——"

"Have you absolute proof of that?"

"No. She might, too, not have been your wife. Just some woman engaged in a mild love affair with him . . . Spring and Autumn. These things happen. The roses could have been a gallant gesture. The envelope in the book just a message. His wife, I should say, was with him in Glasgow. And her presence at the funeral would need no explanation except the romantic one. He was dead and this was her final adieu."

"You believe that?"

"At the moment I don't know what to believe. She is your wife, you say. She disappeared over two years ago. She could have lost her memory and could have started a new life. From that premise she could well have found herself cultivating an innocent friendship with this man . . . nothing more than that. The only oddness, coincidence . . . is that it was him. He was a listed man. Not to be touched. Allowed to run because he was small beer. Could turn out to be more valuable to us free than inside. I'm prepared to speculate with anyone, but I'm not prepared to admit anything without proof. That's why I'm here—under instructions."

I finished the whisky and went and poured myself another. With my back to him, I said, "You're going to ask me something, aren't you? Eventually you're going to get round to it."

"Yes I am. But there are a few details first that——"

I turned. "Damn the details! They can wait. She's my wife. I've lived in a vacuum for over two years. Tell me what you want."

He stubbed his cigarette out nervously in an ashtray, making a clumsy job of it. His fumbling, embarrassed movement touched me through my anger. I knew he was hating himself.

He said, "I want you to do exactly what you would have done if the police had come and informed you that they had found your wife. She may or may not have lost her memory. She may have had a good, bad . . . any sort of reason, for going away. That's your problem. Just go to her and handle it your own way. The way you would have done if you'd never seen me or the films."

"And that's all there is to it?"

"I very much hope so, Mr. Rolt. Your wife has been found. Just handle it from there. It may take some time, but nobody's going to bother you."

He drew his briefcase towards him, opened it and pulled out a sheet of paper which he slid across the table to me.

"You'll find all the details you need on that, her address, the name she has adopted and so on. And there's this."

He placed a key on top of the paper.

"What's that for?"

"She often spends some time away from her flat. That's a duplicate key."

"What the hell would I need that for?"

He stood up, and his eyelids flickered. "I don't know, Mr. Rolt. I was instructed to see that you have it. If you wish I could leave the projector and the film."

"No. Take the bloody things away!"

I watched him motor down the drive and, just before he reached the oaks, a magpie flirted, black and white, across his path. I waited for another, but the bird was solitary.

I sat down with the sheet of notes he had left. I looked up at Sarah's portrait and then around the room. It was here at the end of our respective day's duties we had always come for a drink before dinner. She kept her needlework here in a small octagonal table—her last, uncompleted tapestry still rested there. One of the bookshelves held her favourite books; romantic novels, and a collection of stuff about the occult and nonsense about visitors from outer space, flying saucers, and theories of intelligent life existing on other planets. The sight of the books made me smile. For such a practical woman the extreme fancies she cultivated—against all my teasing—seemed bizarre and out of character.

I closed my eyes. She was coming back. Charles Vickers had never been here. The sheet in my hand had been left by some sympathetic police inspector. She had been found and I was going to bring her home. Just that. Nothing more than that. No bunch of roses. No envelope in a book. No mourning for the passing of a middle-aged civil servant. No poison in the mind.

## CHAPTER TWO

I WAS ABSOLUTELY certain that the information left with me by Vickers was by no means complete as far as his people were concerned. Even so, it was very detailed and in a rough chronological order. Reading it, the whole thing held a remarkable remoteness for me. I wasn't reading about my wife but about a stranger and there were only the briefest and most tenuous links between the two.

She went under the name of Mrs. Angela Starr, widow, aged thirty-six. No details were given of any deceased Mr. Starr. Vickers' record of her began in the July just over fourteen months after she had disappeared. Since then she had lived in a large country house close to the banks of the River Deben, near Woodbridge, in Suffolk. The house had been divided into large luxury flats and she occupied the topmost. The telephone number was given. From my knowledge of her it was not a part of England with which she had had any connection previously.

Her profession was described as Property Developer. She specialised in buying country properties, none above the thirty thousand pound mark, and then restoring or converting them for resale. She had done this in Cumberland, North Wales, Northamptonshire and Lancashire. Her latest bank statement showed a deposit account of seventy thousand pounds and a substantial current account. So far as the bank knew—and I guessed that strong official pressure must have been put on the bank to get the information—she had no investments in stocks or shares. The number of her British passport was given. It had five years of its ten still to run and all the details and documents which had supported the application for it—which had been made from the address she now occupied—had been proven to be false or forged. She drove a German car, an Audi saloon, insured by the Norwich Union and registered with the Suffolk County Council for the last year. There was no record of any previous car registration in her name with the same authority.

The previous occupant of the flat—for four years—had been a Mr. Albert Martin Chinn, English, whose present whereabouts and past history were unknown.

It was stated that she spoke fluent Spanish, Italian and French, which I well knew because she had lived and travelled for many years on the Continent with her mother. Her mother, whom I still visited twice a year, lived in Italy. She had been married twice—the first time, when she was very young, to a Brazilian politician, and Sarah was the only child of that marriage which had ended with the death of the father in a car accident. The second marriage was to a Greek banker who had been long dead before I married his stepdaughter. That Mrs. Angela Starr, widow—for the time being I was holding back all emotion knowing its hour must come—and my wife should be successful financially was no surprise to me. Her mother was worth far more than a million, and my wife was worth almost half as much in her own right. I had never had anything to do with her financial affairs. There had been no marriage settlement nor any financial arrangements. Over seven years of marriage had made it clear that Sarah was—no matter how wayward and compulsive she could be in other respects—more than capable of handling her own affairs. For this in a mild way I was glad because the management of the Rolt interests was as much as I could comfortably deal with.

(Writing this now, I realise that I must sound stiff and self-contained and a bit of a cold fish. Well, even after quite long acquaintance that is how I appear to people. It is an aspect of my character I can do nothing about. I know that my true friends—the ones who have passed this character barrier—say openly that there are two Robert Rolts but only a few people know about the second one, the one that is hidden behind the barrier. In my younger days I used very often to drink too much, deliberately I see now, to help myself to the courage to escape over the barrier for a while. It was never very successful.)

After I had read the information left by Vickers, I called Mrs. Cordell and told her that I would not want lunch. I was leaving on a business trip and might be away a few days. I was not, I said, sure where I would be staying, but I would telephone her and let her know. I then rang the estate office and told my farm manager the same and asked him to pass the message to my agent when he saw him.

I collected up a few things from my study which I thought might prove useful and then went up to my bedroom to pack a small case. When this was done I opened the connecting door to the other bedroom and stood in the doorway and looked round. Nothing had been altered since the day she had driven into Shaftesbury. Everything was kept as it had been and in readiness for her return. The wide window looked westward across the small park plateau to the brook-fed lake which I had had made for her because she loved water so much. The brook was spate-fed and dried quickly in the summer, so we had sunk an artesian well higher up the plateau which could be used to maintain the water level in times of drought. Everything had been of her own choosing: the blue curtains, the Italian tiled floor, the low white bed overhung by a blue silk *baldachino*, the gold-panelled white walls and the single picture which old Bordino had painted for her of a blue-robed Madonna holding a goldfinch in her right hand while the Christ-child lay in the crook of her left arm ... Everything as it had been, waiting for her, because I had never ceased to believe that a day would come when she would return. . . .

It was late afternoon before I got to Woodbridge. I had driven fast, but not impatiently; without feeling; cocooned in a vacuum from which I was content to await the moment of

19

release, knowing that it would be dictated by forces and circumstances beyond my control. In the long past months I had often felt that death would have been better than not knowing. No man or woman, no matter how much love they hold in trust for others, can claim other than God's season for their going. But to vanish into thin air, taking love with you, is to leave behind only a slow hell whose agonies can never dull the anguish of the one who stays to watch and wait. But now I knew that there could be other agonies. Vickers had brought them in his train like a cloud of devils.

I got myself a room at the Ship Hotel and directions from the reception clerk of the way to Otwell Park House which was the address given in Vickers' notes. It was three miles from Woodbridge and a good half-mile from the nearest village. It stood on high ground overlooking the River Deben, but set well back from the river. Elms flanked the entrance frontage and there was a short, curving driveway up to a pleasant, square, Georgian mansion. There were three cars parked in front of the house, none of them an Audi. At the side of the main entrance steps there was a notice-board, giving the name of the house and underneath arrowed directions to the entrances of the four flats. The ground- and first-floor flats had their entrances through the main doorway. The second-floor flat was away to the right of the house. The top-floor flat was arrowed to the left and around the side of the house. A small pathway led across a stretch of rose-bordered lawn. A narrow green door in the side of the house was open. A board on the wall inside read, FLAT FOUR. PLEASE WALK UP.

I went up three flights of carpeted stairway. In the old days I guessed that it had probably been a servants' back entry. At the top was a wide landing which held an antique chest with a Chinese vase on it. Opposite this was a large doorway. Over a brass bellpush at the side was a card in a holder: *Mrs. A. Starr.*

I stood outside the door, holding my briefcase, and hesitated.

Deliberately since Vickers had left me I had pushed away all thought of this moment, all consideration of how I should handle the situation. She would open the door and I would have to rely on the sequence of events, and that sequence was utterly unpredictable.

I pushed the bell and kept my finger on it for a few seconds. I waited. Half a minute went by. I pushed the bell again, this time holding it longer. I pushed the bell and waited five times and no one answered the door. My mind a cold blankness which I did not want to reject, for I felt in some way that it was all the protection I had at the moment, I went down the stairs and around to the main entrance. I was completely unaware of the interior of the entrance except for a small desk behind which sat an oldish man in a green porter's uniform who was sorting out and counting change from a large tin cash-box. As I stood in front of him he looked up at me, his mouth moving silently with some calculation, one hand going to enter figures on a paper at his side, and said, "Yes, sir. Can I help you?"

I said, "I can't get any reply from Mrs. Starr's flat. Would you know where she is or when she is expected back?"

"Mrs. Starr . . . let me see." He pulled open a drawer and drew out a clipboard with papers attached to it. "Usually they tell me or leave a note if they . . ."

He thumbed through his papers and then shook his head. "Nothing here. . . . Let me think. . . ." He looked up at me, fingering his chin. "Yes, I saw her go out this morning. She was getting her car from the garage as I came by. She's often out most of the day."

"But she's not away?"

"Oh, I wouldn't think so, sir. If any of them is going to be away any time, they always let me know. Would you like to leave a message for her, sir? Or perhaps come back later? Or perhaps it would be better to 'phone before coming all out here again."

"Thank you. I'll come back later."

21

I went out and got into my car. I drove down a rough side road beyond the main gate and in a few moments found myself on a small, disused quay by the river. I sat in the car and stared out at the water. Waiting was not hard. I had waited long enough. It was thinking that was the true torture.

I sat there and went through all the things I had brought with me in my briefcase . . . the evidence to establish with her a bizarre claim. That it was going to be so for her I had no doubt. Across the river there were low fields and slowly-rising slopes to wooded ridges. The tide was moving in fast, rapidly covering the mud flats and swirling in a brown spate along narrow reed-lined creeks. A flock of black-headed gulls rode up on the breast of the flow, and oyster catchers and redshanks worked the water's edge. Needing a cigarette, I reached for my lighter and found in my hand with it the key of her flat which Vickers had given me. Forgetting the cigarette, I stared at it. Men like Vickers did nothing on impulse. Behind every action lay deliberate design. He would have known that I would waste no time in coming to Suffolk—and he could have known that my wife would not be in her flat, known that she was away. He wanted me to go into the flat on my own. Not, necessarily, because he knew there were things there—papers, evidence, the tags of past activities—which he wanted me to see because in some way they might help to bind me closer to some project or half-formed plan of his own. No, not that, but solely because he wanted me to commit myself with a first comparatively simple action, an intrusion on another person's privacy, and so begin the process of further committals.

Frankly as a Rolt, as the man I was, and the way I had been brought up, the idea of violating another's privacy in this way was unthinkable. But sitting there, holding the key in my hand, there was no instant rejection of the idea. Mrs. Angela Starr was a stranger, a fiction created by I knew not what circumstances, but Mrs. Angela Starr was also my wife and I could have presumed, indeed I almost started to do so, some right to excuse its use.

I got out of the car, went to the water's edge and tossed the key into the river. I drove back to the hotel, had dinner, and then returned to Otwell Park House as the last of the summer light was fading from the sky.

I went up to the flat and rang the bell. I rang it four or five times and nobody answered. I left without consulting the porter in the hall. Before I slept that night I had made up my mind that no matter what troubles, problems or personal anguish lay ahead I would deal with them in my own way, following my own code. The first step towards the losing of honour is to become another man's creature.

(Writing this now it still sounds as pompous and old-fashioned as it did then. But I do not care a damn for that. If to have sound principles and believe in and act by them is out of fashion, then I am content to be out of step with the world. To have faults and weaknesses of character is common to us all, accord them house-room we all must, but to make welcome guests of them only strengthens their arrogance. As a very young man I was considered stuffy and humourless. In many ways I was, but it was mostly only an appearance which arose from beliefs firmly held but awkwardly displayed. Now that I am no longer a young man but by no means an old one I have learned the art of a quiet presentation. There is no need to shout when one gives thanks to God.)

The next morning I deliberately held back my visit to Otwell Park House until eleven o'clock. When I got out of my car I knew that she must be in the flat. There was an Audi parked on the drive by the side entrance.

I went up the stairs and rang the bell and she answered it within seconds. The door opened and she stood there, framed by the wall sconce lights of a small hall behind her. In some odd way, seeing the hall lights burning stirred me as much as the sight of her did. She hated any shadows or darkness about a house and was prodigal with light. The light touched the crown of her ash-blonde hair and the plane of one side of her face. She looked exactly as she had looked when she had left me. Untouched, unchanged by absence or time. She wore a loose, long-sleeved tunic blouse that flowed down to her thighs over black trousers. On her feet were red leather slippers. All this I saw while for a few seconds I looked into her deep, violet blue eyes, now dark and almost colourless in the shadow. Her clothes were unknown to me, but the faint movement of scent that reached me from her was familiar. She stood facing me, tall, composed, her head slightly tilted with unspoken enquiry for a brief moment in time. And in that moment I had to hold myself in rock-hard immobility. This should have been a moment for instinctive emotion, the sudden sweep of sunshine bursting through livid, nightmare clouds. For long hours now I had anticipated the moment. But now, I found those few seconds the most difficult ones to live through of my life.

I said, "Mrs. Starr?"

"Yes."

I hesitated for a moment, waiting without hope, but forced to it, for some sudden, miraculous expression of recognition to touch her face, or maybe some slight shadow of a frown to herald the stirring of ghostly memory in her.

Before hesitation could become awkwardness, I said, "Mrs. Starr, my name is Robert Rolt. I'd be very grateful if you could spare me a little of your time?" To help myself and her, I handed her my card.

She took it, read the inscription and then turned it over to look at the blank back before raising her eyes to me.

I said, "It's not a business matter. I'm not a salesman, or anything like that. It's purely personal."

She raised her left hand and glanced at the wristwatch on it. It was a small crystal-faced affair with a gold strap and I had never seen it before. But I knew the gesture. It was one of her ways with unexpected, unknown callers to indicate that although she was prepared to listen she had no time to waste. She was a good business woman and knew the value of time.

She said, "Please come in." She stepped aside and then

24

closed the door behind me and went on, "Go straight through."

The door at the end of the hall was open and I went into a large lounge. The room was full of sunshine flooding through a large spread of windows. It was a comfortable, richly furnished room, but the details meant nothing to me. I was schooling myself hard against the wild instinct to turn and loose some dam-breaking outburst that would magically make the formality and stiff-paced passage of courtesies between us suddenly flower into recognition, into a joyous, heart-shaking explosion of passionate understanding and acknowledgment.

She passed by me, indicated a chair and said, "Do sit down, Mr. Rolt." She went to the fireplace, looked at the card still in her hand and then placing it on the mantelshelf said, "Rolthead Manor . . . Dorset. It's a nice county, though I don't know it very well."

She dropped, with a slow, graceful settling motion to the edge of a settee and I sat down and put my briefcase on my knees.

I said, "The Rolt family have lived there for donkey's years. My father, Sir Henry Rolt—he's dead now—was in the Diplomatic Corps. Ambassador—though he never had any really plum appointments. . . ." I heard my voice going on calmly, amazed at its steadiness against the ferment that churned inside me. "I should tell you that this may take a little time, so if I have come at an awkward moment maybe you would be kind enough to make an appointment for me——"

"There's no need for that, Mr. Rolt. I'm quite free at the moment." She smiled, and now her long, beautiful face, slightly sun-tanned, her eyes unshadowed, was the face that for years had looked down from Bordino's painting. Maybe it was this, the well-known, well-loved face, and the woman herself sitting there on the edge of the settee as I had seen her sit a thousand times, that broke me down momentarily. The simple vividness of her presence, the sure knowledge that she was my

25

wife, that we had spent happy years together, that hundreds of times she had shared my days, that we had loved each other, slept in each other's arms countless times, hit me with all the disrupting force of a physical blow.

I stood up and said, "Mrs. Starr . . . apart from the fact that you know I'm called Rolt—isn't there anything else about me that means something to you? Look at me—doesn't anything move in your mind? Have you never seen me before?"

She looked up at me and her smooth brow wrinkled with thought or fear. I could not tell which but I realised that I might have vaguely frightened her which was the last thing I wanted. Before I could do anything to remedy this, she said, 'No, I'm afraid not, Mr. Rolt. I think it would be best for you to say what you came to say."

"I'm sorry. Forgive me. For a moment I stepped out of line. I'll try to explain as simply and quickly as I can. Over nine years ago I married. My wife was twenty-seven and I was thirty-two. We lived at Rolthead, which is the family house. We were happy, we loved one another, and there was no shadow between us. Just over two years ago my wife motored one morning to a nearby town to do some shopping. She went as she had gone a hundred times before and there was no discord or any sign of trouble between us or in her or me. She never came back. Her car was found abandoned by the roadside. It gave no clue to her going. She just vanished into thin air and nothing the police could ever do, or I myself privately, ever succeeded in tracing her. From the day she went I have never given up hope that I would find her . . . and I . . ."

The effort of speaking like a family lawyer, like a court witness making a deposition, was too much for me momentarily. I broke off and turned towards the window. Outside there was all summer; a great chestnut tree was covered with pink spikes of flower, each leaf lacquered and burnished in the still air, and the hall porter in shirt sleeves was hosing down someone's car on the concrete outside the garages, the hose spraying a

26

wide fan of silver in the air. Against the summer outside there was a winter in my mind. I had walked into a cold, an icy, fantasy.

Slowly I turned and looked at her. She was still on the settee, almost as she had been before, but now her hands had moved from the placid pose in her lap and were at her side and the long fingers were gripping the edge of the settee, tensed, and from her face, unchanged, I could not tell whether she sat there suddenly afraid because of something that rested within her or simply from a sharp concern that she should not so trustingly have invited me into her flat.

I said at once, "Please don't be frightened or concerned. You've only to say the word and I'll go. But I ask you not to do this. It would mean only that, for the sake of my peace of mind and yours, I would have to send someone else in my place—and that would be very much against my nature."

Suddenly she smiled and gave her head a little shake. "Don't worry, Mr. Rolt. The last thing I want you to do is go. You see, I think I need to know everything you want to tell me."

Her fingers relaxed on the edge of the settee and she stood up slowly and walked to a cabinet at the far end of the room. As she opened the door she said, "Usually at this time of the morning I have a glass of sherry. I'm sure you'd like a drink, too."

"Thank you, Mrs. Starr. Yes."

"Smoke, too, if you wish."

I lit a cigarette while she poured the drinks. The moment she had said that she needed to know everything I could tell her, hope had stirred in me, but it was a small growth, so small that deliberately I would not allow myself to take more than a fractional comfort from it because a cold fantasy held us both prisoners still. She came across the room and set a tray with the sherry glasses on it carefully on a small table. I watched her long, capable hands and there was no tremble in them. On her left hand she was wearing a wedding- and an engagement ring.

27

They were not the ones I had given her. She picked up her own glass and went back to the settee.

She made a little movement of her head to me and drank from her glass. Her hair, her face, her body, the pose and set of arms and legs, were all so familiar, and once part of the pattern of my happiness—and for the last two years the pattern of my anguish.

Quite unexpectedly, she said, "You're the type who believes in being very much in control of himself at all times, aren't you?"

"Yes, I am."

"So am I, Mr. Rolt. Particularly at this moment. But the point is that . . . well, I don't think I have quite your strength."

"If you want me to, I'll go and come back some other time. Or even write to you before I come."

"No. You must stay and you must say what you have to."

"Thank you, Mrs. Starr." I reached for my briefcase at the side of the chair where I had left it and began to open it. The thing to do, I told myself, was to keep it straightforward and unemotional. I had a brief to deliver, a statement to make, and for the time being there could be no speculation. To dwell on the possibility of success or bitter disappointment was idle. The time of one or the other would come.

I took out a large envelope from the case and put it on the settee at her side.

"There are some photographs and documents in the envelope. They all concern my wife and myself."

She nodded, the loose fall of her hair moving against the line of her neck and she put the envelope in her lap with one hand. She looked down at it, looked across at me, and then slowly drank some of her sherry. I had a feeling that she wanted to put off the moment of opening the envelope. I was wrong. That she had passed that moment already was clear when she said unexpectedly:

"You have come because you think I am your wife, haven't you?"

"Not *think*. I know. I know as surely and utterly as I know myself, my own body and my own mind."

"As simply as that?"

"Yes."

Her face went grave and for a moment she bit gently against her lower lip.

She picked up the envelope and turned it over almost as though she expected to find some inscription on it. I watched her and sipped at my sherry, not knowing I had done so until it touched my palate. And when it did there was no surprise in me to recognise it. She always drank Tio Pepe. The dryness and the aroma belonged to her, to summer mornings on the terrace at Rolthead.

She pulled the flap free and slid the contents on to her lap. There were four photographs, all of them in colour, our marriage certificate and a letter which she had written to me from Italy when she had been staying with her mother a week before she had disappeared. It was a loving letter announcing her return but there was nothing in it which could possibly embarrass her before me now, I had made sure of that before I had chosen it. Neither had I brought it in the hope that it would convince her of our relationship.

She picked up a photograph. From the angle at which I sat I could see enough of it to know which it was. It was of her, her mother and myself, taken in the garden of her mother's villa. I watched her face as she studied it. Nothing moved on it. It was as still as marble. She put the picture down and went through the others. There was one of her on horseback in the stable yard at Rolthead, on a bay gelding called Minto which had been a favourite of hers. The next one was a group on a beach taken in Devon on Braunton Sands. She sat in a bikini between my younger brother and his wife and I was kneeling behind her. My father had taken it the month before he died. The last one was of our wedding. It showed bride and bridegroom just outside the porch of Rolthead Church. For the first time her hand trembled as she held it and she lowered her head so that

I could not see her eyes. I would have given everything to have known then what thoughts or emotions were going through her mind. Then, with an abrupt movement, she dropped the photograph and picked up the letter which was in its opened envelope. She read my name and address which was on the outside and then slipped out the letter, a single sheet, and read it. Then she folded the sheet and put it back in the envelope.

Not looking at me, she took the letter and the photographs and put them back in my large envelope and handed them over to me.

As I took them she looked full at me and there was no life in her face, no shade of movement, nothing but the well-known beauty now fixed, graven and still. Then slowly she closed her eyes and I saw the slow movement of her shoulders as she breathed deeply, hungrily, as though she were desperate with sudden exhaustion. Slowly her shoulders began to shake. Her head dropped and she put up a hand, holding her brow, shielding her face from me. I made a movement towards her but she sensed it. Before I could reach her she stood up and turned away from me and walked to the window, keeping her back to me.

After a moment she said, the quietness of her voice emphasising the fight she was making to regain control, "Please . . . just let me . . . Just stay there for a moment."

I stood and watched her, helpless, longing to be able to do something, wishing that I could have had some god-given power to dissolve this moment in time, prove it a nightmare, and wake us both to the peace and security of a spring morning two years in the past.

Suddenly, she began to sway and then she collapsed. I caught her as she crumpled to her knees and I lifted her and carried her to the settee, and I knew that it was a stranger I held in my arms, that the moment of true return was still far away in the future.

\*　　\*　　\*　　\*

30

I found the bathroom, soaked a small towel in cold water and came back to her. I bathed her face, clumsy with my own anxiety. There was too much water in the towel and it dripped down her face and splashed on to her blouse.

After a moment or two she came round and slowly sat up. I knelt on the floor at her side and realised that I was holding her hand. She took it gently from me and gave a small smile.

"That was silly of me. . . ." She looked down at her wet blouse and absently fingered the material.

"I was rather clumsy, I'm afraid."

"It's nothing. And thank you."

She rose to her feet and I stood up and put out a hand to steady her, but she moved away.

"I'll just go and change my blouse. I shall be quite all right."

She left the room and I stood there, wondering where on earth we went from here. Then I noticed that her half-finished glass of sherry on a small sidetable by the settee had been knocked over. I began to clean up the mess with the wet towel which was still in my hand, remembering how she hated mess of any kind and couldn't bear to have things about her in a muddle. My mind went back over the years to when Bordino had painted her. She had wanted to change her wine-stained skirt but Bordino had teased her and talked her out of it because it was that skirt and no other he wanted her to wear. She could be wild and impulsive and carefree, sometimes with a suddenness that had taken me by surprise, but she was always fresh and cool even in abandon.

I wiped my sticky hands on the sticky towel and stood there not knowing what to do with it. For a moment I thought of dropping it in the waste-paper basket but decided against it, and then forgot the towel completely as my eye caught the envelope which held the photographs and the letter. I realised then how clumsy I had been. The evidence of the photographs and the letter was undeniable—and so was the shock which they had produced. To walk into someone's life and lay before them without warning, brutally, the evidence that they had once had another life, a life clearly forgotten, undreamt of, maybe wiped from the memory completely . . . God, I couldn't have handled it more stupidly, cruelly and selfishly. For the first time I put myself in her place, tried to imagine the effect such a revelation would have had on me. . . . Angry with myself, I went to the window, thinking that it had been a typical Rolt move, charging bull-like and heedless along the first line which suggested itself. I should have done it all through an intermediary, a doctor, or a lawyer, or my sister-in-law. . . . But no, I had to come myself, brashly, like some damned insurance salesman. Just walked in out of the blue, saying to a stranger, someone who had no memory of me or my life, our life in the past, someone who now lived another life, all memory of the past gone, that I was her husband and I had come to take her back. For the first time then I realised that love had hidden powers that could make a man wound without thought no matter how strongly the spirit in him claimed only the desire to cherish and restore.

From behind me she said, "You can't stand there holding that dirty towel in your hand all day, Mr. Rolt. You can get rid of it in the bathroom."

Without a word I went into the bathroom, wrapped in cold fantasy still. I was Mr. Rolt. I had to remember that. I dropped the towel in the linen basket and washed and dried my hands. Looking at myself in the mirror, I realised my lips were tight-set and I was scowling, my face the face of a pugnacious intruder not that of a lover.

When I went back she had refilled the sherry glasses and set them on another low table between two armchairs. She sat in one of them with my envelope on her knees.

She motioned me to sit down and said, "I think we both need another drink. And clearly we have a lot of talking to do. This has been a shock to me as you must know, but I'm all right now." She smiled. "After all, it's not every day that a man walks into your flat, into your life, and tells you that he is your

32

husband and produces the evidence to prove it." She paused and looked levelly at me, and then went on, her voice strained but deliberate, "You must forgive me, Mr. Rolt, if I make this clear to you—you are a complete stranger to me. I have no memory of you at all. There are some things which I can tell you in a moment which may make the situation a little more rational, but first there are a lot of things I want to ask you."

"Ask me anything you like."

She was far more in control of herself now than I was. I recognised the manner. She had decided to be businesslike, logical, leaving all emotion aside. It was the same directness with which she had managed Rolthead and all her business affairs. She had always kept her emotional life clearly apart from the precise obligations of managing her financial affairs.

She took the photographs and the letter from the envelope. She held up the letter. "This—you brought because of the handwriting?"

"Yes."

She nodded. "Unless it is a very clever forgery, it is mine——"

"Of course it's no forgery. I——"

"Mr. Rolt," she interrupted me, "you mustn't be like that. I am trying to decide what to do, what to think. You come out of the blue into my life and——"

"I'm sorry. Please forgive me. Yes, of course, it could be a clever forgery. But there are the photographs."

She dropped the letter and picked up the photograph taken at Braunton Sands. "It looks like me and it is clearly you kneeling behind me. Who are the others?"

"It was taken the year after we married. My father, now dead, took it. The others are my brother and his wife."

"And this one?"

"That was taken at Rolthead. The horse was a favourite hunter of yours called Minto."

She shook her head. "The world really is upside down this

33

morning. So far as I know I've never ridden a horse in my life."

I smiled. The world was upside down and no amount of protest was going to right it just yet. I said, "You were a very good rider—if anything almost a thruster. You know what that is?"

"Impetuous?"

"Yes."

She picked out the one taken in the garden of her mother's villa. "This is me again and you. Who is the other woman?"

"It was taken in the garden of a villa near Amalfi. The other woman is your mother. As you can see, you are very like her. Extraordinarily so."

She put her hand to her forehead and gave a little shake of her head. "My information is that my mother died when I was three or four years old. I have no memory of her."

"If you say so. But that is your mother. She is still alive, still living in Amalfi and she would have no doubt that you are her daughter. You were an only child. Your father—a Brazilian politician—died soon after your birth. Your mother is an Argentinian of Spanish extraction. After your father's death your mother came to Europe and eventually married again. To a Greek banker. He died about fifteen years ago. After his death your mother—although she still lives most of the time in Amalfi—obtained British naturalisation papers for you and herself."

She reached for her sherry, drank and then shook her head, saying, "This morning is real, isn't it? We are not both bewitched . . . waiting for the moment to awake?"

"This morning is real, and I'm real and so are you. You may not believe it, but we are man and wife, we lived for years so and loved one another and my prayer is that one day we may do so again. I should explain that your mother was, at first, very opposed to our being married. You were, in fact, engaged to someone else. We eloped and were married at a register office in London. Your mother changed her attitude then and—to please her and my father—we went through another ceremony in church." I reached forward and spread out the church marriage certificate for her. "There's the certificate of our marriage. I can take you to Rolthead Church and show you your signature in the register and there are a hundred people——"

"Please . . ."

She took up the photograph of the two of us standing in wedding dress outside Rolthead Church. It was some time before she said anything, then as she put the photographs, the certificate and the letter back in the envelope, she said, "The marriage was nine years ago—did we have any children?"

"No."

She handed me the large envelope.

She said, "Mr. Rolt, you are absolutely convinced that I am your wife?"

"Absolutely. This——" I tapped the envelope—"is only a fraction of the evidence. There is no doubt in my mind at all. Hold out your left hand."

Very slowly she did so, and I smiled at the hesitation for in all the years I had known her she had developed the subtlest ways and habits of avoiding an obvious display of the hand. That she should do so had been a joke between us and the reason of no importance for me because her beauty was unimpaired by the small blemish. In fact my father had said that great beauty always needed some small imperfection to complement its uniqueness. The middle finger of her hand was considerably shorter than her ring finger and about the same length as her forefinger. It was an inherited characteristic, her mother had told me, that always skipped a generation and was confined to the female side of the family.

I said, "Your grandmother's left hand was the same. You were, as you still are, very good at concealing it."

"It's true that I am a little sensitive about it."

"You said a short while ago that there were some things which you could tell me that might make the situation seem a

35

little more rational. Does that mean you know something or that something has happened to you which might make . . . well, all this, have some logic, some explanation?"

She stood up slowly, her face thoughtful, and she said, "Something very strange happened to me once. Not a very comfortable thing. Because I'm a reasonably methodical person I wrote a record of it. I'm not the type that keeps a detailed diary or anything like that, but this was so unusual that I decided I must do it." She moved away towards a bureau in a corner of the room. "I think the best thing I can do is to let you have the account. But I would much rather you took it away and read it and then came back to see me. Just for the moment I don't feel that I can face going into it personally. Would you mind?"

"No, of course not. I'll do anything you want."

She opened one of the bureau drawers and pulled out a long white envelope. She came back and handed it to me. There was no superscription on the envelope and it was sealed with a little blue blob of wax.

"Are you staying around here?"

"At a hotel in Woodbridge."

"Don't read it until you get there. Perhaps after that and when we've both had time to think things over, you would like to come and have dinner with me tonight?"

"I should be very happy to."

I made a move to go, but she stopped me. "Tell me something before you go. What was your wife wearing on the day she disappeared?"

I said, "You mean what were you wearing." I regretted saying it but it was out. To my surprise she took no objection to it.

She smiled, a touch of warmth moving into her expression, and said, "I'm beginning to appreciate one or two things about your character, Mr. Rolt. I asked what your wife was wearing and I meant just that."

"All right. She was hatless. She was wearing a light grey

flannel coat over a blue linen dress which had a white leather belt. Brown nylon stockings and brown crocodile shoes with a silver buckle. She had a brown handbag on a shoulder strap. So far as could be told the handbag contained her purse with a few pounds in it and her cheque book. The bank was the Westminster at Shaftesbury. There were other small items undoubtedly, but nothing significant that was ever missed after a check of her belongings at Rolthead. The only jewellery on her was her wedding-ring, a plain gold band with our initials inside, and her engagement ring, also gold with a large sapphire mounted in an oval of small diamonds. Substantially what I have listed is what she went away with. I am never likely to forget any of it. Or that day."

"I can quite understand that." She moved past me into the hall and opened the flat door for me.

Outside I turned and there was no power on earth which could keep the words from me.

I said, "I mean nothing to you? Looking at me now, have you no flicker of memory . . . no slightest . . . well, feeling about me?"

She looked at me unemotionally and said calmly, "I have a great many feelings about you, Mr. Rolt. Why should I not? The world has done something strange to both of us. Please, just go away and read what I have written. I wrote it for myself. Shall we say a little after seven?"

Before I could say goodbye, she turned her head from me and drew back closing the door.

I went down to my car and drove to the quay which I had visited the day before. I hadn't handled things in the way I would have liked to. I sat there and watched the river, seeing the flight of swallows low over it and the occasional movement of duck and gulls, thinking about her. She had handled herself well except for her one brief moment of collapse. And, in everything she had done and said, I had recognised the shadow of similar things from the past of the woman who was my wife. The left hand which she had held out for me had once carried her engagement and our wedding-ring. Today it had held rings which were strange to me.

Remembering that now, I was taken back to my father. After his first meeting with her he had asked me if I had noticed her left hand. He had eyes like a hawk and had seen the mild oddity of her middle finger. As it came back to me now I recalled that that was the first time I had heard the phrase the Saturn finger. My father was well read and a lover of old lore. He had called it the Saturn finger. Because it was something to do with her, and anything, particularly at that time, which touched on her was precious to me, I had always remembered his quoting from Ben Jonson to back up his erudition:

> The thumb, in chiromancy, we give to Venus;
> The fore-finger to Jove; the midst to Saturn;
> The ring to Sol; the least to Mercury.

No matter what had happened to her, I knew that there was no power on earth that could ever move me from the absolute knowledge that she was my wife, or that she would not come back to Rolthead and know it herself.

I started the car and began to drive back to Woodbridge. The road was narrow for about a mile and then made a sharp right-hand bend. As I approached it a car—I had no idea what kind it was, my mind was full of other things, my driving automatic—came around the corner and down towards me very quickly. I had to pull over to let it pass. The other car skidded a little and threw up a shower of grit from the freshly surfaced road. Some of the grit or a heavy stone must have hit my windscreen because it shattered.

I stopped and got out. The other car had gone. Swearing, I pulled on a driving-glove and punched the windscreen clear. I drove to a garage in Woodbridge where the proprietor said he would fit a new windscreen for me, but he would have to get one from Ipswich. My car would be ready by the next morning. In the meantime he kindly offered me the use of one of his cars which I accepted. Except for anger at the way the other car had been driven, I scarcely gave the incident a thought. I had had windscreens shatter before. By the time I reached my room and settled to read the contents of the white envelope I had forgotten the whole episode.

## CHAPTER THREE

THE ACCOUNT WAS handwritten on sheets of lined foolscap paper.

It began:

*It is now quite a long time since it happened. I have decided to write all this down because I know how memory can fade, how hard it can become to recall things exactly.*

*I came back to myself, or awoke—it's hard to say which—in a bedroom. The details of the bedroom are of no importance personally because I learned later that it was in a rented villa on the coast between St. Jean-de-Luz and San Sebastian. I was lying in bed and feeling tired but not ill. Subsequently I realised that I had a large bruise on my right temple.*

*The window of the room was partly open and the white curtains were moving in a strong current of air and I could hear the sound of the sea. I was wearing a blue nightdress of silk with red ribbons threaded through the neck and sleeve openings. I did not know who I was or where I was. I remember that in a curious way this did not worry me. Later on, when things were explained to me, it did not worry me, but this I know is because I had to accept other people's word for it, and still do have to. Sometimes now, if I begin to think about it, it almost frightens me. I just woke and could remember nothing of myself or my previous life at all. So far as I am concerned I was born in that room in a French villa at that moment in time.*

*There was a man sitting at the side of my bed. There is no need to describe him for I see him often still. I had no idea then who he was.*

She went on to describe how from this man—who was her

brother, some ten years older than herself—she learned what had happened and who she was. All this information she had to take on trust from him at first, though some details were substantiated later by other people. The man was called Albert Chinn. First of all he explained to her that she was a widow, Mrs. Angela Starr, and that they had been holidaying together in the villa which he had rented. They had only been there four days. On the evening of the second day they had been walking across the rocks at the sea-edge below the villa when she had slipped, fallen and struck her head against a rock. He had carried her up to the villa and called a doctor from St. Jean-de-Luz who had treated the bruised cut on her forehead— she was still unconscious—given her an injection and sent out a private nurse from the town to be with her. (This nurse, with her name, she described in her account.)

*All that my brother told me was completely unknown to me. I had no memory of anything except waking in the villa bed. He was very worried about all this, and, I know now, rather frightened. He called the doctor who talked to me and explained that the blow on my head had caused a temporary form of amnesia. Everything would come back to me gradually. The fact that nothing ever has come back to me is one of my reasons for writing this. I live in hope and, quite why I don't know, feel that it is important to remember everything about the first moment of existence I knew and the people and circumstances which surrounded it. The details of myself which I learned in the next few days (we stayed two more weeks before my brother took me back to England) I list below. . . .*

I had to smile at this—although there was no humour in me —because one of her characteristics was a passion for listing and tabulating things, her personal belongings, jewellery, pictures, furniture, and also her business affairs. She kept an immaculate portfolio of her investments and her expenditure and receipts. She could have run the Rolthead estate far more efficiently than I did. Although she was the most generous person in the world, she just had to know where everything

42

was and have an exact picture of the state of all her affairs.

Her maiden name, she had been told, was Angela Chinn. Her mother had been French from Algiers. Her father had been an Englishman of independent means with a passion for gambling and travelling. Her mother and father had been killed in a car accident in Spain—on the Madrid–Burgos road—when she was five, and she and her brother had been brought up by an aunt (also now dead) in Birmingham. At the age of twenty-two she had married a Mr. Franklin Starr, fifteen years older than herself, who was a Liverpool businessman, and they had lived close to the small town of Formby, north of Liverpool. There had been no children and her husband had died of a heart attack two years later. (Three years before she had married me! And I had known her for six months before our marriage!) He had left her a great deal of money. Two years after his death she had left Formby and had spent two years travelling with a woman friend and finally they had settled together in a flat in Florence. There had been a quarrel between them after some years and her friend had left her. She had come from her Italian flat to share a holiday with her brother at St. Jean-de-Luz. She had never gone back to the flat. Her brother had insisted on taking her back with him to his rented flat at Otwell Park House. She gave meticulously all the names, addresses and dates which had been supplied by her brother. There were lists, too. She specified the clothes, jewellery, money and so on that were at the villa with her.

Her account finished:

*Nothing of anything I did or was before that moment of waking in the villa has yet come back to me, but often I get the feeling that it is there, just out of grasp and that it will come one day. But there are things with me which belong to the past. Not only can I speak and read English, but also French, Italian and Spanish. I have a good mathematical brain and understand figures and legal, financial and women's matters. But of the world and what happened in it before I woke I am ignorant and now having to learn with the least embarrass-*

43

*ment to myself. It is not a situation I would want anyone else to be in. To wake one day and look into the mirror and find the face of a complete stranger looking back at you is frightening. Soul-destroying.*

The private agony in those last two remarks touched me deeply. Not for one moment while I had been reading had it seemed as though I were reading the report of a stranger. This was my wife. She had left Rolthead and all this had happened to her—or so she had been told. Birth, childhood, parents, the details of her life, her marriage and all the rest up to the moment of waking just could not be true. Were not true. Some of the facts, I knew already from Vickers, were not true— her passport had been forged. But that she had lost her memory and awakened in that villa I was prepared to believe. From that moment of waking, for reasons which I couldn't know, but meant to find out, a new life and identity had been assigned to her. All this, however, was far less important than the immediate business of restoring her to Rolthead and bringing her back to the paths of her true life.

It was not going to be easy to handle. I knew that I would have to school myself to all the gentleness and persuasion I could muster. I was going to have to face bitter days and disappointments, and, while all this was being done, I was determined to keep the interests of Vickers and his people out of it. That to me was a side issue. It could be faced when she had recovered. Albert Chinn, I was convinced, had used her, might even still be using her. Next to restoring her to Rolthead, I wanted to meet him.

I drove out to Otwell Park House in the car the garage proprietor had loaned me and reached it just before half-past seven. She opened the door for me and, although I gave her a greeting, she just nodded her head and let me in.

She was wearing a long, golden velvet dress and her hair was tied back on the nape of her neck with a ribbon of the same colour. Except for a thin necklace of small pearls she wore no jewellery except for her rings. She looked pale and, I thought, was a little nervous. She waved me into an armchair and asked me what I would like to drink.

"A whisky and soda, if I may."

She turned to the cabinet and said, "Please don't think it rude of me, Mr. Rolt, if I don't join you. Later, maybe."

When I had my drink she sat down on the settee across from me. I handed her the long white envelope with its broken blue seal.

I said, "Would you mind sometime if I had it back to make a copy? Perhaps also permission to show it to other people?"

"No." She gave a little smile. "I don't see how I can refuse you that."

"Or if I now ask you some questions?"

"In the circumstances how could I possibly refuse? All I am interested in is the truth."

"So am I. But I must say this first. I am absolutely certain that you are my wife."

She spread her hands and gave a little shrug of her shoulders. It was the gesture of a small child who feels it has no reply to make.

I nodded at the envelope which she had put on the settee at her side.

"Have you ever checked any of the facts about your life before you lost your memory?"

"Oh, of course. Quite a few but not all, naturally. In the statement where I list my possessions you will see my passport mentioned. Also the return half of my rail ticket to Florence."

"What happened to the flat in Florence?"

"I never went back. It was rented unfurnished. Albert went over and cleared things up. The furniture and so on was sold. I have a sale statement in my bureau. He brought back some clothes and a few other things that he thought I might want to have."

"And the friend you lived with?"

45

"I never heard from her again. Albert tried to trace her but she was not to be found."

"Where is your brother now?"

"He's been abroad for some time. This flat is still in his name. He works for a group of American oil companies. He's a biochemist, or was. He's now in an executive position. He was in London for many years but was recently transferred to America. He was dead against this because he didn't want to leave me. If I hadn't persuaded him that I was perfectly capable now of looking after myself I think he would have resigned."

"Where in America is he?"

"His office is in New York, but he travels. He phones me from time to time. The last call I had was a few days ago from Montevideo." She smiled. "He's a wealthy man and hates letter-writing. The thought of what some of his calls must cost horrifies me at times."

"Have you ever checked any details of your marriage?"

"Naturally. The marriage certificate—it was a Register Office in Liverpool—came to me from Florence. And a couple of months after Albert brought me here he got in touch with my husband's sister and she came to see me. She told me quite a lot about the marriage, and brought photographs of the house we lived in at Formby and some photographs of my husband and myself—both together and singly."

Before I could help myself, I said, "This is crazy!"

To my surprise she gave a laugh. "Mr. Rolt, I agree. But it happens to be a very real kind of craziness which concerns us both. You come here telling me that I am your wife while everything I have been told—and so far as I can, have checked —tells me that I am not. It is so crazy that I think I will change my mind and have a drink."

As she began to move I stood up. "Let me get it for you."

"Well, thank you. I'll have——"

"Don't tell me what it is."

I walked away from her and opened the bar cabinet and

46

made up her drink. I brought it back and handed it to her.

She looked at it and said, "How did you know?"

"Because you are my wife. Because that is what you always drank before dinner. Just as you always had Tio Pepe before lunch. Not everything is lost in the past. You yourself have written that English, French and other languages came naturally to you, and a flair for mathematics and business details. Your mannerisms persist, your way of speaking and your character—so far as I have been able to judge it. If all these things remain then the others can't be forever lost. I refuse to believe it."

She sipped at her drink and, although she liked it, I waited for the first slight wrinkle of her nose as the bitter Campari taste took her palate. It came just as I had seen it hundreds of times before.

I said, "I've mixed that drink hundreds of times for you before. There are other things, too." I nodded at a small bookshelf at the side of the fireplace. "You've got half-a-dozen books there on life on other planets, flying saucers and space ships. In fact, the afternoon of the day you disappeared you were going to a meeting of a local society which believes in all that stuff. I used to tease you about your interest in such things, such——" I broke off.

She smiled at me. "Such what? Such nonsense?"

"If you like. What else is it? But the point is there is no doubt in me that you are my wife."

She said, "You're a very determined man, aren't you."

"Yes, I am."

"And at this moment I am a very confused woman. What is there to be done about it?"

"Everything. After your brother brought you to England did you have any kind of treatment for your amnesia?"

"Of course. My brother took me to a famous neurologist in Manchester who could do nothing and he arranged for me to consult Sir Hugh Gleeson, a professor of Experimental Psychology at Cambridge. I used to go once a week for a while,

47

but now I only report to him every other month. Sir Hugh has now retired but we have become friends and I visit him still . . . as a patient and a friend."

"And what did he have to say about all this?"

"Well, I don't clearly understand these things, but he says that I have no organic amnesia—that clears up gradually with treatment. Mine is psychogenic amnesia. And that clears up suddenly and unexpectedly. I've tried to read about it, but it is all a bit beyond me. Basically, although I bumped my head, he is sure there is no damage to the brain. But you must really ask him about all this. He's a very charming man. I'll give you his card." She went across to her bureau and brought me back the card which I put into my wallet.

"I certainly shall see him." I paused. I was unable to resist the temptation of testing her. I went on, "I gather from your statement that you are a wealthy woman. But do you do anything now? I mean how do you fill your time?"

I felt unworthy of her and myself, but she could not know that I had information about her from Vickers which I had no intention of revealing to her. Much as I loved her, though, I just had to explore all the avenues open to me, distasteful as this was.

"I have plenty of money, yes. But I don't like to be idle. I spend most of my time buying old properties, country cottages and that kind of thing. I do them up and resell them. I find it very pleasant and stimulating—and reasonably profitable."

I said, "I imagine your brother has photographs of the two of you . . . well, before all this happened. Photographs when you were young. And letters from you that go quite a way back."

She laughed and stood up and took my empty glass. She looked down at me, and I had the quick impression that abruptly something in her had changed. Maybe it was only a phase of awkwardness that had suddenly passed, or a quick movement into some kind of acceptance of this whole tangled affair. Some weight, however small, had lifted from her, and

48

in that moment she was more than ever the woman I had loved and married.

She said, "I like you, Mr. Rolt. I like the way you talk and manage yourself. I like the way you always talk of photographs. Other people say photos. And you've got a nice kind of pompous manner. Do you mind my saying that?"

"Not at all. I've got a good picture of myself. I don't altogether like it. As for the way I use words, well, my old man was a bit of a stickler about language."

"So is Albert." She went to the cabinet to get me another drink and, half over her shoulder, said, "Yes, Albert's got a few old photographs. Not many. He believes in travelling light. There are no letters that I know of. But he has shown me a card I sent him on his twenty-first birthday with a silly school-girl message on it. I was at a school in Florence at the time." She came back, holding the glass carefully. "I keep meaning to go back to Florence sometime. When I see pictures of it I get . . . well, this feeling of something near me, just out of reach."

I said, "You were in Florence just over three years ago with me. We stayed a night at the Excelsior Hotel while we were motoring down to see your mother."

She put the glass on the table at my side and sat down on the settee. She just looked at me and said nothing for a moment or two.

I took my glass and drank and over it I saw her deep violet-blue eyes steadily on me. Her face and body were very still as though she were looking at me and through me to something a hundred miles away. Then slowly she gave her shoulders a little shake, and said, "You've asked me a lot of questions, Mr. Rolt. Now I want to ask you one. How did you come to find me here?"

It was almost with a shock that I realised that this question had not been asked before. Since so many others had now been asked, the inevitability of its coming had gone from my mind. I couldn't tell whether she was aware of my slight hesitation or not.

49

I said, giving myself time at first, "When you disappeared it was a public matter. The police took it in hand and the newspapers published the details. There were the odd rumours of your being seen but they never came to anything. You won't know, but we had a wide circle of friends. At one time I was briefly in the Foreign Office and knew many people from other government departments. Some weeks ago a friend of mine from the Ministry of Defence, who comes to Woodbridge to sail, saw you in the town, just getting into your car. He took a note of the registration number and after that it was easy to trace you. He couldn't be certain it was you but the moment I was informed I came right up here. You opened the door to me and I knew it was you."

Although it was only the shadow of a lie, it was the first time that the mildest deceit has passed between us. Expediency is an easy god to serve. I should have made nothing of it. Instead, I felt like dirt.

She said, "There is absolutely no doubt in your mind whatever, is there?"

"None. You are my wife. You've seen our marriage certificate. You were born Sarah Peralta—the name of your mother's first husband. Your mother is living still in her Amalfi villa. Her name is Alexina Vallis. Vallis was your stepfather's name. He was a very wealthy Greek banker. Your mother was born in a small town called Rosario not far from Buenos Aires. For all I know there may well be a person called Angela Starr. But you are not that person. You are Sarah Rolt . . . once Sarah Peralta."

She sipped at her drink, then gave a small laugh and said, "Sarah . . . It's a nice name." She was silent for a moment, running a finger around the rim of her glass and that, too, was a gesture I recognised. In our private talks at Rolthead it was always the signal for some frankness, the moment of deep concentration before she posed some straightforward question. The question came now. "Mr. Rolt, were we very much in love?"

50

"We were. So much so that you were willing to break your engagement and marry me. You were the first woman I ever loved, and the only one. You are the only woman I've ever known. When you went away I would not honestly say that it was the end of my life. There were still things I could and had to do. But if all the meaning did not go from my life something else did . . all the magic and the joy. My brain and body went on working, but my heart was empty. I know this sounds . . . well, fanciful. But that's how it was."

"It doesn't sound so to me. It's a straightforward honest statement." She stood up. "I think we should go and have dinner. It's all cold, I hope you don't mind?"

"Not at all."

"And over dinner you can tell me how you came to meet me . . . or rather this Sarah Peralta."

"It was you I met!" I said vigorously. "You are my wife. I can tell you not only what your favourite drinks are but what your favourite flowers are, your favourite composer. I know the things that set your teeth on edge. I know your likes and dislikes and all the other thousand and one things that a man knows about his wife which few other people can ever learn."

"And what are my favourite flowers?"

I handed her my silver pencil. "Write the name down on the back of the envelope."

She picked up the white envelope that held the statement she had written and wrote on the back of it and then held it to her breast, hiding the writing from me.

"Well?"

"Roses. You took over the old rose garden at Rolthead and made it a show place. In your private sitting-room at home you have four paintings of individual roses."

She held the envelope out to me and turned it round. On the back was one word. *Roses*. She went past me without looking at me and from the door said, "I need five minutes to make things ready. If you would like, help yourself to another drink."

51

I sat there, staring at the white envelope which she had dropped on to the settee.

We sat over dinner for two hours and we talked. Or rather I did most of the talking. I told her how I had met her while I had been staying in Amalfi with my father and, through a friend of my father's, had managed to be introduced. She was very curious about these early stages and asked many questions. Later, when it came to details of our life together at Rolthead, she was full of interest but it was of a different category from the attraction the early days had clearly had for her. Overall I noticed particularly that, although she wanted to know everything she could about her mother and other people like my father and my brother, it was of herself that she was most inquisitive. Not only did this seem natural to me, but I had the feeling that from one or other of the questions she put about herself she was hoping that something would be said, some mental chord touched which would awaken, if only faintly, a response from her. I could understand this, too, and because of it I tried to remember some of the host of small things that had happened between us, knowing quite well that it is often the small details of a shared life that carry the seeds of significance.

When I told her about her wealth and the way she had always managed her affairs she showed no surprise. This was something she could recognise in herself now. That she could —in those days—ride and play a good game of golf and tennis did surprise her. At no time did I in the slightest way try to put any question to her which might even remotely touch on any of the activities I had seen on Vickers' films. I was not interested in her present friends or acquaintances and wanted to know no more about her business affairs than she had already told me. Above all—having been forced to deceive her mildly about the way she had been recognised—I did not want to put myself in the position of having to dissemble again. The only thing I cared a damn about was that she was

52

my wife, and that there must be some way to bring her back to a complete understanding and acceptance of that. Nothing else was of any importance.

In the end we came to a sensible arrangement. She could not ignore the weight of evidence which I had brought with me to prove that she was Sarah Rolt. On the other hand she had evidence that she was Angela Starr. She could do nothing, make no promises nor commit herself until she had had time to consult with her brother. She said that she would telephone his New York office and try and get in touch with him. She told me that she had already tried to do this since my morning visit, but there had been no reply to her call. I left her with the understanding that I would come back the following afternoon to find out what had happened between herself and her brother.

By the time I left her she was looking pale and was clearly very tired. Seeing her like that, knowing the strain she had been put to—and all this by me—it was hard to keep my feelings for her in check. Standing at the doorway, I had to fight hard not to put my arms around her, draw her to me, and hope that some magic in the contact would dissipate the dark shadows of the fantasy that surrounded us. Maybe from the confusion that clearly possessed her, she recognised this, but could find no convincing impulse to seek what I so strongly wanted to offer. For a moment we looked at one another and then, without a word, she put out her right hand and just touched my arm with her fingertips. It was the lightest of contacts and then her hand was gone and she closed the door on me. I stood outside without moving, suddenly possessed with a black desire to hit something or somebody violently . . . anything to ease the anguish in me. As I stood there I heard quite clearly the sound—brief, quickly choked back—of a woman's sobs from the other side of the door.

I drove back to my hotel in a quiet, useless rage of frustration.

To some extent it was with me when I woke, and stayed with me right through breakfast. After I had eaten I went into the

53

lounge to read my newspaper. It was hours before I could go back to Otwell Park House and they were going to be hard hours. A man came into the lounge and sat down in an armchair a couple of feet from me.

He said, "Good morning, Mr. Rolt."

It was Vickers in his blue suit and red tie, his chin still unshaven. I made no attempt to hide my surprise or anger.

"What the bloody hell are you doing here? You said you were going to leave me alone!"

Fortunately there was no one else in the room.

He shrugged his shoulders, his eyes flicking nervously. "Sorry—but I'm only doing what I've been told to do. I thought perhaps you'd care for a stroll down by the river . . . that you might like someone to chat with."

I said, "I don't want to talk to anyone. I just want to read my newspaer."

"Of course. I'm never very chatty after breakfast either." He picked up a newspaper from a table and began to read it.

After that it was impossible for me to read my newspaper. I had only picked it up, anyway, to avoid casual chat from any other residents who might have been in the lounge. There was far more on my mind than any newspaper could make me forget. Sitting there, too, I was suddenly reminded of the rows which had come my way with my friends and my family because I had a habit—to a large extent now cured, I liked to think—of speaking first and thinking afterwards. Just seeing Vickers and remembering the films had made me want to damn his eyes. Now I realised that if there were anything in the world I did want to do, then it was to talk about it to someone. Vickers was only doing a job. He was concerned with the whole affair. In fact without him I might still have been at Rolthead never having heard of Mrs. Angela Starr.

Lowering my paper, I said, "My apologies for flying off the handle. The world's a bit upside down at the moment."

"That's what they thought, Mr. Rolt. That's why I was told to come. However, nobody's pressing you." He grinned, self-assurance returning. "You'd know how to deal with that. But if there is anything . . . any way we can help—just name it."

"Thank you." I reached into my inner pocket and pulled out the long white envelope with its broken blue seal. I was breaching no confidence. I had had Sarah's permission the previous night to make a copy of it and also to be allowed to show it to other people at my discretion. I handed it to him and said, "Read this."

He pulled the statement out and began to read. I lit a cigarette and watched him. Once or twice he scratched at his growing beard, and twice he turned back to check something he had read. He then put the statement back in the envelope, glanced at the word 'Roses' pencilled on the back and said, "There's an interesting old tidal mill here and quite a pleasant walk by the river."

We strolled through the town to the river and along a short stretch of raised bank and found a seat to ourselves. It was June and there were a few people mucking about with boats. The tide was running out fast, slap-slapping along the sides of the moored craft.

Vickers said, "I'd like to take Mrs. Starr's statement back with me. That's the first thing."

"You can make a copy. She's given me permission for that, and for other people to see it."

"No, I'd like the original. I'll get a copy made, too. You can have the original back very soon."

"Why that way round?"

"Just take my word for it—the reason is sound. Also it might be a good idea to let me have the key of her flat back. You won't have any use for it now."

"I never did have any use for it. I threw it in the river."

He chuckled. "I'm glad to hear it. You've won me five pounds. I bet that you would never use it."

"For God's sake—this isn't any game!"

"Of course not. It's a very vital part of your life—but it's an equally vital part of my profession. Whether you like it or not, you've got to accept that. However, so far as I'm concerned all that doesn't mean that I can't take time off now and then for a joke or a simple bet. Even you have to eat, drink and sleep. The world isn't stopping because you and I and a few others have a big enigma on our hands."

I realised then that I had made too hasty a judgment of him. Behind his apologetic and nervous manner lay a quiet strength. He held out his hand and I gave him the white envelope. As he put it away, he said, "She is your wife—you haven't the faintest doubt about that?"

"None?"

"Neither have I. She's Mrs. Robert Rolt, your wife. At the risk of having you throw me in the river, I'm going to be frank. So far as she is concerned there are only two ways of looking at things. Either, until the moment you walked in on her, she genuinely believed she was Mrs. Angela Starr and is now a very confused woman. Or, she knows perfectly well that she is your wife but for her own reasons prefers not to acknowledge it——"

"I can't accept that!"

He shook his head. "You're not a fool, Mr. Rolt. You must have reasoned as far as that. It won't do you any harm to admit it."

"As a possibility it has crossed my mind—yes. And I kicked it out because I know it can't be true. I think this man . . . this bastard Chinn found her after she'd lost her memory and she fitted some bill . . . God knows what . . . and he took advantage of her state."

"It's a strong possibility, I agree. If it's any comfort to you I'm sure when we come to check the facts in this statement, and anything else that she may have told you she has learnt of her so-called past, we shall find them either false or unprovable. That's why I'd like you to tell me everything you've learned from her. The more we have to check the sooner we shall arrive at the truth. I'm willing to bet, for instance, that this Albert Chinn is not at the moment readily available or that

56

she has any photos or letters or what not to prove his identity."

I said, "He's in America, works for some oil company. She's going to telephone him."

"There won't be any answer. We've been looking for him. We knew, too, he was supposed to be with an oil company in America. But nobody knows anything about him. And it's been a very thorough investigation, Mr. Rolt. I don't have to tell you what that means. I think the wisest thing at the moment is for you to tell me what you have learned from her and we'll go into it all. She's your wife. We're not over-concerned about all that stuff you saw on film. Until you say otherwise— bluntly—she's your wife and she's lost her memory and accepted another identity. That's your problem and a pretty hellish one, but you will deal with it in your own way. We shan't interfere. But if at any time you want our help . . . well, you know how to get it."

We sat there and I told him all that had passed between Sarah and myself, and I did it gladly because I wanted everything about Mrs. Angela Starr to be proved false. If they could do that and Sarah could be convinced, then I felt that it was the first and maybe the biggest hurdle passed. But the fact that Vickers had said it was my problem and that I had to deal with it in my own way was not something I accepted blindly. His card carried four blue stars. I knew the Foreign Office and other government agencies. If it ever suited them they wouldn't care a damn about me or Sarah. No ties, no loyalties of any kind would stop them from taking over.

When I had finished we walked back to the hotel together. He was not staying there. As we stood outside, he said, "I'll let you have your wife's statement back as soon as possible. Before I go, there's one point I'd like to make though. Like you, I believe your wife is being used. How the opportunity arose and how it was all fixed up we'll find out in time. We'll turn up Mr. Albert Chinn one day——"

"When you do I hope I'm there! By God—I'd like to have him here this moment!"

57

"No doubt. But the point is that your wife hasn't been used for any innocent purpose. You've seen the films. Mr. Chinn's applecart is being upset. He—and no doubt others—won't like that. People who have done a lot of planning don't like their work knocked sideways. Sometimes they hit back."

"You mean I should keep my eyes open when I cross the road?"

"All the time. Everywhere. It's a sensible precaution. Your car's up the road now having a shattered windscreen replaced, isn't it?"

"How the devil do you know that?"

"Because I was here yesterday. In the bar having a drink while you were having dinner at Otwell Park House. The garage bloke mentioned it——"

"You've been watching me. Or somebody has."

"Was it an accident?"

"Yes."

"Perhaps it was. But it could have tipped you over into a ditch, say. All it needs then is one good smack with a spanner to make it a fatal accident. For your own safety it wouldn't hurt, Mr. Rolt, to think a little more dramatically than the ordinary driver does. No?"

He walked away. When I collected my car after lunch I asked the garage man if he had found a stone or anything amongst the shattered glass when he had swept up the inside of the car. He said that he had not.

## CHAPTER FOUR

WHEN I ARRIVED at Otwell Park House that afternoon it was no surprise to me to be told by Sarah that she had not been able to get Albert Chinn on the telephone. When I asked her for the name of the oil company for which he worked she handed me a piece of paper on which the name was written and also their addresses in London and New York.

I said, "Have you got their telephone numbers?"

"No. But they would be in the book."

"Did you ever go to see him at the London office, or ever telephone him there?"

"No. I never had occasion to. Why?"

"To be frank, while I obviously accept your word that there is an Albert Chinn and that you know him, I don't think he works for this oil company or has anything to do with it."

"I'm sure that's not so."

"Why are you so sure?"

"Because of something Albert told me and also——"

She broke off and I waited for her to go on. Today she was completely composed and I had the feeling that since I had seen her last she had done a lot of hard thinking. Quite possibly she might have come to the conclusion which Vickers and I shared that Chinn had taken advantage of her loss of memory to foist a new personality and background on her for his own purposes.

"What did Albert tell you, Sarah?"

At the use of her name, her head jerked up and for a moment I thought that she was going to be angry with me.

59

I went on, "If you object to being called that, you must say so. But to me you are Sarah, my wife. I can't call you Mrs. Starr or Angela."

She gave a little shrug of her shoulders. "If you prefer it that way." Although her manner wasn't cold it was certainly distant.

I said, "What was it that Albert told you?"

"That he preferred it if I never tried to phone him at his office. Or even write through them. It seemed odd to me, but he explained that he did a lot of confidential work for them. Secret and confidential work which made it politic if he were not openly or officially known to be connected with them. In fact, he said that if they were ever challenged they would deny that they knew anything about him."

"Didn't you find that odd?"

"No. I know enough about business to realise that everything is not done through official channels. Big companies are in competition with one another—they have to have some kind of information system. You must know that, surely, Mr. Rolt. All businesses keep an eye on one another, want to know what developments are in the air. I always presumed that Albert did something like that."

"Did he ever ask you to help him at all?"

She went to the window and stood with her back to me. "You sound like a policeman."

"I hope not. I'm just trying to sort this mess out. I know you are my wife. You don't know for certain who you are. You've accepted that you are a Mrs. Angela Starr, and you have proof of it. I'm going to have that proof examined and I know that it will turn out to be false . . . faked . . . God knows what."

She turned. "But how can you do that?"

"In many ways. You're on the police files as a missing person. We can tell them your story and they can check it. Or, more discreetly, I could get it done by my friends in Whitehall. But if you don't for the moment want it that way . . . well, I could try and do it personally. Whichever way you choose it

60

can only be for your good. . . . You want to know who you are without any shadow of doubt. I know already, but that doesn't help unless you know. So for the moment let's keep things between ourselves. Did Albert ever ask you to help him in his work?"

"Just now and again."

"What did you do?"

"Sometimes I would go and meet people . . . collect things for him. Business things. A letter or a note. These I would pass to Albert or sometimes hand on to someone else for him."

"What did you make of that?"

"I didn't like it at first. But he explained that there was nothing illegal about it. They were just people he didn't want to be seen with. He explained that when it came to companies making big deals it could be enough for two particular people to be seen having lunch together for rumours to start which could upset things."

"I suppose it could, yes."

"I'm sure that there was nothing illegal about any of it." She smiled. "Sometimes I thought it was probably all unnecessary. Grown-up men playing some sort of secret business game just to make it all seem more exciting than it was. At least I got that feeling from Albert. He loved things to be dramatic . . . to be different. For instance, if I were meeting him for dinner somewhere he was quite capable of walking in wearing a suit and clothes I'd never seen before and a false beard or moustache and a wig. . . ." She giggled suddenly, and it was a sound right out of the past, striking hard at a hundred memories. "Sometimes I'd sit in a bar or lounge and he'd be there, some way from me and then he would wink and I'd know at once. He liked to make things fun, you know."

"What did he look like?"

"Oh, I don't know. Just ordinary. Middle height, a sort of straightforward squarish face, a bit solemn, even sad. But he was full of jokes and laughter."

I stood up and lit a cigarette and walked to the window.

Two small boys with rackets were knocking a shuttlecock to one another on the lawn beyond the garage. From a group of trees a wood pigeon took off from its nest, rose high, gave a quick flap of wings and glided out of sight. The whole thing was a damned mess. Somebody, somewhere, had compounded a sadistic joke. I wanted to hit somebody, and hit somebody hard . . . I wanted an explosion that would blow the whole thing sky-high.

She must have sensed how I was feeling. I heard her move up behind me and felt her hand touch my arm for a moment.

She said, "What are we going to do?"

I turned and I had to fight to keep myself from reaching out for her. Her face was drawn and pale, the spirit had gone from her body and her eyes were half-closed.

I said, "We're going to sort it out between us. I want you to come back to Rolthead. See it. See the house where you lived for years. It might spark something off. If it doesn't—then it doesn't. After that I want to take you down to Amalfi to see your mother. Through an accident, illness, God-knows-what, you lost your memory and it hasn't come back yet. You're living with a fictitious past. I've got to say that because that is what I believe. I'm not accusing Albert Chinn of anything. I just don't know where he fits in all this. But one thing is clear—you've got to find out who you really are. I know. But that's not enough. You've got to know. There's no reason at all why you should stay here———"

"But there is. I've got to get in touch with Albert."

I put my hands on her shoulders and held her firmly. Anger was still in me and I was in no mood for other than plain speaking.

I said, "I don't think you're ever going to speak to Albert again. That you're fond of him is obvious, but so far as I'm concerned I'm sure that he is not your brother. He found you when you were wandering about with a blank memory and for some purpose, good or bad as he saw it, he made up a life for you that is a complete myth. Your real life is waiting at

Rolthead. The least you can do is to come back there and give yourself a chance to acknowledge it."

I dropped my hands from her shoulders. I had gone over the mark, I knew, but there was nothing that could have stopped me. I was ready for her to resent my manner.

She didn't. She just shook her head gently and said, "You know what you want, don't you? But I'm not saying yes or no to you at the moment. I'm going to spend the rest of the day trying to get Albert. Come back after dinner tonight and I'll give you my decision."

"Very good . . . and, well I'm sorry if I flew off the handle a bit."

She smiled unexpectedly. "Are you, Mr. Rolt? I'm not. There's always a lot of truth in a man's anger."

*       *       *       *

Driving back from Otwell Park House, I stopped at the spot where my windscreen had been shattered and had a look around. The road had been recently tarred and gravelled and there were loose drifts of gravel at the verges. For the first time I noticed that there was a fairly deep ditch on the left-hand side of the road and my tyre marks had gone within a couple of inches of it. In a mild way I was annoyed with myself for stopping to look. I wanted no part of Vickers' world. My own was more than enough confused at the moment.

At the hotel I telephoned Rolthead and spoke to Mrs. Cordell, telling her where I was and that I hoped to be back very soon. I had a drink and then an early dinner. After dinner I strolled down to the river for half an hour. I wanted to give Sarah as much time as possible for her telephoning. It was a warm night, the light fading from the sky, and there were quite a few people about. Vickers' words about thinking "dramatically" came into my mind but I pushed them away. That was his world, not mine. There was nothing sinister in the evening or about the people who passed me in the streets or on the quay and riverbank. Anyway, I found myself half wishing

63

that something would happen, that someone would attack me. There was a core of frustration in me which would have welcomed the opportunity for violence.

It was half-past nine when I got back to Otwell Park House. I parked the car at the side of the building and went up to the flat. There was no light on the outside landing and I had to grope to find the switch at the head of the stairs.

I rang the flat bell. There was no answer. I rang it three times, keeping my finger on the button. There was still no answer. I tried the door. It was locked. I banged on it loudly. Anybody inside must have heard my angry blows, but nobody came to the door. For a moment I was tempted to put my shoulder to the door and charge it, but I held myself back and schooled myself to contain the crowd of anxious thoughts that were sweeping through my mind.

I went around to the main entrance. The porter was sitting behind his desk reading an evening newspaper. I asked him if he knew whether Mrs. Starr had gone out. He didn't know. Had she left a message with him for anyone? No, she had not.

"Do you keep duplicate keys of the flats?"

Although I was speaking quite calmly he must have sensed some of the tension in me. He said, "Yes, sir. Why? Is there something wrong?"

"I don't know. But she was expecting me this evening and I can't get any reply. Her car is parked in the garage. I think it would be a sensible thing if you came up and unlocked the flat for me. She may have had an accident and——"

"She might just have gone out for a walk, sir. It's a nice evening."

"So she might." I had to bite down on my impatience. "But if I kick my heels around here for an hour it could be that she is up there all the time needing help. Come on, man, get the key and take me up there. I'll accept full responsibility."

For a moment he looked like arguing. Then he got up and reached to a key-board at the back of his desk. We went up to

64

the flat. He rang the bell twice and when there was no answer he unlocked the door. I went in and he followed me.

The place was in darkness. He switched on the lights as we went through the hall and into the big lounge. He stayed close with me and together we went through the flat. It consisted of the hall, the lounge, a dining-room, a kitchen, a master bedroom with its own bathroom, and a guest room also with its own bathroom. The two bedrooms had small balconies fronting their main windows. Although the windows were shut the porter opened them and looked on to the balconies. There was no sign of Sarah anywhere. The beds were made and the one in the master bedroom had been turned down for the night. There was no indication that any meal had been cooked in the kitchen and the dining-room table was not set for any meal.

Back in the lounge, the porter said, "There's nothing wrong here, sir. I suppose really it was a sensible thing to look and I know Mrs. Starr will understand. She's a very nice easy-going and understanding lady. Fond of walking, too. It's a nice night. She's probably gone off for a stroll. . . ."

I scarcely heard him. I just knew that she had gone. She would never have gone out for a casual stroll knowing that I was coming back—certainly not with the situation as it was between us. I did not know the flat. I had no way of checking whether any clothes or personal belongings had gone. So far as I could tell everything was as it had been when I was last there. The ashtray on the table by the chair in which I had sat still held two of my cigarette ends. I would have liked to have been left on my own, to have gone round the whole flat again methodically by myself, but I could see that this was something which the porter would make a fuss about—and quite rightly. He didn't know me from Adam and he had a responsibility towards the tenants.

He locked up the flat and we went down and it now occurred to me that I might have started a train of thought with the porter which could lead to trouble. The comings and goings of the tenants were no concern of his. But I had now made Sarah's movements of special interest to him. If she did not return he might feel it his duty to tell the police. At the moment I did not want that. It could mean publicity and all sorts of awkwardness. And Vickers I was sure would not want it.

I said, "I expect you're right and she's just gone for a stroll. I'll call her later tonight and check up. If you don't hear from me you'll know that everything is all right."

"Very good, sir."

I handed him a pound note and he went off back to his desk.

I drove back to the hotel not knowing what to think or what to do. She could have gone for a walk. She certainly had enough on her mind to think about . . . more, perhaps, than I could know if she had succeeded in getting Chinn on the telephone. Maybe so much that she had just not felt like facing me that evening. I decided to ring the flat before going to bed and if I got no reply I would go out in the morning and see whether she was there.

I parked my car in the hotel garage. As I came through the hotel hallway, the girl at the reception desk called out, "Mr. Rolt."

I went over to her.

She handed me an envelope. "This came for you a little while ago."

The envelope was addressed to R. Rolt, Esq. I knew the handwriting well. I ripped the envelope open. Inside was a small sheet of paper. On it, unsigned, but in her handwriting, was the message 'Please go back to Rolthead and be patient. I have spoken to Albert.'

I said to the girl, "Who brought this?"

"I don't know, sir. I came in about half an hour ago and it was lying on the counter here."

"Thank you."

I went up to my room and sat on the edge of the bed staring at the sheet of paper.

\*     \*     \*     \*

I left Woodbridge early the next morning. I went out to Otwell Park House. The Audi was still in the garage. I went up to her flat and rang the bell a couple of times but there was no reply.

Before leaving I went round to the porter and told him that Mrs. Starr was all right. She had gone for a walk the previous evening. Also, I said that she was going away and would be gone for some days. He accepted all this without any great show of interest. My only concern was to make certain as far as possible that the events of the previous night and now her absence did not lead to any busybodying on his part with the possibility of the police being called in.

I decided to go to London on my way back to Rolthead. I got there just after mid-day. I garaged the car and went round to my club for lunch. On the way down I had done a lot of hard thinking. Although I had no intention of lending myself to any course of action which Vickers might secretly have in mind, I had decided that it was only proper that he should know of this latest development. For myself—hate it though I did—I was prepared to accept Sarah's request to be patient. The phrase held a note of hope for me. I would have given anything to know what had passed between her and Albert Chinn. Whatever it was it had been of such a nature, I guessed, to make her want to have a few days' peace and quiet to sort things out for herself. I could accept no other construction. However, I considered it only reasonable to let Vickers know the present situation. I called him on his Foreign Office extension and caught him just as he was on his way out to lunch. For a moment I was tempted to invite him to lunch with me, but decided against it. The less time I spent in his company at the moment the better, I thought. I asked him to come round and have some coffee with me at the club after he had had lunch.

The club servant eventually called me out to him in the hall. His face was untidy with his growing beard, but he was wearing a dark city suit and held an umbrella and a bowler hat in his hand. I took him up the main stairway and found an empty alcove in the wide gallery just under the glass rotunda which lit the hall below.

When the coffee had been served and we were alone I described what had happened the previous evening and then handed him Sarah's note. He glanced at it and then dropped it onto the table.

I said, "What do you make of that?"

He scratched his chin and said hesitantly, "There could be various explanations, naturally. Which one do you favour?"

I said sharply, "What the hell do you mean—which one do I favour?"

He sighed, tugged nervously at his tie-knot and gave a bleak smile. "Sorry—but it's a perfectly reasonable remark. From where I sit, Mr. Rolt, I could present you with two or three hypotheses. You mustn't bark at me because you're only prepared to accept one. What we're both after is the truth?"

"Of course. And it seems clear to me that Sarah—I can't go on damned-well calling her Mrs. Starr—got in touch with this Chinn fellow and he had to come clean, to confess that he had used her, invented a false life for her. That would be a devil of a shock for her and the only thing she wanted to do then was to go off for a few days and think it over and get used to the idea that she was certainly not Angela Starr. That she was Sarah Rolt. In similar circumstances I think that's what I would have done. By God, I'd like to get my hands on that bastard Chinn."

"No doubt." He smiled. "I hope you do one day. Yes, I think it's a very credible interpretation. But there could be others. Anyway they are of no importance at the moment. The thing is that Mrs. Rolt has gone off into the blue. All you can do is to sit at Rolthead and wait for her to turn up. I'm sure she will."

"So am I."

"But I should warn you that that doesn't necessarily mean she'll come back with her memory restored. She will then be relying on your word and all the evidence you can bring—

entirely conclusive, we know—to start building a new life for herself."

"She'll get the best treatment I can give her. Sooner or later she'll be cured. I won't even begin to think of any other possibility."

"Naturally. All I ask is that you keep an open mind." He pulled a long white envelope from his pocket and passed it over to me. "That's her statement you kindly let me have. We've made a copy. We haven't started to check up on the facts stated in it yet. But I'm certain when we do they will all be false. A clever Chinn concoction, shall we say. But there is one thing I must tell you—in fairness to you."

"What in God's name have you got up your sleeve now?"

"Another piece of Chinn's cooking, maybe. Our lab boys did a quick analysis of the paper, writing and ink this morning. They'd go on oath in court and testify that that statement was written not earlier than two months ago."

"Well, why not?" I demanded. "She didn't say when it was written."

"Would you—if you had had such an experience and wanted to remember it—have waited all that time?"

"How the devil would I know what I would have done? Are you suggesting this statement is something she's invented—that she's a liar?"

"I'd be a rash man to suggest it in your present mood, Mr. Rolt. All I can put to you is that—against her will—she may have done things and said things which . . . well, which she was forced to, possibly for her own protection." He stood up. "We'd be glad if you would let us know when your wife turns up at Rolthead. We shan't interfere. But if you need any help you can always call on us."

Although I was angry, it wasn't anger against him. It was against the whole tangled, confusing situation. Following an impulse, I said, "You or your people know a damned sight more than you're prepared to tell me at the moment, don't you?"

69

He considered this, one hand dangling his coffee spoon over his cup. He nodded. "Yes, we do. But there's nothing we know which would be of any help to you or Mrs. Rolt at the moment." He paused, fingered his chin nervously, and then said, "I'm not giving away any secrets if I tell you that there is a great deal more behind all this than the original disappearance of your wife and her loss of memory. All I can tell you is that there are two schools of thought as to the real truth—and there isn't a penny to choose between them at the moment."

"And what about Sarah? If you think she's not innocent of any underhand business, then you'd better say so frankly. It'll clear the air and I'll know where I stand!"

To my surprise he grinned, and nodded towards the iron-work balustrade that ran round the edge of the rotunda gallery, and said, "With that drop down the stairwell only six feet away? I'm not crazy. But I will be frank. I could easily dislike you, Mr. Rolt. I expected to when we first met. But I don't. I genuinely like you. So I'll tell you what I believe to be the truth about your wife. I think—without any choice on her part—she strayed into no-man's land and for the time being she is still pinned down by the crossfire from either side."

"That tells me a hell of a lot. But thank you anyway for your frankness."

When he was gone I went into the bar and had a large brandy. As I pulled out my wallet for a note to pay the barman, a visiting card slipped free from one of the smaller pockets on to the counter. I retrieved it. It was the card which Sarah had given me with the name and address of the professor she had talked about and whom she still saw once a month.

'Sir Hugh F. Gleeson, Abbey House, Upper Chute, Wilts.' I knew vaguely where Upper Chute was, and that it would not be a long detour on my way back to Rolthead. As I sipped my brandy I realised that I was not in a hurry to get back. There would be no Sarah there.

When my brandy was finished I went into the club library and looked up Upper Chute on a map. I got down a copy of

*Who's Who* and found the entry for Gleeson. Against the simplicity of his private visiting card I had to smile when I read the entry under his name. He was Sir Hugh Frank Gleeson, K.B.E., and there was a good four-inch entry under his name. He had been born in 1895 which made him close to eighty years old. He was an M.A., D.M. (Oxon) and a F.R.C.P. (London) and had been educated at Rugby and New College, Oxford, and had trained at Guy's Hospital, London. He had been in the First World War (Médaille Militaire) and there was a whole string of appointments, qualifications and publications. He had at varying times been, among many other things, the Medical Registrar of Guy's Hospital, the Visiting Neurologist to Johns Hopkins Hospital, a Sims Travelling Commonwealth Professor, Harveian Orator, a Membre Correspondent de la Société de Neurologie de Paris, and a Director of the Psychological Laboratory, Cambridge. His recreations were given as astronomy and fly-fishing. His address was as on his card, but unlike the card it gave his telephone number.

My first intention was to telephone and ask if I might call in on him on my way. I decided against that. He would not know me from Adam and if I mentioned Mrs. Angela Starr some professional ethic could well make him close up on me. It is much easier to put down the telephone quickly than it is to shut the door in the face of a man who stands on your front step. I wanted to see him and I was not in the mood for any rebuffs. If he were not at home I could always come back. Sarah had said that she liked him very much and I had a feeling that, if he were at home, he would not turn me away.

\*     \*     \*     \*

It took me two and a half hours to reach Upper Chute. Abbey House was a bleak, stone-built house standing in a small area of parkland on the ridge of the downs and facing southwards.

A dark-suited manservant answered the door to me. I gave

71

him my card and said that I would be glad if he would ask Sir Hugh Gleeson if he could spare me a little time on a private matter. I was lucky. He was in and he was willing to see me.

The manservant took me down a long hall hung with oil paintings and into a large, mullion-windowed study which looked southwards over the falling downs and forest sweeps. I didn't at first pay much attention to the furnishings of the study, but I did notice a desk in the window which had a small fly-tyer's vice clamped to it and a litter of feathers and silks spread around. From the way the chair in front of it had been half pushed back I guessed that Sir Hugh had been tying flies.

He stood by the fireplace now, held out a hand and welcomed me, and then waved me to a chair. He remained standing. He was a tall, grey-haired man and despite a slight stoop to his shoulders there was an almost military bearing about him. His face was lined and heavily dewlapped and his eyes under shaggy brows were a bright china blue. In private he was clearly disregardful of his dress. He wore a shabby green velvet jacket and wrinkled cavalry twill trousers.

He looked at my card and then put it on the mantelpiece behind him and said, "Are you Henry Rolt's boy?"

I said, "Yes, Sir Hugh, I am. Did you know him?"

"On and off. Not close friends. But I always liked meeting him. Always had some good story to tell. You got the same knack?"

"I'm afraid not, Sir Hugh. At least, not any amusing story. But I have got a story I would like to tell you."

"A sobersides, eh? And why, out of the blue, do you come here and want to tell me a story? I was just in the middle of tying a Green Highlander. Going to Scotland next week. Still fish, you know. Though everyone tries to tell me I'm decrepit, and the ghillies have heart failure when I take a wading stick and get in the river."

"I want to tell you this story because, frankly, I hope you can help me."

"Is it a long story?"

"I'll keep it as brief as I can. Some of it you will know already."

"Will I now?" He looked at his watch, and went on, "Too late for tea, too early for whisky. We'll have to make do with sherry."

He went to an untidy sidetable, picked up a house telephone and called his manservant. "Martie, bring us a bottle of sherry and a couple of glasses. Don't muck around with silver trays and decanters." Putting the telephone down, he said to me, "I take it you're the one who took over when your brother died."

"Yes, I am, Sir Hugh."

"Foreign Office, weren't you?"

"Only briefly."

"Regret leaving it?"

"No, I don't, Sir Hugh."

"Very sensible."

He eased himself stiffly into an armchair, pulled out a battered packet of cigarettes and lit himself one. He jerked his head at me and said, "Smoke if you want to. You wouldn't like these. They're herbal but that doesn't stop 'em from making me cough like hell at times."

I lit a cigarette and began to tell him my story. At some time during the telling his manservant came in with a silver tray on which were a decanter of sherry and two very fine Waterford glasses.

I made the telling as plain and short as possible. I left out a great many things, mostly about Vickers and the Foreign Office, and I glossed over the episode of the films which I had been shown which had led to the discovery of Sarah. But I did make it clear that I thought Albert Chinn had taken advantage of Sarah's loss of memory to impose a new identity on her.

He listened to all I had to say without interruption, leaning forward in his chair, cupping his hands on top of an old knob-ended hickory stick which had rested against the side of the sherry table. When I had finished, he leaned over and refilled his glass, looked at mine which was practically untouched, and then said, "Do you know the good book well?"

"The Bible?"

"What other good book is there? When Martie brought your card in I was busy. Busy and happy doing a small but pleasant work. I guessed you could be Henry Rolt's boy, but that didn't make you a good reason for not getting two or three salmon flies tied before dinner. I was going to have him tell you I was out—and then I remembered something from the good book. Somewhere it says, 'Be not forgetful to entertain strangers; for thereby some have entertained angels unaware'."

"I'm no angel, I'm afraid, Sir Hugh."

"How do we know what we are? Anyway, I won't press the point. You're obviously a practical, logical man. No nonsense. But don't give up hope. Some day you might understand. More things in heaven and earth. That kind of thing."

Frankly I didn't know what the devil he was talking about, but he had been kind to me and I wanted his help. Old men may be full of wisdom, but they often stray from the point. In my present mood I only had one concern.

I said, "I'm grateful to you for seeing me. And that's the story. Frankly, I don't know whether I'm on my head or my heels except that I know without any shadow of doubt that Mrs. Angela Starr is my wife Sarah."

"And you're going back to Rolthead now to wait for her to turn up?"

"Yes."

"You have no doubt she will?"

"Absolutely none."

"That's a demonstration of faith. A good sign. And what do you want from me?"

"God knows, Sir Hugh. At some moments I'm completely adrift. I suppose I want hope from you—I'd like you to go on treating her. Or advise me who should. But most of all I need some explanation, some promise—or hope anyway—that she will eventually come back to herself. This is not selfishly for me. It's for her."

He nodded. "Don't mind if I speak like some old sage of the mountains, my boy. But I can see that you're a stiff, obstinate character when you bite into a problem. You'd damn the eyes of any man who got in your way if you thought you were on the right path, wouldn't you?"

"Well, yes—I suppose I would. If I knew I was right."

"The trouble, Rolt, is that there are many paths of truth. And they often cross one another and people find themselves face to face, each sure of his own truth. Who gives way then?"

I held down my impatience. I hadn't come here for moral philosophy. I wanted help. If all he could do was to beat around the bush I was wasting my time.

He clearly guessed my thoughts because he smiled and said, "I'm sorry. I'm confusing you. That's unpardonable. So, I'll be quite straightforward. Yes, when your wife returns bring her to see me. I know all about her as Mrs. Starr. In my files I've got her case history—and from a professional point of view it's a very unusual one, but not unique. I'm not going to try and explain it to you. There are many forms of amnesia and brain damage—by the way, I am quite sure that there is no brain damage as far as your wife is concerned. That was established by her Manchester neurologist. It would do no good to you to talk of fugue states, pathological wandering or the long- and short-term effects of psychogenic amnesia or any other forms of memory loss. You wouldn't be a penny the wiser. All you want to know is whether she'll ever be herself again. Right?"

"Yes, of course."

"Well, I'm not God. He's the top consultant, but I'm prepared, arrogantly maybe, respectfully to anticipate him. Yes, I think she will return to normal."

"When?"

"The obvious question. But you may not like the answer. I think her loss of memory could well be a form of self-punishment which she has inflicted on herself out of guilt feelings."

"Guilt! In God's name what should she have to be guilty about?" I was sorry for the outburst but it was done.

He was silent for a moment or two and then said quietly, "Did two paths of truth cross then? Did another traveller get in your way?"

"I'm sorry, Sir Hugh. Please forgive me."

"Forget it, my boy. As for the guilt—if one knew what it was it would make things easier naturally. But, if it will put your mind at ease, I must point out that there are a thousand forms of guilt which have nothing to do with the law and are in no way indictable offences. You can be guilty of giving or taking too much love. You can be guilty of being helpless or of ignorance. Arrogance, pride . . . hundreds of 'em. Some people even feel guilty of being too happy. Do you get me?"

"Yes, yes I do." And I suppose I did in a general way, but I couldn't see how it could have anything to do with losing one's memory, or deliberately throwing it away. I certainly at this moment in time didn't want to get involved in metaphysics or whatever. It was enough that he thought that Sarah would get her memory back. That was hope. That was what I wanted. There were other things too. I said, "Do you mind if I ask you a few questions, Sir Hugh? If I step over . . . well, the bounds of professional ethics?"

"If you do, I'll just shut you up, Rolt. So ask your questions."

"There's this man, Albert Chinn, who says he's her brother. Did you ever meet him?"

"Yes. I knew him in a very casual way. That's why, when she'd finished with her neurologist and all the obvious forms of treatment, he brought her to me.'

"May I ask how you knew him?"

"Through dealing. . . ." He smiled and rubbed the knob of his stick against the side of his nose. "You don't know it, but I have a passion for portraits. Old portraits and not done by any famous painters. Just the kind of thing you still can find in old country houses like this. England and the Continent are stuffed full of 'em. Some of them are very good and some awful,

76

but it pleases me to collect such as I can afford. I first met Chinn at a country-house sale. He arrived just too late to bid for a painting I had bought. He tried to buy it privately from me afterwards, but I wouldn't sell. I saw him then at various times at other sales and . . . well, we had a limited acquaintance. Eventually he brought your wife to me."

"Was he a professional dealer?"

"I gathered not. An amateur like me. So far as I knew he was something to do with some oil company and he lived near Woodbridge. I know you're not going to accept this in view of the circumstances, but he was a nice fellow. I liked him. But that means nothing. I like a lot of dubious characters."

"You thought he was dubious?"

"Not at the time. But from what you tell me it would seem so."

"Have you seen him lately?"

"Not for well over eighteen months."

"I'm sorry to persist, but could you describe him?"

"Of course. I'd say he was getting on for his fifties. Middle height. Well built. Well spoken. Biggish face. He had dark, very straight hair and a very close-clipped moustache and well-trimmed beard. I always assumed he was English but that he had a touch of vanity about him so far as his appearance was concerned. Wanted to look a little Continental. He was a very intelligent man. Widely read. You may not know it but I'm a bit of an amateur astronomer. He had the same interest but he knew far more about it than I do."

"Can you think of any reason why he should have invented this fictitious past for my wife?"

He shook his head. "I find it very odd. But then there is no end to the oddness of human beings. For some reason it suited his book."

I asked him a few more questions and then took my leave of him. He came with me into the hall. It was a lofty, gloomy place with a wide stone stairway running up from it. He stopped when we were half-way down it. He looked at me in silence for a moment or two, almost as though he were debating

77

the wisdom of some course that had suddenly occurred to him.

Then, clearly making up his mind, he said, "You're good, solid Dorset stock, Rolt. A no-nonsense family. Feet firmly on the ground. And an admirable thing, too. But here you are suddenly right up to your neck in a situation you could never have dreamed of for yourself."

"Well, I won't argue with that."

"Let me show you something—not to further confuse you, or even to suggest anything. Just something which I found most intriguing. Take a look at that."

He raised his stick and pointed to an oil painting which hung to one side of the hall fireplace, one in a row of others and brightly lit by an overhead light at the top of the frame. It showed a dark-haired woman. Her hair was drawn back in two smooth wings on either side of her head and then tied with a ribbon behind her neck. She was wearing a long, dove-grey dress that hid her feet as she sat on a high-backed chair. There was a diamond cluster, star-shaped, on a black narrow band around her neck. Behind her chair was a wide window with rose-red curtains drawn back. Through the window there was a conventional piece of parkland showing and a man on horse-back in the distance. She sat on the chair holding a fan in her right hand. Her left arm was along the side of the chair, her hand resting on the moulding at the end of the arm. At her feet was a small King Charles spaniel type of dog. On the bottom of the frame was a gilt plaque with an inscription on it in black lettering.

I stepped forward a pace to read the inscription and Sir Hugh said, "It's by a man called Hever. I know a little about him. Although he was only a journeyman painter he had something. He made a living travelling around the country doing family portraits. I've got a couple more of his. They fetch somewhere between fifty and a hundred pounds. That's the painting which Chinn wanted. He offered me a great deal more than I'd paid for it. For my own reasons I wouldn't sell. Do you like it?"

"Yes, I do. It's very pleasant. She looks a calm, peaceful sort of woman." As I spoke I was reading the inscription: 'Miss Evangeline Santora of Great Park in the County of Worcester. 1820.'

I stepped back, my eyes going up to the painting again. It was then that I saw something which made me turn quickly towards Sir Hugh.

Before I could say anything he shook his head, silencing me, and said, "Good—you're an observant man, Rolt. So am I." He jerked his head at the painting. "There it is—and I can tell you it's not due to bad draughtsmanship. Hever was a good draughtsman if nothing else. Now then, off you go and let me get back to my flies. When your wife comes back, just give me a call."

I drove down the drive, wondering why he had given me the chance to see it. Miss Evangeline Santora's left hand resting on the chair arm was exactly the same as that of Sarah's, the short Saturn finger clearly showing.

## CHAPTER FIVE

ON THE WAY back to Rolthead I decided that for the time being it would be wise to say nothing to any of my family or Mrs. Cordell about Sarah. (I had a younger married brother who farmed two thousand acres about twenty miles from Rolthead. He had two children, both boys, one still at preparatory school and the other at public school, Marlborough to be exact. I had also a sister, two years older than myself, who had married a naval officer. At the moment she was living in Plymouth where her husband was based. They had one child, a daughter of nineteen. There were, of course, more distantly related Rolts spread through the county and elsewhere.)

There was no point, I felt, in saying anything to them. The situation was puzzling enough to me without their conjectures and curiosities being added to it. But there was one person who I felt had to be told, and that was Sarah's mother.

So, that evening after dinner I went into my study to write to her. Before beginning I looked at the painting which Bordino had done of Sarah. As she leaned against the balustrade of the stone steps her left arm fell loosely at her side and part of her skirt masked the fingers of her left hand. Bordino had posed her like that and I knew that he had been too observant an artist not to have noticed her Saturn finger. He had said nothing about it. Sir Hugh Gleeson's honest journeyman painter Hever, I had a feeling, would have been equally observant and tactful, but Miss Evangeline Santora obviously had not cared a damn about her peculiarity being portrayed. She was clearly a woman of some character.

I wrote a long letter to Sarah's mother telling her what had happened. I didn't give her all the facts, any more than I had done with Sir Hugh. Nevertheless it was a pretty fair overall account except for the involvement of Vickers and the implications that arose from his professional interest in Albert Chinn.

When I had finished I sat there thinking about her mother. I had always felt that Alexina Vallis had never been sincerely reconciled to our marriage. There was never any discord between us now, but there was always an awareness in me that I was not the type—perhaps not the character—she had cherished in her mind when she had day-dreamed of—or, more likely, practically considered—the kind of husband that Sarah would one day marry. (In fact the man to whom Sarah had been engaged was—so Sarah had told me—really her mother's choice. He was an Italian, a self-made man, who had perfected certain new processes in the development of plastics, had started his own company for their manufacture, and had become very successful.) Even after Sarah and I had been forgiven by Alexina for eloping and marrying, her manner had for a long time worried me and I had mentioned it to my father. He had dismissed it as imagination. He got along very well with her, but then he did with all women, having a quiet charm and an instinctive gallantry which were foreign to me. Anyway, as he pointed out, it was a well-known psychological thing that all mothers were basically antagonistic towards the men who wanted to take their daughters from them. I was amused when he told me this because it clearly worked in reverse, too. I knew that through his Foreign Office connections (although he was retired at this time) he had made it his business to learn all he could about the dead banker Vallis, Sarah's stepfather. His standing had been impeccable and his fortune had passed to Sarah and her mother.

After I had finished the letter, since there was still some light left in the evening sky, I called up the house-dog, Frannie, and went for a stroll through the grounds across to the lake which I had had made for Sarah. There was a small island in the centre on which a summerhouse had been built. Trout were rising to a hatch of flies along the line of sedges that fringed the island. In the air above the water a few bats were hawking in erratic flight. Suddenly, on the far side of the lake, a nightingale began to sing from a thick growth of tall hazelnut stands. The bird's sudden music brought a lump to my throat. Sarah and I had often walked this way after dinner and heard the nightingales suddenly greet the closing dusk. I turned away and went through a wicket gate and along a path that led up to the first slopes of the downs. I let the dog run ahead, questing in the bracken and gorse clumps for rabbits. To the side of the path, about fifty yards ahead of me, there was a clump of fir trees, their silhouettes dark and metallic against the pale sky where the stars were now beginning to strengthen. When the dog was about ten yards from the trees, it suddenly stopped, its hackles went up and it began to growl, its lowered head pointing towards the firs. As I came up to it, Frannie suddenly rushed forward a few yards, stopped, and began to bark furiously.

I put my hand in my pocket and felt for the torch which I always carried on any evening walk. Although the land on this part of the downs was mine, the path was a public right of way. I called the dog to heel and it came, reluctantly. Then I went forward. There were only four or five trees, the trunks bare for about six feet above the ground before the foliage began. The light was good enough for me to see anything which might break cover in any direction from the clump. All I had in mind was the possibility of a poacher. There were always a few of the last season's pheasants hanging about and I knew that they sometimes roosted in the clump.

I flicked on the torch and walked into the trees with the dog at my heels. As I passed the first tree, I swung the torch about and saw a black shape, clearly that of a man, edge out from the cover of a tree and begin to move away from me. I called to him and swung the torch sideways to cover him with the light. As I did so the torch went out either because I'd clumsily released the press switch or because the movement had temporarily jerked the battery inside the case, breaking the contact. I banged the torch on my thigh and pressed the switch hard. The light came on. I walked forward, swinging the beam from left to right, but there was no one to be seen. On the far side of the trees I crouched down so that I could bring the whole sweep of the downside into silhouette against the pale sky. I must have been able to see anyone running away clearly against the sky. But there was no one and no sound of anyone running. I was pretty sure that it must have been a poacher. Whatever he was he was a fast mover and had known how to take advantage of the cover of the bracken and gorse growths on the down. I went back through the trees, flashing the torch along the ground which was covered with pine needles, but the place had been used by walkers and picnic parties so that it was not possible to pick out any new prints, not even my own.

It was then that I realised that the dog was not with me. It had stayed on the far side of the trees instead of coming in at my heels as it should have done. I went back to it. It was lying on the ground a yard from the first tree. It was stretched out on its side, its eyes open, and its tongue hanging out as it panted hard as though it had just finished a long chase. For a moment, seeing the stiffness of its front legs I thought it had had a fit. It was a pretty highly bred spaniel that had never been much good with a gun but I had kept it as a house-dog. I crouched down beside it. As I did so, it slowly rolled over and then stood up. I fondled its head and ears for a moment or two and then rose and called it to follow. It came obediently to heel and we walked back down the path to Rolthead together.

I was not unduly concerned about Frannie. Some spaniels are very excitable and can throw a brief fit, but I was annoyed about the torch. I like the things about me to work properly and clearly the torch had become faulty.

It was only much later, remembering Vickers' advice, that it occurred to me to think dramatically. But when I did I couldn't give it much importance . . . an expert poacher, knowing how to use ground and fast on his feet, a faulty torch, and an unreliable overbred dog. I had enough mystery on my hands already without trying to make more.

*    *    *    *

For the next four or five days, I occupied myself with my usual affairs at Rolthead. It was a busy time of the year and there was plenty to do. But it would be idle to say that I immersed myself in my work. Work was only a partial anodyne. I had the utmost faith that Sarah would come back soon. Although—to me—it was a drastic step she had taken I could understand that the bombshell of her true identity, plus whatever Chinn might have said to her on the telephone, could easily have made her want nothing more than a week or so to be alone and to sort things out in her own mind.

However, during those days, in each morning's post I looked first for a letter in her handwriting. Whenever the telephone bell rang there was a moment of high hope in me before I picked it up. And sometimes I would find myself standing at the study window, looking down the drive, waiting for the sight of the Audi or a taxi to come clear of the trees by the lodge gates.

During this period Vickers telephoned me twice to see if Sarah had returned. Our conversations were brief. But he did tell me that his department had put a man to watch Otwell Park House. Nobody had been back to the flat since Sarah had left. He made no mention of any investigations into the details of the past life of Mrs. Angela Starr which Albert Chinn had created, and I did not ask about them. For me Mrs. Angela Starr never had existed.

The telephone call I constantly hoped for came from an unexpected quarter, eight days after my return, when I was in my study at eleven o'clock at night. It was a long-distance call, from Sarah's mother in Amalfi. I recognised her voice

85

at once and, since I had had no reply to my letter to her, I at first felt that she was calling to discuss it. But I was wrong.

She said, "Robert?"

"Yes, Alexina?" It had taken us a long time to come to first-name calling. "How are you? You had my letter safely?"

"Yes, I did, Robert. I think you should come out right away. Sarah arrived here this morning."

I was speechless. It was the last thing I had anticipated— but at once it seemed obvious to me. Why the devil hadn't I thought of it?

I said, "Thank God for that. How is she? Is she all right? Put her on, I'd like to speak to her."

For a moment there was silence on the other end and then her voice, precise and a little accented, came: "You can't speak to her now. She's sleeping."

"What about her memory? Does she know who she is?"

Very deliberately, she said, "She accepts who she is. But her memory is no better. When will you come?"

"Right away. I'll motor up to London tonight and take my chance of getting a flight."

"Good. She knows I'm calling you. I'll tell her in the morning you're coming."

"Thank God she's with you. . . . Give her my love and tell her I'm on my way."

"Of course."

She rang off without saying any more, but I was well used to her rather abrupt manner on the telephone. The only thing that concerned me was to get to Italy as fast as possible.

I called Vickers' number at the Foreign Office. The duty clerk answered. Vickers was not there. I said I had to get in touch with him urgently and would like his home telephone number. The duty clerk said he couldn't give it to me, but if I hung up he would arrange for Vickers to call me within half an hour. I then rang Dorchester and arranged for a car to

86

come out right away and take me up to London. I saw Mrs. Cordell and told her that I had just had a message from Sarah's mother asking me to go out at once and see her.

Mrs. Cordell, who had been at Rolthead since I was a boy and knew to a fine point what liberties she could take because of it, said, "Is it something to do with Madame, sir?"

"Yes, it is, Mrs. Cordell. But I'd like that just kept between us for the time being."

"I'll go up and pack a bag for you, sir. If there's anything special you want to go in you must let me know."

"Just pack the usual things."

Ten minutes later Vickers called me. I told him that Sarah had turned up at her mother's villa. I was leaving for London almost at once and would he book a flight for me on the earliest plane I could catch for Rome or Naples. Whichever one he got I would like a hired, self-drive car waiting for me. He promised that he would arrange it all and would himself be at the airport.

When I got to Heathrow it was four o'clock in the morning and sure enough Vickers was there. He had me booked on a held-over flight to Rome that was leaving at five o'clock and had arranged the hired car.

As he handed me the flight tickets he said, "One of our men will be at the other end, Mr. Rolt. He'll fix you up with any *lire* you want . . . in fact give you any assistance you ask for."

"That's kind of you."

"Not at all. Part of the service. Do you know if your wife has regained her memory?"

It was the first personal question he had asked me.

"I'm told not."

"I see. The man who will meet you in Rome will give you his phone number. If you want any help of any kind at any time just ring him."

By ten o'clock that morning I was driving fast down the A2 to Naples. I knew the route well because I had driven down it

87

many times with Sarah . . . Frascati, Frosinone and Capua where Pompey had wintered his troops . . . I could smile at that thought because it had first been told me by my father who was passionately fond of all history.

Alexina Vallis' villa was off the coast road between Positano and Amalfi. It was called the Villa Mendola and was set about two hundred feet up in the hills overlooking the sea. It was reached by a short length of twisting loose-stoned road which turned into a torrent in the bad weather. There was a large terraced garden which ran almost down to the coast road. The villa itself was set back on a small plateau that had been blasted out of the hillside. Although the gardens and the setting high above the sea were beautiful, the house itself was almost ugly. It was two floors high, capped with a shallow-pitched slate roof and the walls were covered with a hideous dull-red-colour wash. Vallis, the banker, had bought it some time before he married Alexina, as a summer house. He had married late and had died within ten years of his marriage. Alexina had kept it on—although they had a permanent house in Athens and another on one of the islands. In the end she had sold all her Greek property and retired to the Villa Mendola which she refused to alter in any way. It was kept just as it had been in Vallis' days. Alexina lived there with a small staff. She had visited Rolthead only rarely since I had married Sarah.

It was well past two o'clock when I drove up the twisting hill road and through the open wrought-iron drive gates. The terrace which fronted the house was cut with a row of arches covered with a growth of bougainvillaea and plumbago. A wide flight of steps came down from the semi-circular formal garden that fronted the house.

As I got out of the car, I saw that Alexina was waiting for me at the top of the steps. I gave her a wave of my hand and began to go up to her. Driving down in the car and thinking things over, I had, with difficulty, forced myself to acknowledge that although Sarah had come back, her return—since she still had no memory of our life together—could not mean any change or advance in the relationship which had been established between us at Otwell Park House. The exercise of any lover's spontaneity was denied me. It was a damned difficult thing to accept.

Alexina held out her hands to me and, as I took them, I leaned forward and kissed her on the cheek. It was a greeting long established. She was always friendly, cool—but immutably remote. And this not only with me. Even with Sarah, in public, there had always been an undemonstrative politeness and reserve which had surprised me at first until I realised that there was a strong bond between them.

After our first words of greeting, I said, "Where's Sarah?"

"She's in her room. She'll be down in a moment. Have you had lunch?"

I lied. "I stopped for a quick bite on the road. How is she?"

"Very much, I imagine, as she was when you last saw her. Now, Robert, you must, before you see her, make me a promise. This is a difficult situation for both of you. But I know you. You think if you go charging into a problem it will be solved by the sheer force of your attack. Well, clearly, this one won't. You've got to be patient, and then even more patient . . . I'm sorry, Robert, but I have to say that. Remember, although she's your wife—she's also my daughter."

I wasn't angry with her. She had a right to speak as she did. I said, "You needn't worry, Alexina. At first I might have been like that. But I've had time now to adjust."

"Splendid. I'll have Tino take your things up and then bring you some coffee out here. Later we can have a family discussion, but I think it better if you see Sarah alone first. I'll make myself scarce."

She gave me a cool smile and walked away. She was a tall, attractive woman, well preserved for her age. Anyone would have put her at an easy forty rather than well into her fifties. There wasn't a touch of grey in her hair. (Sarah's ash-blonde had come from her father. But in looks mother and daughter were very much alike and both had the same dark violet-blue eyes and the same way of holding themselves and moving.)

I sat down in the shade at one of the terrace tables. Tino, the elderly house-servant, came out, greeted me and brought my case up from the car. A little later, in his white jacket and white gloves, he served me with coffee.

I drank some, sitting there looking out over the garden and the drop to the sea. Dark cloud shadows raced across it. A couple of lizards flirted about the terrace steps and the sun burnished the young growths of the vines on the distant slopes of the hills. I loved the place, not only for its beauty, but because it was here that I had first properly met Sarah and it was in the garden below that I had eventually under a purple-dark night sky asked her to marry me and had been accepted. Thinking back to that moment it was hard to accept the reality of the present. But it did seem fitting that it should be here, where we had first met, that the first steps of her return to me should be taken. We were to begin again and—as we had done before —learn to know one another and to share and face the problems that our life together would bring.

Even as I was thinking this, Sarah came out from the house. I stood up, but held back the instinctive desire to run to her. She paused for a moment looking towards me. Her hair was loose about her neck and she was wearing a plain short-sleeved white cotton blouse and the blue skirt which she had had on when Bordino painted her. (I don't know whether this was from design or accident, or whether perhaps Alexina had obliquely influenced the choice. Sarah always had kept a well-stocked wardrobe permanently at the villa. Accident or design, it seemed a good omen to me.)

She came across to me and I held out both my hands to her.

"Sarah."

Without any embarrassment she took my hands, held them briefly and said, "Robert . . ."

The use of my name filled me with happiness.

She sat down in the chair opposite me and went on, "You

90

got down here in good time. Are you tired?" Her voice was calm, a natural calmness, no sign of its being forced since she was schooling herself to accept the situation of our being man and wife because it could not be denied.

"No, I'm not tired—just happy."

Seeing my empty coffee cup, she picked up the pot and refilled it for me. With her head lowered a little as she did so, she said, "I was sorry to go away from Otwell Park House like that. But I just had to. After what happened I just had to be on my own and decide what to do."

"After what happened?"

"I told you in my note. I spoke to Albert. Or rather he spoke to me. I'd tried to get him two or three times at the New York number and there was no reply. Then out of the blue, he called me——"

"Where from and what did he say?"

"I don't know where from, but I had a feeling that it wasn't a long-distance call. The phone just rang and I picked it up and it was Albert speaking. And then almost before I had begun to tell him why I wanted to speak to him he told me that he didn't want to hear. That he knew all about the situation."

"How the devil could he have done?"

"I don't know. I wasn't concerned about that because I asked him point blank whether it was true that I was really Sarah Rolt and not Angela Starr. He said that I was Sarah Rolt."

"Didn't he explain things? You must have asked him."

"Of course I did. But he said that explaining things wouldn't help me. He just said, 'You are without doubt Sarah Rolt. Just go back and start being her again.' Then he rang off. The whole thing was very odd. He didn't seem angry or disappointed . . . or anything. It was just Albert as he always was. 'Just go back and start being her again' were his words and then he gave a little laugh and rang off."

I said angrily, "I'd like to meet Albert Chinn one of these days. The man's a monster."

91

Sarah nodded. "He must be. But somehow I can't make myself think of him except as . . . well, the man I knew and liked. Anyway, when he rang off, I just felt that I wanted to go away and sort things out in my mind. I did . . . I mean, I went away—but I didn't get very far with sorting things out. So—" she looked at me and smiled—"I decided to do what a lot of girls in trouble do—go home to Mother."

"When you got back here and saw her, talked to her and couldn't be in any doubt that she knew you were her daughter —didn't anything come back? Any trace of the past?"

"No. Nothing at all."

I stood up and said, "Sarah, come with me."

"Where?"

"You'll see." I reached out and took her hand. I led her down through the garden to the exact spot where one evening years before we had stood. It was a little round garden with small beds of herbs enclosed by dwarf hedges of box. In the centre was a shallow ornamental pond with a piece of sculpture in the centre showing Triton surrounded by dolphins. Tall, graceful eucalyptus trees sheltered one side of the garden.

We stood together by the pond. A fountain that sprang from one of the dolphins' mouths sent a thin, silvery curve into the air and the sun touched the spray with yellow fire.

Still holding her hand, I said, "This is where I asked you to marry me all those years ago. As much as you loved your mother, knew her disapproval of me, you abandoned your engagement and ran away with me. We loved one another and we were married. We were happy. This is where it all began."

"And I can remember nothing of it."

"You will one day. But this is where I want it all to begin again. I love you and I can be patient. All I want to know is whether you feel that you can make a beginning from here. Even though you are my legal wife nobody can force you. Without any memory of the past, you must look inside yourself and then look at me and say either Yes or No."

She was silent. She looked away from me, raising her eyes to the narrow, rustling leaves of the eucalyptus trees as though in the wind murmurings there might be some message for her.

Then she looked at me and said, "Yes, I want to begin again." Her voice broke for a moment with a deep, body-racking sob. "Dear God, I must begin again!"

\*     \*     \*     \*

After dinner that night we had a family conference. Alexina and Sarah were practical women, they liked their affairs to be in order and if they could see problems ahead they had to make immediate plans to deal with them. Of the two, though, it was Alexina who, in her firm manner, was more dominant and forthright. In the interests of truth she could be embarrassingly outspoken when it suited her. Before dinner, while Sarah was still up in her room changing, and we were having a drink together, she had made it as much as I could do to control my anger with her.

Out of the blue she said, "Because Sarah has accepted the situation between the two of you, it doesn't of course mean that you can resume your old relationship as though it had never been interrupted. You know what I mean?"

"Of course I do! For God's sake, Alexina, what do you take me for?" I really was angry.

She shook her head, smiling. "You don't, you know. Naturally you wouldn't expect it to be that way now. But you do feel that fairly soon, as you get to know one another again, it will happen. Possibly you feel that the sooner it happens the better —that physical intimacy might in some way be part of the process of bringing her back to herself."

"Alexina, I don't know that I really want to discuss this with you."

"I know you don't. It's not done. Well, I won't discuss it with you further. But I will tell you what I think, whether you like it or not. Until Sarah has her memory back—anything you take or she gives you can never be real. The gifts will come

93

from kindness on both sides. Don't glare at me like that, Robert. Until Sarah has her memory back nothing can be real between you as far as being man and wife is concerned. You must face that and act by it."

"Thank you, Alexina, for reminding me that I mustn't act like a damned caveman!" And there it ended. It wasn't the first time that we had had our flare-ups.

It was decided that we should stay for a week at the villa. Sarah and I could quietly get to know one another without the small pressures which might arise at Rolthead where it would have been impossible to be alone because of my family and friends. The time too would give Alexina a chance to talk to Sarah about her father and stepfather and the life she had known with Alexina. There were photographs and mementoes, too, in the house of her past life. God knows, if the loss of her memory could be inexplicable, then its recovering might be just the same. Who knew? Some chance remark from Alexina, some old photograph, the playing of some well-worn favourite record, or the sight of a shabby, once-beloved toy or doll (Alexina had kept a stack of childhood things belonging to Sarah) might bring it all back. It was at this point that I suddenly remembered Sir Hugh Gleeson saying that Sarah's loss of memory might have been a form of self-punishment inflicted out of guilt feeling. That was a bloody nerve on the old boy's part. But the memory stuck with me for a while as the two women talked. What guilty feeling could Sarah possibly have? If there had ever been anything in her life which had worried her—eventually to the point of making her reject her past—I would have known about it, or sensed it in seven years of marriage. Anything so big would have had to manifest itself one way or another and given me some warning. But it never had. There had been no flaw in our marriage whatsoever—unless it had been the lack of children for whom we both wished, and there we had been in God's hands because, sensibly, we had both been examined by a specialist and he had said that we were both capable. In fact just before Sarah had disappeared we had decided to give it another year and then adopt a child.

At the end of a week in the villa we were to make our way back to England by road in my hired car because Sarah wanted to see more of Italy and there were places I wanted to show her.

I was to write to my brother and tell him about the coming return of Sarah. He could let people know about it discreetly and a word from me to Vickers would kill any publicity in the press. We would just move back into Rolthead without fuss. So far as it could be managed—except for immediate members of the Rolt family—no one was to know that Sarah was still suffering from a loss of memory. When we were back we would decide what treatment she would have for this. Remembering what Sir Hugh Gleeson had said, I doubted whether I would want her to continue with him. But at this family conference the point was not raised. It was something I could talk to Sarah about privately and later.

So, the week began and a quiet routine was adopted. I was always up early, but the two women seldom put in an appearance before eleven. When Sarah appeared we would go down to the small private beach below the coast road and have a swim before lunch. Then there was lunch, a siesta, and we would go for a drive along the coast or for a walk up into the hills at the back of the villa. The evenings we spent quietly. Alexina had plenty of friends in the neighbourhood but she asked none of them to the villa. Although the days passed pleasantly I could not help feeling impatient to be back at Rolthead. I had the feeling that since it was there that Sarah belonged, that it had been from there she had disappeared, then it would be there that she would finally recover herself. But I said nothing about this to either of them. Maybe this growing impatience in me was stronger than I knew and, when the chance came, expressed itself more forcibly than I could have wished.

The little cove from which we bathed was privately owned.

It had half a dozen changing cubicles which were let out by the proprietor along with the right to use the place for bathing. Alexina always hired two of the changing cubicles each year. Below the cubicles was a flat expanse of concrete platform with a few bollards for tying up small boats, and then a flight of steps down to the water. There was no beach at all. The little quay went straight down into deep water. If you wanted to sunbathe you used the concrete platform.

Both Sarah and I were strong swimmers. We liked to swim out almost to the mouth of the cove where the sea ran free of the shelter of the tall cliffs, and there we would lie on our backs being swung high and low by the strong swell that came rolling in.

On our third morning we were both well out in the cove, lying on our backs. There was no cloud at all, the sky a pale, hazy blue and the sea was like moving silver. I dropped my legs and trod water. Coming in from the open sea very fast was a speedboat towing a water-skier. The boat was curving sharply from side to side and I could see the skier swinging far out in long arcs, the spray pluming up from his skis. I watched with only mild interest at first. Then the boat straightened up and headed in for the little quay. Sarah and I lay in the direct line of the boat's approach. Knowing what dangerous fools some of the drivers of these craft could be, I raised myself in the water and waved an arm to signal our presence. The boat came straight on and I saw that there was a man at the wheel. He was wearing a blue shirt open down the front and a blue peaked cap with a round white tassel on top of it. I waved again and shouted but the boat just kept coming at top speed straight for us as we rose and dropped in the rolling sea swell. I turned to Sarah who was alongside me and shouted to her to dive and at the same time made a downward motion of my arm, plunging it into the water to make clear what I meant in case she could not hear me. To my relief I saw her duck under porpoise-fashion and go out of sight. I followed her. We went deep down together. I rolled over on to my back and looked upwards. The keel of the boat flashed through the water four or five feet above my head, followed by a milky turbulence of exploding water as the screw bit into the sea. I didn't know whether the bastard had seen us or not—but he had gone right over the spot where we had been swimming.

I came to the surface furious with rage. The boat was moving into the small quay now. Its speed slackened and the skier dropped low into the water. Sarah surfaced a few yards from me. The thought that the boat might have ploughed into her made me see red.

I turned and swam as fast as I could for the quay. By the time I reached it the speedboat was tied alongside. I went up the steps. There were two men on the concrete. One was the man who had been at the wheel. The other was the skier, a youth of about eighteen in bathing trunks. He was squatting on the ground, just lighting a cigarette. The man in the blue cap was a tall, well-built fellow in his thirties.

I went straight across to him and said, "Do you know you damned nearly killed me a minute ago? What the bloody hell do you mean by racing in here at top speed when people could be swimming around?"

He looked at me for a moment without speaking and I thought he might be Italian and had not understood me, but then a look came over his face which was one of sheer insolence. He said in an American accent, "Sorry, buddy—guess the sun-dazzle must have blinded me." He gave me a little nod as though that were the end of it and raised a lighter to his cigarette. His manner sent me right over the top.

Holding my voice steady against the fury in me, I said, "If there's sun-dazzle on the water you should handle your boat sensibly and not like a bloody maniac! You could have killed me or my wife and neither of us would have been interested in your being sorry. The next time you're in that speedboat of yours—keep it in mind! And here's something to help you remember it!"

97

I stepped forward and I hit him hard with my right fist on the jaw. No power on earth could have stopped me from doing it. I knew it was wrong, primitive, that I should have controlled myself—but there was no controlling the thought that he could have killed Sarah. He fell backwards and went clean over the edge of the quay into the deep water. When he came to the surface I expected him to start shouting or swearing at me. To my surprise he just looked up at me, felt his jaw with his hand, then grinned and began to swim round to the steps. When he reached them he stood up and, looking up at Sarah who had arrived at the quay a few moments before, said, "My apologies, *signora*. I seem to have upset your husband." Then, signalling to the youth who was still sitting on the ground, he called, "Come on, Giorgio—we're not wanted here."

A few minutes later the boat was heading out of the cove. As we watched it go, Sarah said, "Robert, did you have to do that?"

"Yes, I did. He might have killed us. But I'm not particularly proud of it. It's a long time since I really gave way to anger."

She touched my arm, and gave me a quick smile.

"It was anger on my account. That makes it forgivable. Come on, let's get changed."

We never mentioned the incident again and I said nothing to Alexina about it. Neither did we see the speedboat again. But that night, before I slept, I found myself thinking about it. If someone had knocked me off the quay as I had knocked the American I would have come back up the steps wanting to return as good as I had got. From the little I had seen of the man he looked like the type who should have done that. I would have betted on it. Thinking about him and of the few moments when the boat had gone threshing over me, I remembered Vickers and his caution that I should think dramatically . . . and then the shattered windscreen and the odd incident in the fir copse above Rolthead drifted into my mind.

Not understanding clearly why I should do it I had a private talk with Tino the next day. I had always got on well with Tino, who spoke far better English than I did Italian. I told him about the speedboat and the American and, as I hoped he would, he knew him. His name was John Chambers and he rented a small villa in Positano each year for a couple of months. He had plenty of money apparently and was known locally as a playboy. I was almost on the point of telephoning Vickers' man who had met me at Rome and telling him about the incident but I decided against it. I had enough on my hands without looking for further complications. Once you started thinking in the way Vickers and his kind did then there was an assassin behind every tree and you had to get a food-taster to avoid being poisoned. But the real trouble was that the moment you came into contact with Vickers' world personally, then it could be very hard at times to avoid its particular contamination. It became so easy to see mysteries where no mysteries existed, and to mark down quite innocent behaviour as odd or prompted by some esoteric motive.

Neither Alexina nor Sarah appeared until late in the morning. I was usually up by about six. To pass away the time until Tino brought me my coffee and breakfast on the terrace at eight I sometimes strolled around the garden and then went down to the bathing cove and smoked a cigarette. There was seldom anyone there and I was alone with my thoughts.

Sitting there, I remembered the first time I had ever seen Sarah. My father and I had been staying with one of his friends in a villa quite close to Amalfi. I had gone for a long walk over the hills behind the villa and had lost my way. In the end I had come down to the coast road along the rough track which led past the Villa Mendola. When I was within a hundred yards of the villa Sarah had come out of the drive gates and begun to walk up the track towards me. I might have taken another track down from the hills, or Sarah could have been five minutes later in coming out of the villa. A hundred small daily incidents could have intervened to upset one pattern and substitute another. But nothing had. She came out of the gate

99

and walked towards me. When she was five yards from me she looked up. I saw her face for the first time. As we passed I gave her a small, half-nod which she barely acknowledged with a polite smile.

We passed and I knew that she was the one. I can be arrogant and obstinate and self-willed. But I was none of those things at that moment. I just knew that someday she was going to be with me at Rolthead. And so it had been. She had come to Rolthead and for years I had known a happiness which had made my life flower . . . which had made me bless every day we shared, and which I knew spread to her too. And then she had gone from me—into some private agony or limbo of her own—and I had known only black days, but never a loss of faith that the day would come when she would return . . . completely and utterly to me.

One morning the early light got me out of bed long before my usual time. Instead of strolling around the garden I decided to take the rough roadway which ran up into the hills behind the villa to see if I could get high enough to have a vantage point which would give me a view of the island of Capri miles away to the south-west. For some way up, the hillside was cultivated with vine terraces and little groves of olive, fig, and almond trees. Now and again small paths ran off the main track to a farmhouse or a cottage. Eventually the cultivated ground gave way to the rocky higher slopes and the main track dwindled to a rough path. After a while I began to realise that it was going to take me a long time to get to the top which was well over a thousand feet. I sat down on a boulder and lit a cigarette, looking back down the hill to the dwarfed villa far below and beyond it the great spread of the sea.

As I sat there I saw a figure coming up the track from the villa. It was a woman and I watched her movements idly for some minutes before I suddenly realised that it was Sarah. Her clothes were unmistakable. She wore a red scarf tied over her head, a yellow shirt and a pair of blue slacks. Some way above the villa she turned off the main track along a path to one of the farmhouses and I lost sight of her. I was delighted to see her, guessing that she had decided to rise early for a change, and I at once gave up any idea of climbing to the top of the hill. I started to move down to find her, thinking that for once we could have breakfast together on the terrace. It took me a little over five minutes to get to the farm.

It was a pretty poor sort of place built partly into the hillside. The roof was covered with red tiles, a great many of them broken and the plaster of the walls was peeling away. The first floor was taken up by a stable and a storeroom. The living quarters were reached by a flight of wooden steps lined with old cans in which grew geraniums and petunias. Picturesque and not a penny spent on it for years.

There was a small boy of about ten sitting on the bottom step tossing pieces of stick at a group of hens that scratched away in the yard. So far as I could see the pathway ended at the farm.

Languages had never been a strong point with me, but I did know a few words of Italian and could string them together in an execrable way which always made Sarah laugh.

I said to the boy, *"Dov' è la signora? In casa?"*

He looked at me as though I were an idiot.

I pointed down the hill and said, *"La villa Mendola. La signora della villa Mendola."*

He just shook his head, clearly not understanding me. It occurred to me that he might be half-witted. So I stood at the bottom of the steps and shouted, "Sarah—are you there?"

After a moment or two a woman came through the house door at the top of the steps. She was middle-aged, buxom, wearing a crumpled old black dress and had a black shawl over her head.

She said, *"Buon giorno, signore."*

I said, *"Buon giorno, signora. Vengo de'lla villa Mendola . . . Mia moglie—la signora Sarah . . . è venuta qui?"*

She shook her head. *"No, no, signore. L'ho vista passare di là."*

101

She pointed across the yard to a small opening in the wall that led out on to one of the vine terraces. *"È passata due minuti fa."*

I had enough Italian to understand that. I said, *"Grazie,"* gave her a nod and went across the yard. Beyond the gap in the wall was a path that led alongside the terrace and then dipped down through patches of cultivated ground and into a grove of olive trees. I followed it down quickly, hoping to overtake Sarah, but without success. After about a hundred yards the path swung back to the main track, and I made my way down it to the villa.

Tino was on the terrace setting the breakfast. I gave him good morning and asked him if he had seen Sarah. He said he had not. As he spoke Sarah came through the main gate and up on to the terrace. She gave me a smile and dropped into a chair.

"I'll have breakfast here, Tino."

"Very good, *signora.*"

As Tino went off, I said, "You're up early this morning?"

"I know. I couldn't sleep."

"I was up the hill and saw you. I came down to join you when I saw you go to that farmhouse up there. The old woman said you'd gone by but I couldn't catch you. I must say the small boy up there is either half-witted or my Italian is much worse than I imagine it is."

Sarah grinned. "From the little I've heard I wouldn't give it a very high rating. I'm sorry you missed me. What a lovely morning."

It was a small incident and of no importance at all. But the odd thing was I couldn't help being puzzled. I was a countryman born and bred, and I had a good eye for country. From the terrace in front of the farm there was a good, clear view of the hillside down to the main track and the villa. If anyone had been moving down to the villa I was sure I would have seen them. But somehow I had missed Sarah and she had arrived after me. As I sat there with her then, a thought crossed my mind to which I should never have given the slightest house-room. The fact that I did—even though I dismissed it almost at once—I was sure sprang from the corruption (and I use the word deliberately) of even my meagre contact with the kind of world Vickers and, no doubt, Albert Chinn inhabited. Had Sarah been *in* the farmhouse and not wanted me to know?

## CHAPTER SIX

IN THE END we did not drive all the way back to England. We went up to Rome and from there crossed to the Adriatic coast and motored up to Venice. We stayed three days and then flew back to London.

Sarah was relaxed and easy with me now, but we were far from being man and wife again. That would come, I never doubted, but until it did my only allies were time and patience and an understanding which enabled me to see clearly all the difficulties and hesitancies on her side.

From Rome I had thought we might go to Florence. Deliberately I had planned to stay as far as possible at places we had known before. When I mentioned going to Florence— and apart from anything else there was the thought in my mind that we could see the apartment in which she was supposed to have lived with her friend—Sarah said she did not want to go there. She said—and at once I understood and supported her reason—that she wanted nothing to do with any place which had any connection with the spurious life of the Mrs. Angela Starr she had once been.

She said, "Mrs. Starr, for some reason that served Albert Chinn, was a myth. Something he created. I know who I am now—even if I have no memory of it. I don't want to think about Mrs. Starr. She's dead. All I want to do is to find my way back fully and completely to being your wife. It's not going to be easy, but we can do it together."

I entirely agreed with her, and as we drove up Italy we discussed without any embarrassment the situation that awaited us at Rolthead and the difficulties which would have to be dealt with. So far as relations and friends were concerned her disappearance would be explained as a loss of memory due to a nervous breakdown. Beyond that there need be no further explanation. They could speculate, nothing could stop that, but it was no concern of theirs. To my immediate family, we agreed, the whole truth should be told. There was not the slightest fear that any of them would take anyone else into their confidence. The Rolts were a solid family. We had had in the course of our history scandals and critical episodes like any other family. But to the limit of our ability we had kept them to ourselves.

The days spent at the Villa Mendola, and the days driving through Italy, gave me plenty of time to brief Sarah on all the people she had known at Rolthead and in the county and to go into details of things that had happened which she would be presumed to know. It amused me to see how eagerly she took this information, sometimes laughing and joking as I built up the characters of her past friends. And it was clear to me that now we had left her mother, her manner to me was changing rapidly. At the villa there had been a reserve in her which now thawed. We were not husband and wife, but we were at least good friends. If there were any intimacies between us they were those of a brother and sister and I did nothing to alter this. She kissed me goodnight before she went to her hotel room and when we walked together we sometimes held hands, and I now and then put my arm around her so that a slow acceptance of physical contact grew between us.

From Venice I wrote a letter to my brother, explaining matters as fully as was necessary to him, and warning him of our return. The day before we flew home, I telephoned Mrs. Cordell—who had already been half-warned—and told her that I was bringing Sarah back with me. Mrs. Cordell, as I knew she would, accepted this with the same calm as she would have done had I been telling her that there would be four extra for dinner that night. When I got back I intended to have a talk to her and explain enough to satisfy her that she knew more of the real situation than most other people did.

In actual fact when it came to our settling in again at Rolthead there were far fewer difficulties than either of us had imagined there might be. People were kind and tactful without making it obvious and the few embarrassments that arose were of the smallest nature, quickly covered and quickly forgotten.

One of the things we had discussed before coming home was the question of what treatment, if any, she should have for the loss of her memory. I was in favour of making a fresh start with somebody new. Sarah was against this. The specialist in Manchester was a first-class man and so was Sir Hugh Gleeson. She felt that everything which could be done by any professional had been done. Time, and Rolthead, and the taking up of the lines of her past life—these she regarded as the best hope for a recovery. However, since she had become more or less a friend of Sir Hugh's and had always felt that her periodic visits to him did her some good, she wanted to continue to visit him. Naturally, I agreed. I did not, however, mention to her his opinion of the reason why she suffered from this peculiar form of amnesia.

The only person I ever mentioned this to was my brother, Harold. He was thirty-six, younger than I by five years. Like me he was on the short side of middle height, heavily and stockily built and with the same kind of battered pugnacious looks as mine. We were both solid types who could never have won any prizes for good looks.

Shortly after we were back he and his wife came over for the week-end and both of them were marvellous in the way they handled the situation. They drew Sarah to them right away and any stranger listening and watching would have been hard put to know that for Sarah this was tantamount to meeting them for the first time.

On the second day they were with us Sarah and Harold's wife Isabelle went off to bed before us. We stayed down in the study and had a few nightcaps before going up and naturally

I talked to Harold about the whole extraordinary business. For the first time I gave someone the full story. I did it because he was my own blood and nearest in relationship to me.

After I had finished, he said, "It's curious old Sir Hugh What's-his-name should have said that . . . about her loss of memory being a form of self-punishment because of some guilt feeling."

"You think so? I thought it was damned presumptuous. Typical psychological claptrap."

Harold chuckled and helped himself to another whisky. "You would, Bobby-boy. But you've always been so besotted with Sarah—and why not?—that you'd take it as an insult if anyone so much as said she had a smut on her nose. To you she's a goddess and can do no wrong."

"Are you suggesting she could have a guilt feeling, because if you are——"

"Hold it, Bobby. I'm not suggesting anything. I was merely considering Sir Hugh's statement. Most of us have guilt feelings. All of us, I'd say. You can't live without picking 'em up. But that doesn't mean you're actively guilty of anything."

"That's a bit over my head. If you've got a guilt feeling it means you've been guilty of something."

"Not quite. It could mean that in all innocence you have walked into a situation, been presented with a set of circumstances from which you can't escape without taking some kind of guilt with you—whether you like it or not."

"Don't be ridiculous. If Sarah had ever been caught up in anything like that, I'm the first one she would have come to."

"After you were married, yes. But what about long before she knew you? You're not the only one she has a loyalty to, you know. There's her mother, dear Alexina. She's a pretty remote, cool fish, isn't she? Always felt there was a little bit of mystery there."

"You're talking through your hat."

"No, I'm not. I'm only saying that what Sir Hugh said could be a possibility. Sarah might have had some kind of trouble long before she met you. When she married she brought it with her and it wasn't something she could get off her chest to you. She had to bottle it up and that would have been hell for her. A strain that in the end made her crack."

Angrily, I said, "I'm damned certain there could never have been anything like that. And I must say it's not the kind of fancy theory I ever expected to hear from you."

Harold grinned. "Don't glare at me, Bobby. I'm a hundred per cent on your side. But the fact is that I'm growing up and each day I take the world and the people in it less and less for granted. Know what I'd do if I was in your place?"

"I don't know that I want to know."

"I don't mean about Sarah. I think you're handling that absolutely right. I mean about this fellow Vickers and all that Albert Chinn business. I wouldn't put up with that. I'd go right to Vickers, take him by the scruff of the neck and shake everything out of him. And if he wouldn't come straight I'd go higher. Right to the top and raise a stink until I did know. You know your way around Whitehall. You've got all the old man's contacts, too. You could clear that side of it, at least. You'd be that much freer then to concentrate fully on Sarah's recovery."

"The last thing I want to do is to get further involved with that lot."

"Up to you." He stood up, drained his glass and went on, "Sorry, Bobby-boy, if I inadvertently put your back up a little—but you know the Rolts. Plain speakers. That's why the old man never got a plum Embassy."

I sat and had another whisky after he had gone and thought over what he had said. The fact that we had almost stood up to one another like a pair of fighting-cocks meant nothing and was soon forgotten. We had quarrelled and fought all our lives, but nothing could alter the loyalty and affection we had for one another. One thing he was right about was that Alexina was a remote, cool fish—but I couldn't conceive of Alexina being in any kind of past trouble which she herself or Vallis, her banker husband, could not have handled. Old Vallis had handled plenty in his time, I knew that from my father. And the last thing I could imagine Alexina doing was to involve Sarah in anything. In her cool composed way she doted on her. Sir Hugh Gleeson was welcome to his theory but I was damned if I was going to share it. And if Sarah wanted to go on seeing him then there was no question of my opposing her. Actually, although I didn't hold with his theory, I liked the man myself very much.

I went up to my room and found there reason enough to send me off to sleep happier than I had been for a very long time.

On the pillow of my turned-down bed was a red rose pinned to a note from Sarah which read:

> Dear Robert,
> Thank you for a lovely day.
> I feel as though I have known Isabelle and Harold for years. Sleep well—
> Sarah

*     *     *     *

Two weeks later something happened which made me even happier. Sarah, in her practical way, had decided that the time had come for her to tackle the management of her considerable financial affairs again. During her absence these had been looked after by her lawyer and her accountant and Alexina—with occasional references to me. In fact little had been done except to keep them on ice. By this time, of course, both the lawyer and her accountant knew that she had returned because I had spoken to them on the telephone— though I had not gone into any great detail. At first I had suggested that I should go and see them before she did and put them more completely in the picture, but she had been against this.

She said, "No, Robert. I've got to learn to act and handle

things for myself. I'll go alone. You say they're both nice, understanding men . . . well, I shouldn't have any trouble. I'm sure they won't be tactless enough to ask me awkward questions."

"I'll come up with you, anyway. We can stay the night in town."

She shook her head. "No. You've enough to do here. I don't need a nursemaid. I'm Sarah Rolt of Rolthead and I can stand on my own two feet. That's how it was and that's how it is going to be." She leaned forward and kissed me on the cheek and the gesture was as simple and spontaneous as it had so often been in the past.

Sarah went to London and stayed the night. The day she was due to return I had to attend a committee meeting of the Dorset County Council at Dorchester in the afternoon. The meeting dragged on longer than I had anticipated. On the way back I decided that I would call on Harold and Isabelle and take a drink from them. I also wanted to settle a business matter with Harold. We jointly owned a large piece of woodland in Somerset and had been having trouble with the syndicate which rented the shooting rights. While I was there I telephoned Rolthead to see if Sarah was back. She was coming down by train and having a taxi from the station. Mrs. Cordell said she was not back. Knowing the times of the trains, I knew that meant she could not be back before about half-past nine. I told Mrs. Cordell that I was staying for dinner with my brother and would be back by half-past nine.

In fact, because of Harold's hospitality and our family and business chatter, I left late and it was just gone ten o'clock when I arrived at Rolthead. Mrs. Cordell met me in the hall.

"Where's Mrs. Rolt?"

"She had dinner on the train coming down, sir. She went out a few minutes ago to take a stroll round the gardens."

I went out into the dusk to look for her. The light was almost gone. The evening was warm and windless. I went around the house and to the place where she was most likely to be—the rose garden. She liked to go there after dinner, sometimes with me and sometimes alone. On these warm, still nights the scent from the roses could be almost overpowering. Personally I didn't care for it much but I would never have said so.

The rose garden was bounded by a tall red brick wall on three sides. On the fourth there was a high, clipped yew hedge with an entrance archway cut into its middle. In the centre of the garden was a circular bed of roses, surrounded by a path which had long stone benches spaced around it.

As I went through the yew-hedge entrance, I saw Sarah coming towards me up the path from the circular bed. She was walking slowly and had her hands pressed against her forehead, her head hung low.

"Sarah."

She did not look up at my call but came straight on towards me and would have walked past me if I had not put out a hand and held her by the arm. She half-turned to me and dropped her hands from her forehead and looked at me. I had a feeling for a moment that she had no idea who I was, that she was hundreds of miles away from me. Then she slowly said, "Oh, Robert. . . . Oh, Robert. . . ." Her face was drawn as though she were fighting pain.

I said, "For God's sake—what's the matter? Are you ill?"

She breathed deeply once or twice and then shook her head. "I'm all right. . . . Please . . . let's go inside."

I took her round the front of the house and into my study, sat her in a chair and got a glass of brandy for her. She just touched her lips to it and then put it away from her. Then she leant back in the chair and looked up at me and slowly smiled.

"What on earth happened?"

"It was most extraordinary. . . . No, don't look worried, Robert. I'm quite all right."

"You're sure?"

"Yes, quite sure."

"What happened?"

"Well, when I got back Mrs. Cordell told me where you

were. I went for a stroll. Into the rose garden. The scent of the roses was wonderful." She made a wry face. "Perhaps it was too wonderful. Intoxicating. Anyway I sat on one of the benches in the middle of the garden . . . and suddenly it was as though I had begun to float away——"

"You mean you fainted?"

"No, no, not that. I just floated—no, that's not it. It was as though something had wrapped itself around me. A lovely feeling of softness and happiness and promise. . . . Robert, I don't want you to make too much of this. But honestly, just for a moment or two, I felt it was coming to me, that it was going to be suddenly all so clear. I knew it."

"Knew what?"

"Knew that I was going to know all about myself . . . that my memory was coming back. I could feel it coming—and then suddenly the next thing I remember was coming up the path and turning to you as you took my arm." She stood up and came close to me and I put an arm around her as she went on. "I'm sure of it. I know it was all going to come back to me— and then suddenly it went."

I said, "I know it's going to come back. Nothing will ever make me believe otherwise. Maybe this is the beginning."

"I know it is. For a moment someone or something out there made me a promise."

Sitting by myself after she had gone up to bed, I thought about it. Quite clearly something had happened to Sarah, but I couldn't accept the rather fanciful way she had described it— not that I would have ever said so to her. Women translate things into terms of emotion far more than men. I didn't object to that. A little dressing up of ordinary things held no harm. But for myself I was sure of what I had always known would happen. Once back here at Rolthead among all her old friends and the places she had known so well there just had to be echoes and impulses from the past which would work on her mind. It was a natural healing process. Nature was wiser than a thousand doctors. I had no doubt in my mind that this was the first sign of recovery. I felt happier than I had done for years, but I was worried, too. For a moment Sarah had looked ghastly in the rose garden, old and drawn and exhausted. I decided that for my own peace of mind and for her protection she ought to have a thorough medical check-up. In the old days she had gone twice a year to her London physician. I would have to get her to start the habit again. Before I went to bed I made up my mind that I would go and see Sir Hugh Gleeson and ask him if he would tactfully suggest to her on her next visit that she have a complete medical check.

I went to bed, happy and without any doubts that the day was coming when Sarah would be completely restored to me and to Rolthead.

*　　*　　*　　*

Two days later Vickers telephoned me.

He said, "Mr. Rolt—I'm sorry to bother you, but I want a directive from you about the flat at Otwell Park House. The lease is in Albert Chinn's name. He can't be traced and has stopped payment. I may say he always paid monthly in cash. Notes by registered letter."

"So what do you want from me?"

"Well, there's Mrs. Rolt's car and furniture and other odds and ends."

"Yes, I see. Well, I don't care what you do with them. Sell them and give the money to charity. I certainly don't want any of it back here."

"Very good. But there will be business papers and so on. Mrs. Rolt was in the property-developing business. No doubt she owns property still."

"Yes, of course. I'll speak to her about it. I've no doubt she'll get her lawyer or accountant to send someone up to Otwell Park to deal with it."

(I did speak to her later but I wasn't surprised to find that she had already given instructions to her lawyer on her visit to

114

London about the flat. He was to go up and sort things out and incorporate any of her recent business affairs into her long-established holdings. She entirely agreed with me that she did not want the car or any of the flat furniture. She wanted them sold and the money given to a charity which she would nominate.)

Before Vickers rang off he said, "You may like to know that, so far as we have been able to check, all the Mrs. Starr details have turned out to be false or rigged. We haven't got round to them all. However, whoever set the details up did a very good job. I suppose you haven't said anything to your wife about the statement she wrote—the possible discrepancy in time, I mean?"

"Of course I haven't said anything to her. I don't propose to go round spying on my own wife, for God's sake! I'm quite sure there must be a very sound and straightforward reason. My wife is back here now and I don't want to be badgered or fussed about anything that happened while she was with Albert Chinn."

Afterwards I had to admit that I had been pretty offhand with him, considering that he was only doing his job and, even more, had been instrumental in finding Sarah for me. But I knew Vickers and his kind, and from my father and some slight experience of my own I knew the involved and—when needed —heartless expediencies some twilight government agencies could employ. They could do whatever they liked about Chinn, for whatever good reasons they had, but if they started to come near Sarah now then I wouldn't hesitate to go bald-headed for someone or other in Whitehall. Nobody was going to come barging into my life at Rolthead with Sarah.

And nobody did. For the next month life moved peacefully along its course. At times it was difficult to imagine that Sarah had ever been away, or that her memory for our past was still a blank. She went once or twice to see Sir Hugh but from her accounts these visits were clearly more social than professional. She had a medical check-up in London and her physician cleared her. Apart from her loss of memory there was nothing wrong with her. Once a fortnight she went to London to deal with her financial affairs, clearly taking the same interest in them now as she had done before.

At the end of July her mother came over and stayed a week at Rolthead, and then went off to pay visits to a round of friends of hers in London and the country. I carried on with my business of running the estate and my duties as a County Councillor and my involvements in odds and ends of committees and organisations which being a Rolt made almost obligatory for me.

Sarah and I were happy, and I never lost faith that the day would come when we would be happier. Man and wife we were not, though a special form of intimacy had developed between us, deeper than any brother and sister relationship, far beyond anything one could call friendship. I was content with it—but it was no good pretending to myself that I could find any lasting fulfilment in it. We were both of a passionate nature. If the ultimate restraint which we both accepted was hard, it was equally hard for us both, but we never discussed this. We accepted the ultimate barrier as being there and, I suppose, we both realised that there would be no lasting balm and bliss in crashing it.

During this period one or two things lifted my hopes a little higher. We rode and played golf together, and the first moment Sarah got up on the bay gelding, Minto, which had been her favourite, she knew exactly what she was doing, everything coming back to her instinctively. It was the same with her golf game—even to the occasional quick hook in her driving which had always troubled her so. She fished for the brown trout in the lake and she handled the rod and put her fly down as competently as she had always done. If her mind was not remembering, clearly her body's memory was unimpaired.

Most evenings after dinner, when we were alone, we would take a stroll through the grounds and always come back

116

through the rose garden. I knew the rose garden held a promise for her and a sixth sense developed in me which told me when she wanted to be alone there. I would make some excuse for going off and leave her there—but, remembering her first experience, I never stayed away too long.

But as so often happens in life, the moment of crisis came when the expectancy of it had become routine, and we had dropped our guard.

Early in August we had taken a stroll down to the lake with the house spaniel, Frannie, and on the way back I sensed that Sarah wanted to go into the rose garden alone. I made an excuse that I wanted to go to the lodge gatehouse to speak to our head gamekeeper who lived there.

I left Sarah and went off. Half-way down the drive I realised that Frannie had remained with her. I stayed with the keeper much longer than I had meant to. He was having trouble with his pheasants and then I had to listen to his problems over a bunch of lads from the village who had taken to using one of the far field barns as a meeting-place, and so creating a fire risk to some early hay that had been stacked there.

I came back as it was getting dark. So sure was I that Sarah would have returned, that I started up the sweep of steps to the front terrace when, for no reason that I could put words to, I just felt an overwhelming compulsion to go to the rose garden. So strong was this feeling that I could not help breaking into a trot over the last few yards to the yew-hedge entrance. As I went through the archway it was to find that because of the surrounding walls and the yew hedge it was much darker in the garden than it had been out on the open sweeps of lawn. I pulled the torch from my pocket and went hurriedly up the path to the centre bed and the circular path around it. I shall never forget the moment. The smell of the roses was strong and cloying. A moth was captured in the jerking torch beam for a moment or two and then came blundering back into my face. Far away down by the lake a little owl suddenly screeched. Low in the darkened sky over the far wall I could make out the smooth profile of the downs and suddenly a shooting star burned brightly low in the heaven. These things I saw, heard, and smelled then without any awareness. But whenever I think back to them now they are sharp in my memory against the shock of that moment when my torch-beam found Sarah.

She was lying on the ground by a stone bench, her legs drawn up as though she had slid or slowly collapsed to the gravel from a sitting position.

I went down on my knees beside her, slid my arm under her shoulders and half-raised her. Her head dropped back over my arm, her fair hair falling free of her face. Her eyes were closed but in the light of the torch in my free hand I could see that she was breathing slowly and steadily so that I could see the regular slight rise and fall of her breasts.

Holding down the anxiety, in fact near-panic, that was in me, I picked her up in my arms and carried her back to the house. In the hallway, I shouted for Mrs. Cordell at the top of my voice. When she came, I said, "Mrs. Rolt's fainted. Call Blundell. If he's not there try and get his partner. I want someone over here right away."

I carried Sarah up to her bedroom and put her on her bed and then switched on the lights. She lay on the bed, limp and relaxed as though she was in a natural sleep. I leaned over and shook her shoulder gently but there was no response. I moved her arms and legs but none of them seemed injured to me. The only mark I could see on her was some gravel dirt and a small graze where her right hand had caught the path as she had tumbled—or so I imagined—from the stone bench.

Mrs. Cordell came into the room as I straightened up from the bed.

"Doctor Blundell was in, sir. He's coming over right away. Whatever happened, sir?"

"I don't know. She was sitting in the rose garden. I think she's fainted. I found her lying on the path."

I don't think I have ever passed a more helpless ten minutes in my life. If you run into trouble and you can see the cause of it then you can do something. But Sarah didn't seem to be injured in any way, except for her grazed hand. She just lay on the bed as though she were in a calm sleep. I shook her gently by the shoulder and spoke her name firmly, but there was no response from her.

Mrs. Cordell made a pillow comfortable under her head and said, "I would just leave her, sir, until the doctor comes. She doesn't seem to be in any pain."

Fortunately Blundell only lived a mile away. I was just about to become impatient when I heard his car come up the drive. Apart from being our local doctor he was an old friend. When I went out to meet him he was already on his way up the staircase. I told him briefly what had happened and he went in to see Sarah, saying, "You stay out here, Robert. I don't want you breathing down my neck. Mrs. Cordell can give me any help I want. Go down and get yourself a drink. I'll join you later."

I went down to the study and poured myself a brandy. My hand was shaking, but with the coming of Blundell the anxiety in me had eased. He was old and old-fashioned but he had been in practice at Rolthead and around for twenty-five years and I had every faith in him.

Twenty minutes later he came into the study.

He said, "Mrs. Cordell and I have put her to bed. She's breathing normally, her pulse is steady and her heart is as sound as a bell. She's just gone off into a deep sleep."

"She's not injured?"

"No. Not that I can discover. She's just sleeping and my advice is to let her sleep until she wakes naturally. Don't worry, she will. If you want to you can stay up there with her. Perhaps it would be as well."

I poured him a brandy and said, "You know her history. Has this anything to do with it?"

He shrugged his shoulders. "I don't know. At the moment the only thing I could diagnose with certainty is that she is sleeping. I think when the morning comes she'll wake up." He sipped at his brandy and then over the lowered glass, he said, "Then you can take it from there. Unless you call me before, I'll be over at half-past nine."

When he had gone I went up to the bedroom. Mrs. Cordell was still there but I told her to go off to bed. After some fussing she did.

I put out all the lights in the room except for a shaded bedside lamp and stood looking down at Sarah. She seemed to be sleeping quite naturally, her cheek resting in the palm of one hand, her hair loose on the pillow.

I went over to the window bay and settled in an armchair with my feet up on the small stool from her dressing table. It was a warm night and I needed no blanket to keep me warm. That night I kept a vigil full of hope. If anyone had asked me why I should be so certain of hope I could have given no logical answer. But somehow, I just knew that when Sarah woke my life would be different.

I sat and watched the stars wheel in the sky and the sounds of the night came to me through the partly open window. A vixen called now and then on the downs and a dog fox answered her. Hearing them, I suddenly realised that Frannie had not come back into the house with me. I didn't worry because she often spent the night out.

The barn owl which lived in the stable block ghosted by the window. From away towards the sea came the swift, melodic call of a curlew. Sometimes Sarah stirred in her sleep and changed her position. Each time I went and looked at her and once I slipped her arm which had come free of the bedclothes back under the cover. I held her hand for a moment and kissed it.

The dawn would soom be paling the night shadows from the countryside and dimming the stars in the sky. There was a great feeling of peace everywhere, peace and love keeping pace with the slow movement of the coming—and, I prayed—the promised day.

Incongruously, proving that there is no conception of

romance in nature, only in man, my body rode imperceptibly over my dedication to a vigil of watching and, knowing that love would be restored, I went to sleep.

When I woke, it was full daybreak. Fast-moving cloud shadows raced across the sunlit sweep of downs and a fresh breeze was tossing the heads of the tall beeches along the garden limits and all the birds were singing and calling.

Sarah, with a blue silk wrap over her nightdress, was standing alongside me. She stood looking down at me, smiling and beautiful. I made a quick movement to stand up but she put out a hand and lightly touched me on the shoulder. Then she came down into my arms, buried her face in my neck, and I knew that she was back. Knew too, as we kissed and held one another, that there were no words which could describe the love and understanding that streamed through our bodies. Everything was said and known and reaffirmed in the passionate contact we shared as she shuddered and trembled against me in the silent ecstasy of her release to freedom.

*    *    *    *

Sarah had little to tell about the incident in the rose garden. After I had left her she had sat there enjoying the evening and the scent of the roses.

She said, "I just sat there. I was feeling a little tired. Relaxed and happy. And then the scent from the roses seemed to become heavier and heavier. Overpowering. My head began to swim a little. I can remember looking up and seeing the stars in the sky, and slowly they began to dance and move about all over the place. Just looking at them made me giddy. I remember thinking, 'Oh, Lord, how stupid. I'm going to faint.' Then Frannie gave a long howl—and I passed out."

Old Blundell came and gave her a check-up and said that there was nothing wrong with her that he could find. Her memory had come back—but not completely. She could remember the whole of her life up to the moment when she had got into her car at Shaftesbury and had started to drive

121

home to me. From that moment on she still could not remember anything which had happened until she had awakened on the villa bed and had been told that she was Mrs. Starr. Blundell thought that this period would eventually return, that the recovery of memory up to that day in Shaftesbury was the beginning of the process of complete recall. At that time, in our delight at her return, our joy because she knew now that we really had been man and wife and still were, it seemed of little importance.

It was the beginning of happy days for us both. Without any embarrassment we recovered a physical and mental passion which it was hard to imagine had ever been broken. In fact our love coloured our lives in a way which it had never done before. There was a richer, wilder element in all we said and did when we were alone. Not easily given to exaggerations of conduct or thought, I had to admit—and gladly welcome—a new dimension about us, one into which we flung ourselves hungrily, not simply in love-making, but in everything. Sarah was my life and I was hers and Rolthead was suddenly a garden of paradise.

For myself, since so much had been restored to me, I did not worry greatly that there still remained a gap in her memory—even though it covered the most puzzling period of her life. She was back at Rolthead knowing she was my wife, remembering the days of our first meeting, our marriage and the years we had spent together. But I knew that the gap still worried her. Almost a year of her life was missing. It was easy for me to ignore that lacuna—no matter how much curiosity I had about it. But for Sarah, I sensed—even though she came to refer to it less and less—that it remained a small flaw in her happiness. Time, I was certain, would diminish its importance for her. The thing now was to forget the fantasy she had lived through and to turn to the future, to the life that lay ahead of us. Time, I was sure, would slowly complete her memory-healing process.

However, in the early days, when it still nagged in her mind and often shadowed some moment of quiet communion between us, I took the opportunity when I was in his part of the world of calling on Sir Hugh Gleeson and having a talk with him about it. He and Sarah were very good friends now and she often went to see him. He knew about the memory gap from Sarah already.

Sir Hugh could put my back up sometimes but overall he was a man I respected. Nevertheless, I knew by now that he was a man of some ideas and convictions very remote from mine. Not being a fanciful type I find it hard to give credence to woolly, idealistic conceptions. The chief business of life is to keep both feet on the ground and to live decently and harmoniously with those around you. It gives me no embarrassment to say that I am an old-fashioned Christian. I am a member of the Church of England. I read the lessons now and then at Rolthead Church and I believe in the Bible. If that sounds pompous and smug . . . well, it may be, but I don't mean it that way. Without sound standards and good principles you are half-way to the devil, and may he be welcome.

I had a whisky with Sir Hugh and after a little chat I brought up the subject of Sarah's remaining memory gap.

He said, "Are you really worrying about it?"

"No, I'm not worrying. In fact I have a suspicion that perhaps she'll never get it back. But I'm a curious type. Tidy, perhaps, would be a better word. If there's an explanation to be found I want to have it."

Sir Hugh smiled. "Wanting to know—that's the history of mankind. But some knowledge always eludes us. Let me ask you something—does it ever worry you that you have a nine-month memory gap in your own life?"

"I don't follow you."

"Because you've ever been worried by it. You were nine months in your mother's womb, my boy. You came into the world a lusty bawling baby, I've no doubt. How much of those first nine months do you remember?"

123

I frowned. He really did come up with some queer angles. "Well, none of course. But why should I? Nobody ever remembers that period."

"It's a big statement. Some people say they can. I wonder? Anyway, people generally don't. There must be a good reason for it. Don't ask me what. The brain with its functions and dysfunctions is still largely a mystery to us. For instance— if I picked a date at random from twenty years back could you recall exactly what you were doing and where you were doing it?"

"Well . . . that depends."

"Of course it does. It depends on whether your memory is that efficient and whether you have a good reason for remembering." He smiled. "When I was a young medical student I sometimes got very, very drunk. I'd black out at a party—and the next thing I would know was that it was morning and I was lying in my own bed. And I would never have any memory of leaving the party, getting home and undressing and going to bed. The memory would be gone for good. All life is dying and recreating. The body renews itself until it can do so no longer. So does the memory. Parts of it die. In my opinion part of Sarah's memory has died. Forget it. If it were something that had to be of importance in her life and yours, God—or whatever power or life force you believe in— would never have let it die. Medical science can answer a lot of questions and solve a lot of problems—but full knowledge is as far away from us as the stars. You have to be content with the fact that man is an odd creature who has the gift of being able to ask questions—but finds answers for only very few of them. Personally, and you might like to consider it, I think we have most of us gone the wrong way—we are looking inwards when we should be looking outwards. Like a true Rolt your feet are planted solidly on the good earth. What you don't understand you find easy to pretend doesn't exist—unless it touches you personally, and then, of course, you're really up a gum tree. For instance, why do you think I showed you that painting of

Miss Evangeline Santora? Have you ever given that really deep thought?"

"No. Not really—except that it was odd about the finger."

He grinned. "There you are. A moment's curiosity and then you go no further."

A little irritated, but hiding it, I said, "That's all very well, Sir Hugh, but I can't see that some old painting has anything to do with my problem. I'm only concerned with my wife. Something strange and inexplicable happened to Sarah. It's not marring her life or our life together—but I know she thinks about it. Nearly a year went from her life—and someone, somewhere, knows all about it. I'd like to get my hands on them. I'd like to know the truth of what happened."

He smiled and shook his head.

"Naturally you would. I used to be curious about my after-drinking amnesic gaps—but I had to accept them. But you're right, practical man that you are. Someone, somewhere, knows about Sarah's amnesic gap. You'll never—in my opinion—get anything from Sarah. So, you've only one recourse if you want to know and have the time to waste: find that someone. But my advice to you is, forget it and enjoy the happiness you've got."

Driving back afterwards, I thought about him. Clearly, at the end of a long professional life full of honours, he saw himself as something of a mystic and liked to talk in riddles. However, I had to admit that his parting advice was sound. From then on I seldom ever gave much thought to the puzzle of Sarah's amnesic gap. From the moment when I had awakened and had found Sarah at my side, and then coming down into my arms, love and happiness and contentment had been restored to me. God had been good—I was content.

That morning, too, when Blundell had come and was alone with Sarah, I had gone out and walked around to the rose garden. As I had reached the yew-hedge arch Martin, the head keeper, had come through from the garden carrying something in his right hand.

He held it up for me to see.

"It's that little ole spaniel bitch of yours, sir. Frannie. I just found 'er in the garden there, dead. Must a 'ad a fit or something. Poor ole dear. Too 'ighly-strung she was anyway, sir."

The spaniel's eyes were open and glassy, and there was a fleck or two of dried foam and saliva on her muzzle. I had felt the moment of emptiness you get when a dog you know passes. She had never been a good working-dog but both Sarah and I were fond of her.

"Bury her. I'll let Mrs. Rolt know."

I told her some days later, and she had said, "Poor Frannie. I'd forgotten she was there with me." Then she had turned away from me to hide the beginning of tears in her eyes.

## CHAPTER SEVEN

WE WERE MAN and wife. We had gone through a crisis and we had survived. But the survival had brought change. When you have come near to losing something precious, and then had it miraculously restored to you, it becomes doubly precious. To take pleasure in simple things was natural with us, but now the simple things were no longer the small, unburnished coinage of life. Every small act shone with a life of its own, carried a glow and new facets which it was hard to accept one had never seen before.

Sarah some weeks after she had truly come back to Rolthead expressed it better and more simply than I ever could.

I walked into her bedroom late one night after I had been working in my study to kiss her and say goodnight—sometimes if she were already asleep I would kiss her without waking her— and I found her sitting in the armchair by her window with all the lights out. She was leaning forward in her chair, staring out into the autumn night.

As I went to her, she half turned to me and in the starlight I saw that her face was wet with tears.

I said, "Sarah—what on earth's the matter?"

She reached out and took my hand and gave a little shake of her head. "Nothing," she said and began to wipe her eyes with her handkerchief.

"But you're crying. Has something upset you?"

"Oh, Robert . . ." She sniffed back her tears and suddenly smiled. "Because I cry it doesn't mean there's anything wrong."

"No?"

"No—you stupid. I was just sitting here, waiting for you to come up, and I was looking at the night . . . and it was all so beautiful and I was suddenly overcome by how happy I was . . . how very, very happy."

I went on my knees beside her, holding her hand, and said, "But that's nothing to cry about."

She laughed then and said, "Oh, Robert . . . always solid and dependable and down to earth. Of course it's something to cry about. Tears are not just for sorrow—they're for joy and happiness, too. At least they are if you're a woman."

I often recalled those few moments, and with the memory there was always sharply in me the remembrance of my own first few seconds of reaction as I had stood there hearing her sobs. It had been a swift primitive anger that anything or anyone in the world could have hurt or provoked her to the point of tears.

*       *       *       *

After the harvest—which was late that year—we went together to Amalfi for a couple of weeks and then motored back along the coast and up through France. At Christmas, as always, we had a house full of Rolts and Rolt relations and the place was alive and noisy and full of carnival and Sarah reigned over it all in a way which sometimes almost choked me with joy and love for her. I had an enormous pride in her, too. Not just because she was beautiful and beloved by me, but because of what she was herself. People liked her. She made friends wherever she went and I was, I have to admit it, almost absurdly delighted with her talents. She was not just a decorative figurehead at Rolthead. She could shoot, ride to hounds, handle a rod and take her part in all country affairs as well as most men. With Mrs. Cordell she ran Rolthead without the least suggestion of strain or fuss and in addition she ran her own private business affairs with a far-sighted efficiency which had made her a much wealthier woman than she had been when we

128

were first married. I knew this, not from her, but from her mother who—proud of her daughter—had told me so when we visited her at Amalfi. Not that Sarah kept her affairs to herself. One or two of her business projects she discussed with me, not because she needed my advice, I knew, but because she felt that it was right that we should be ready to share our activities. If I had wished to know more of her interests or even enter into them to some extent she would have been glad. But running the Rolthead estates—which Harold and I were extending in other counties with the purchase of farming lands and other properties—gave me more than enough to do.

That I loved her and was happy with her was plain for all to see. That I was proud of her and worshipped her and counted myself the luckiest of men to have such a wife I tried not to over-display.

Once while Harold was with me I began to fuss because Sarah had taken the dogs off for a walk and it had begun to rain and I knew that she had no mackintosh.

Harold said, "Don't fuss, Bobby. The goddess Sarah won't get wet. She'll just command the rain to part and fall either side of her."

There were times, I had begun to fancy, when Harold sometimes showed he was changing in character. He had developed an odd trick of saying things which revealed a line of thought I would least have expected from him. But I had in all fairness to admit that perhaps I did put Sarah on a pedestal and worship her too openly. I had to remind myself at times that there is nothing more boring—perhaps, too, embarrassing—than a man making a parade of his love and delight in a woman. Love can blind and delight intoxicate.

Whether this had happened with me I still don't know. All I know is that I was called upon to consider it nine months after Sarah's return to Rolthead.

It was the twenty-seventh of March and a Thursday. I had a salmon rod on the Avon Tyrrell water just below Ringwood in Hampshire. Thursday was my day and the River Avon was a fair drive from Rolthead. The early morning, as I drove over, was full of snow flurries and was as cold as charity, but I was well weather-proofed and as a further precaution—since my pocket flask held only a small ration—I stopped in Ringwood and bought myself a bottle of Scotch as a backstay. I started fishing at nine. The weather and the condition of the river were too bad for a fly so I put up my spinning-rod. I fished for a couple of hours, using a brown and gold Devon minnow. The wind was merciless and the occasional snow-squalls blinding. As I stamped my feet and beat my hands, I remembered my father's favourite remark that only a thin line divided fishermen from lunatics. But the gods have always had a soft spot for madmen and they were good to me. Quite undeservedly I got a twenty-pound hen fish on what I had sworn would be my last cast before an early lunch.

I hoisted the fish on my back and walked towards the fishing hut. As I approached it I saw that a car was parked alongside mine on the track.

I hung the fish outside the hut and went in. Sitting at the table was an old friend of my father, General Sir Maxwell Campbell. He was also my godfather. He was a short, plump, highly complexioned man with an iron-grey moustache. One look at him told you that he was—or rather had been—an army man. Although younger than my father by some five years they had been very close friends. He was wearing a cap and was wrapped up in a thick greatcoat. The lunch basket I had brought was on the table and he had opened it and discovered the whisky. There was a half-empty glass close to his hand.

He grinned and said, "'Morning, Robert. Knowing the Rolt hospitality, I knew you wouldn't mind." He lifted the whisky glass. "Monkey-freezing weather. Do any good?"

"I got a nice hen fish. How are you, sir?"

"Getting older like all of us. I rang your place and Mrs. Cordell told me you were fishing. Thought I'd run down and have a word with you. How's Sarah?"

"She's fine. She's away for a few days."

I poured myself a glass of whisky and sat down opposite him. Although he was retired I knew that he was a busy man. Much too busy, I thought, to motor miles on a bitter day to have a chat with his godchild in a fishing-hut that was as cold as a refrigerator. I lifted my glass and drank to him silently.

He acknowledged the toast, sipping at his glass, and then said, "Haven't touched a rod myself for years."

Quite bluntly, I said, "I'm sure, sir, you didn't choose a day like this to motor down here just for a chat about fishing."

He smiled. "Same Robert. Blunt. Straight to the point. I like it. But it was as well you left the Foreign Office. You'd never have got any of the plums. Your father had a touch of it, but mostly he knew how to hold it back. No, I didn't come down here just to chat. I came to tell you something and to give you some advice. To be frank I was ordered to come and to make it as discreet as possible."

"Ordered? I thought you were retired."

"According to the Army List, yes. But there are times when my seniority and experience are considered to merit a little casual employment."

"What have you got to tell me?"

He pulled a card from his pocket and slid it across to me. "Mean anything to you?"

I looked at the card. It held a printed name and an address. A cold feeling of unease swept through me.

"No, it means nothing to me."

"He wants to see you at eleven o'clock tomorrow morning."

"What on earth for?"

"I wouldn't know in detail—but generally . . . well, it concerns Sarah."

"For God's sake!" I exploded. "Don't tell me all that bloody nonsense is starting again!" I hit the card with my fist. "This is Whitehall, isn't it?"

He lifted the whisky bottle and topped up our glasses. "Yes, it's Whitehall."

"Well, you can tell them I'm not going to see them. I've had my bellyful of them—and I'm not having them mucking up Sarah's life again!"

He was silent for a moment, staring straight at me. Then he said crisply, "Listen to me. I'm here under orders. I'm also here as a family friend. That, I imagine, is why they picked me. First of all let's get the orders out of the way. You'll be there at eleven, Robert. If you aren't, then they're quite capable of coming to you at Rolthead. If they didn't care a damn about you and Sarah they would never have sent me down here."

Angrily, I said, "It seems to me, General, that you're not as casually employed as you would have me think."

He shook his head, smiling. "Robert, my boy, you really are a fighting-cock."

"And why shouldn't I be? Sarah's happy and well—all that Chinn business is dead—and I'm not having her badgered about and upset by a pack of Whitehall snoopers!"

He said, "I came here to give you an order—and some advice. Here's the advice. Let off steam with me as much as you like. I know you. You're the son of a man who was my best friend. I know that when you get back you'll drop me a note apologising for blowing off steam. If I told you that it is unnecessary you would still do it. That's why I'm here. I know your character. They know something about it, too." He grinned suddenly. "Maybe they chose this way because they didn't want someone in their office pitched clean through a window. You're stiff-necked, pugnacious, irascible, and impetuous—oh, yes, you are. But you are other things as well. You're solid, straightforward and honest—and far from being anyone's fool. And the whole of your world revolves around Sarah and Rolthead. God help anyone who tries to interfere. But think this over—and I mean it—it could be that these Whitehall snoopers, as you call them, care as much for Sarah's interests as you do. In that case you owe them a hearing and the courtesy of keeping your temper under control. Do I make sense?"

I nodded. "Yes, you do. I'm sorry, sir. But you can imagine how I feel. I thought this thing was dead."

"I know. You and Sarah have had some bad breaks. But a lot of people do in life." He rose stiffly and turned up the collar of his greatcoat, his red face gleaming with the cold. He went on, "You're quite right to think that I'm more than casually employed, though I say that in strict confidence to you. To give you some comfort I'll break another confidence that I shouldn't. I don't think their interest is centred on Sarah. There are other people who interest them much more. The last thing they want to do is to upset your life and Sarah's. So, Robert—when you meet them—just keep a tight curb on yourself."

"Very well, General."

"Good. By the way, Dora sent her love."

I said, "That's good of her. There's a nice fish hanging outside. Perhaps you'd take it to Lady Campbell with my love."

"Dora will be delighted." He paused at the door and then said, "I'd like you to know, Robert, that if at any time you feel you need help or advice I'm always around—in a non-professional capacity. And remember—before you throw any fast punches, just try to see their point of view."

When he had gone I sat there, in the bleak, winter-cold fishing-hut, and there was bleak winter inside me. In a handful of minutes I had found myself cast out of the paradise of love and warmth and security of my new life with Sarah into a raw wilderness. For a moment or two my hand gripped the whisky bottle and I wanted to sling it viciously against the wall. I wanted to see and hear something smash into small pieces. I damned nearly did, but at the last moment I curbed myself. I sat there sick at heart and slowly began to handle the anger and bitterness in me.

The name on the card was Captain H. Garwood, R.N., Deputy Director Statistical Projects, Ministry of Defence. The address was in Northumberland Avenue. I was there at five minutes to eleven the next morning. It was a tall, shabby-looking building with a uniformed porter at a desk in the small hall. I showed him the card and he pointed to the lift and said, "Fifth floor, sir."

The lift creaked its way upwards. I stepped out into a world that was anything but shabby. There was a long white corridor, the paint work spotless and on the floor a black and white tiled linoleum that had a high shine on it. A girl in a blue dress sat behind a low pinewood desk. I handed her the card and said, "My name is Rolt. I have an appointment with Captain Garwood at eleven."

She said, "Yes, Mr. Rolt. The captain is expecting you. Number seven. Just knock and go straight in." She pointed to her right down the corridor. "The last door on the left."

The night before, thinking things over, I had decided that the advice which the General had given me was more than sound. In fact it was more than advice. It was a reprimand. However much one might dislike the work of people like Vickers and Garwood, there was no arguing against its necessity. Sarah and I had been drawn into that world. My one desire was to get us out as quickly as possible. Being awkward and bloody-minded could only delay that moment. I was going to keep a tight curb on myself. I would, as far as I could, try and see things from their point of view.

I knocked on the door of number seven and went in. The window of the room faced me as I entered. Under the window was a desk and a man sat behind it. As he rose I noticed some pigeons fly away from the window-ledge outside. There was a set of green filing cabinets in the room, a couple of bentwood chairs, and a tall, old-fashioned hatstand. It looked like a room that no one ever inhabited for any length of time, an interview room. It was spotlessly clean, clinical and cold like the corridor.

Captain Garwood was a great deal younger than I was. He was tall and awkwardly built and wore civilian clothes. His fair hair was thin and lay close to his head. His face was high-cheekboned and ran sharply away to a pointed chin. He looked pale and tired. As I introduced myself he reached a long arm across the desk and shook my hand. Then he nodded to a chair which stood by the desk.

He said, "Good of you to come, Mr. Rolt."

I sat down and said without any feeling, "I was ordered to."

He smiled and shrugged his shoulders and said, "Well, yes, I suppose you were. I hope you won't hold it against us."

"No, I won't. I'm quite prepared to be co-operative if you produce good reasons for my being so."

"In other words, don't let's beat about the bush? All right— let's settle for that But before I begin I should tell you that I'm going to have to ask you some very personal questions. They can't be avoided. Some of them you may consider impertinent, but I would like you to answer them because, quite sincerely, it could be in the interests of you and Mrs. Rolt."

"I'll do what I can."

"Thank you, Mr. Rolt." He pulled a green-backed file which lay on the desk towards him and opened it. He said, "How much do you know of your wife's business dealings, and her financial affairs?"

"Not a great deal. She's a wealthy woman and more than able to handle her affairs. I'm glad she is because I have my own hands full enough."

"But you do know about some of them?"

"A few."

"Have you any idea—even roughly—of what she might be worth at this moment?"

"No. A great deal though."

"Would half a million surprise you?"

"No."

"A million?"

"I would doubt it. If she is, then I'm happy to hear it for her sake. But I don't see its relevance. Can we come to the main point?"

Some pigeons had resettled on the sill outside and a drift of sleet was smearing the glass.

135

"In a few moments, yes, Mr. Rolt. Has she ever mentioned to you a company called International Industrial Systems Limited?"

"No."

"Have you ever heard of it?"

"Yes, but I know nothing about it."

"It has a capital of millions. Your wife and her mother are very big stockholders."

"In that case I don't doubt that it's a successful company. Her mother is an even better businesswoman than my wife."

"You don't ask who holds the rest of the stock?"

"I'm not here to ask questions."

"When you feel you want to, I'll answer what I can. You know, of course, that your wife gives a lot of money to charity."

"Yes, I know. So do thousands of other wealthy people."

"Do you approve of all of those charities?"

"I doubt whether I know all of them. But of the ones I do know I think one or two are . . . well, pretty much up in the air. I suppose that no matter how competent and far-sighted a person is there's always some soft spot—perhaps even a blind spot. But it's her money."

"When you say that, have you any particular instance in mind?"

"Well . . . yes, I suppose so. She's very interested in astronomy and I know she's made quite large donations to various astronomical research bodies both in Europe and America."

"That doesn't strike me as being odd, Mr. Rolt. Backing science after all is——"

"This isn't science! This is the rankest kind of nonsense. These are crackpot organisations who believe in little green men from Mars and unidentified flying objects."

"Flying saucers and so on?"

"Yes. Still—" I shrugged my shoulders—"as I say—it's her money. We're all potty about something in some way, large or small, I suppose. But I don't suppose you've got me here to chat about things like that."

"No, that's true." He paused for a moment, the shadow of a smile touching his lips. On the windowsill a pigeon shook its plumage to free it from sleet drift. Then he asked, "How do you get on with your mother-in-law?"

"We're not very close. I suppose you could say we respect one another. Frankly she was opposed to my marriage with Sarah in the first place."

"And her feelings towards her daughter?"

"Outwardly there's a great deal of reserve. But I know they are deeply attached to one another."

He got up and came round the desk and said, "I'm going to play you part of a tape-recording. I should explain that it's not the whole tape. Only as much as I have been authorised to let you hear. Because of the circumstances in which it was taken it's not a good one either. There's a lot of interference and occasionally the whole thing is just an unintelligible noise." He pulled open one of the drawers of the filing cabinet and lifted out a recording machine.

He put it on the desk between us and plugged its cable into a socket below the desk.

He said, "Before I run it I'm going to declare our position in this matter. The whole of this interview and its implications are matters of security. You were in the Foreign Office once. The declaration you made under the Official Secrets Act is still valid. Basically we are not directly concerned with your wife in the sense that she has been a party to any breach of national security——"

"For God's sake, I should bloody well hope not!"

He waited for a moment as I controlled myself and then said with a smile, "Well, at least you didn't try to throw me out of the window."

"I'm sorry. But I wish to God you'd come to the point. I don't like this cat-and-mouse business. I'm not enjoying sitting here. I'd like to hear everything you've got to say hard and straight and quickly."

"All right. Listen to the tape first. It's quite short." He

137

switched the machine on and I sat and listened while winter whistled in sleet squalls down the chasm of the avenue outside.

(Much later on, a transcript of this piece of tape was made available to me. I give the transcript now. Two people, a man and a woman, were recorded. It took me only a few moments to recognise the woman's voice as that of Alexina. The man's voice I did not know.)

*Man:* Well, we always knew there was a risk of the arrangement going wrong. Let's face it, there is an element in Sarah which has always been difficult to handle.

*Woman:* It's always been recognised that as far as possible her natural demands as a woman should be respected. She's my daughter and I wanted for her as much human happiness as possible . . . (noise and static interference) . . . we're a long time here. No matter our first loyalty, it's always been policy to concede these periods of withdrawal from the overall design.

*Man:* They're becoming more complicated to handle as the years go by . . . (noise and static interference). . . . The level of human curiosity has risen. Government agencies have become more imaginative. Also there's a powerful drive from below. Societies and organisations whose voices can't be ignored . . . (noise and static interference) . . . Anyway, in view of the new directive I think a decision about Sarah should be made fairly soon——

*Woman:* As her mother, I object to any drastic interference with her for . . . well, for a considerable time. She's gone through a bad time. She's happy and she's in love and she's entitled to stay that way . . . (noise and static interference). . . .

*Man:* That was one of Chinn's rare mistakes. However, now let's get down to the new directive.

*Woman:* (With a sigh) I suppose we must. . . . Dear Lincoln . . . even with all the time we have on our hands don't you

138

|         | sometimes wonder about it all? Don't you ever get tired? Don't you ever wonder whether the whole thing hasn't been framed wrongly? |
|---------|---|
| *Man:* | A little. But not as much as you do. My breeding was different from yours. You're partly Latin. |
| *Woman:* | Well, what has authority decided now? |
| *Man:* | We've become dangerously vulnerable. Too much violence is being turned against us, you know that . . . (voice distortion, unintelligible) . . . We have only a limited reply. So the directive is: a complete reorganisation of all collecting methods; the closing of most financial outlets and the establishment of new ones; the breakup of all information centres and the . . . (noises and static interference) . . . and these new centres, except for key people, to be restaffed. |
| *Woman:* | That'll take for ever! |
| *Man:* | A year. Far less, if possible. But it has got to be done. Locations haven't all been settled yet, but the emphasis on Europe will be cut down considerably because it's felt that . . . (here a very long period of static interference). . . . |
| *Woman:* | Surely that wouldn't be difficult to arrange? In the circumstances it must be. |
| *Man:* | I agree. But next time the disengagement must appear absolutely natural—and you know what that means. The choice won't be left to . . . (some static interference and the end of the transcript). |

Garwood switched the machine off and then leant back in his chair and said quietly, "Would you like it run again, Mr. Rolt?"

I shook my head. He opened his green file and passed a sheet of closely typed paper across to me. "That's a transcript of the recording. You might like to refer to it here. I can't let you take it away."

I picked up the sheet of paper and stared at it. Quite frankly

I was considerably confused, so confused, in fact, that there was no room in me for any other feeling. What in hell was it all about? What on earth was going on? The typed words on the sheet danced in front of my eyes. I just could not take them in.

Garwood said, "The woman, of course, is your wife's mother. Have you ever heard of the man Lincoln?"

"No."

"The tape was taken some considerable time ago at the Villa Mendola and——"

"I don't much care where it was taken. You've called me up here to listen to it. I don't think there's anything I can say to you, Captain Garwood, until you have said all you have to say to me."

"Yes, of course. You will understand that some things I can't tell you because I am not authorised to. But the broad picture is this. For a considerable number of years now the security forces in this country and others have known that there is a well-organised agency which has been collecting information most of which is of a highly secret nature. The field of operation is very wide indeed. This organisation is not interested in just military or defence matters. Their operations cover government confidential papers which aren't necessarily concerned with defence. They collect industrial secrets, details of new patents, highly technical manufacturing data, and plans for new projects over a wide spectrum. In fact, they seem to want anything which for the moment is not openly in the public domain. Anything. The easiest way of putting it is to say that they are like a lot of jackdaws or magpies who pick up anything odd or curious that may be going around. In fact their range is so broad it is confusing. I mean this in the sense that it is not possible to play a game of probabilities and pick any other country in the world who would want all the stuff they gather in. The conclusion, here, officially —and there's been some proof of this—is that it is a private organisation which collects and then finds clients for its material. An underdeveloped country, a new African state, say, would be in the market for information which all the major powers already have. Because their range is so wide you can see that there has been a reluctance in our individual security forces to accept sole responsibility for tackling these people except when their own particular interests are involved. That led to a lot of wasted time, duplication of investigations and general inefficiency. That's finished now. A combined security body was established some time ago. In fact, just after Vickers approached you. You remember Vickers, of course."

"Yes, I do. But I'm not interested in him, or anything except what all this has to do with my wife."

"You heard the tape. Alexina Vallis is a principal in this collecting organisation which we are pretty sure is sponsored or directed by International Industrial Systems. So is the man Lincoln and so is the elusive Albert Chinn. From the tape it's clear that the organisation is to be reshaped and redeployed. This is largely because we're getting too close to them and also, maybe, because they intend to extend their activities."

I said coldly, "You're still avoiding the subject of my wife. I'm waiting for a frank statement from you."

"Very well. You're not going to like any of this. There are three hypotheses. The first is that—in the past—your wife was used by this organisation without her knowledge. In other words she was innocently involved. The second is that she is involved in this organisation still, but against her will, an involvement that could date back to long before she married you and that she has no present means of disconnecting herself from it. Neither can she confide in you because it would be dangerous for her, or for both of you." He paused and fiddled with the file in front of him.

"And the third?"

For the first time he was embarrassed and said, "You surely must see what it is."

"I want to hear you say what it is, Captain Garwood."

"All right. The third is that she is involved in this organisa-

141

tion, has been for a long time, and works for it of her own free will."

I said nothing for a moment. I was holding myself in, putting on the curb hard. No shouting or table-banging was going to be of any good now. The violence in me had to be contained, but I prayed that a time and day would come when I could release it.

I said, "And what is the official attitude?"

"Divided, fairly evenly, between all three."

"And yours?"

"That she's being used against her will—but at the moment she has no means of escape."

"Blast you!"

He shrugged his shoulders. "I'm sorry but you asked me." He tapped the transcript. "Look at it. The man talks of an element in your wife which has always been difficult to handle. I take that to mean she kicks or has kicked against the role she has to play. Her mother says she doesn't want any drastic interference with her for a long time. That could mean that for the moment she is doing very little for them and her mother wants that period to be as long as possible. And the man says at the end, 'But the next time the disengagement must appear absolutely natural.' I think they've tried one disengagement already—when your wife disappeared—but it went wrong."

I stood up. "You think it's going to happen again—is that it? That these people have such a hold over Sarah that they let her go on a vacation and marry me? Gave her a few years' happiness and then whipped her away? That it went wrong and she came back to me?"

"I hope I'm wrong—but, yes. Remember, they didn't want her to marry you. She was already engaged—to someone far more suitable from their point of view. By marrying you, your wife defied them. She tried to escape, but in the end they took her back."

"I think it's a lot of bloody, fantastic nonsense," I said angrily.

142

"I would in your shoes, too. But I know it is not."

I stood up and looked down at him. So far as I was concerned at that moment I was in a cell talking to a committed lunatic.

I said wearily, "You, or the people you work for, want your heads examined. Sarah is Alexina's daughter. There's a deep love between them. Alexina would never harm her own child. She doesn't care much for me—but for Sarah, yes. And anyway, how could they possibly have arranged all that Mrs. Starr stuff and her loss of memory?" I sat down. "Sorry, but no."

Garwood shook his head, and said, "Why don't you raise the really important point? Don't you want to face it? Until a few moments ago you had no idea that there was any connection between Alexina and this Albert Chinn. There's the real beginning of proof that Alexina was party to Sarah being used. The script says, 'That was one of Chinn's rare mistakes.' I believe that refers to the new identity he created for your wife— no matter for the moment how it was done—when she was originally detached from you. It went wrong. But in good time they may try it again unless we wrap them up."

He sat there watching me, his long face grey in the winter light from the window. He had put to me a truth whose existence, I realised then, my mind, my whole nature, had refused to acknowledge in some instinctive act of mental evasion . . . to avoid a swift and brutal shock which might destroy my life, Sarah's life, our life together.

I said quietly, my voice seeming to come from an unfathomable remoteness of time, "What is it you want from me?"

"Mr. Rolt, we *may* want your help. Just how, at the moment, I can't say. It could be that we may never want it, that we can settle this thing without calling on you. I may say there was considerable opposition from some of our people against letting you know what I have. For a variety of reasons it was finally decided that you should know."

I said, "You've done a good job, Captain Garwood. Or, at least, the people behind you have. No matter how much you might want to deny it, you've come between a man and his wife. You're not interested in me or my wife. You're only interested in doing the dirty little jobs you have to do. You've told me all you have so that I know the brief when you want something from me. I know exactly what you're going to say to me before I leave here. 'Go back to Rolthead and carry on your life as usual. Say nothing to anyone, not even to your wife, but keep your eyes and ears open. One day, if you're obedient and docile and help when asked, and when we've put all those we want to in the bag, we'll see that your wife—guilty or not guilty—is quietly left out of it all.' That's the form, isn't it?"

"It's your way of looking at it, Mr. Rolt. But it's not personally my way, nor of a lot of other people. There are other elements which I can't possibly discuss with you. But this I must say for the people I serve—they're not monsters. They are human beings with a problem that concerns thousands of other people. They want to protect them—and they genuinely want to do all they can for you and your wife and your happiness together. Fundamentally human happiness is their sole concern. As far as we can be at the moment, we are being open and frank with you. Your wife is with you now because of us and we don't want you to lose her again. All we might ask of you is a little help towards that end—and your absolute discretion about all I have told you. Yes, Mr. Rolt—I am saying to you, 'Go back to Rolthead and carry on your life as usual, and say nothing to your wife.' If we hadn't thought you were a man of the character, ability and understanding to be able to do that you wouldn't be in this room at the moment."

I said, "All just as simple as that? You turn a man's world upside down and then . . . All right, I'll try to see it your way. But before I go——"

"You'd like to ask me some questions?"

"Yes."

"Very well. If I can answer them I will."

My first question was the most important one for me. I had for a long time now centred all my anger and spleen on one man.

I held one man responsible for all that had happened to Sarah—
and it was that man I wanted one day to find so that I could
settle my account with him.

I said, "What information have you got about Albert Chinn
that you can pass to me?"

"Very little. We are pretty certain that the *real* Albert Chinn
never comes out into the open. His mantle, as it were, is worn
by different people. We have film of the Albert Chinn your wife
knew. We have film also of other Albert Chinns that other
people knew. They are all different. Your wife's Albert Chinn
has disappeared. He certainly worked for a consortium of oil
companies, but only on the vaguest of terms. This consortium
no longer has any contact with him. We've experienced the
same thing before with all the other—shall we call them sur-
rogate?—Albert Chinns. They pop up, operate for a limited
purpose, and then disappear."

"What did my wife's Albert Chinn use her for?"

"As a collector. Specifically in two fields. One was new
patents and the other confidential papers from companies
within the oil industry. They were mostly concerned with
estimates of residual oil-field capacities and reports on new
drillings. Most of the stuff eventually became a matter of public
record. Though I should point out that a lot of things which are
legally accessible to the public are very difficult to find."

For the first time I lit a cigarette. The window was blurred
with a fierce snow-squall and I suddenly realised that the room
was soundproofed. No noise of the weather or the heavy traffic
in the avenue could be heard.

I said, "Have you anything against my wife for which she
could be indicted in a court of law?"

"No."

"Well, thank you for that, anyway."

"That doesn't mean there isn't anything, Mr. Rolt. She has
a large interest in International Industrial Systems Limited.
There are certainly a few charges we could bring against them
—only it would be premature to do so just now. For all we

know your wife may be quite unaware of their clandestine activities."

"And her mother?"

"You've heard the tape. From other information we have there's no doubt that she's fully aware of these activities and controls some of them."

"How long has all this been going on?"

"For a very long time. An extraordinarily long time, in fact. I wouldn't want to be precise."

"Was old Vallis—Alexina's husband—ever involved in any of this?"

"Not that we know."

I looked at the tape transcript. "Alexina Vallis says in the recording: "Well, what has authority decided now?' Who or what is the authority?"

Garwood ran a lean hand over his thinning fair hair. "That's the big question. Usually after a time one can pinpoint an agency or country. You can tell by the kind of stuff that's being collected and after a while make a reasonably sure assessment. You can say China, the U.S.S.R. or the C.I.A., and so on. Every country has its own intelligence systems—but they can usually be pinpointed. But not with this set-up. You can always, too, eventually isolate the operations of private individuals or groups, double agents, or just criminal opportunists who know their markets and sell to the highest bidder."

I said, "Tell me—you know my wife's private history? I mean about her amnesia."

"Yes, of course."

"You take that to be all part of a plan—which went wrong— to take her away from me so that she could be . . . well, re-deployed in some other place or in some other rôle decided on by this 'authority'?"

"Yes, I do."

"If that's so—how valid does your organisation consider her amnesia to have been?"

"There's a division of opinion."

146

"In other words you don't bloody well want to commit yourself? You don't want to say straight to my face that my wife was a knowing party to everything that happened. That she put on a big act for me as Mrs. Starr—either against her will or deliberately of her own choice?"

"That's not the reason. Quite frankly we have no evidence one way or the other. And anyway, you've overlooked a third possibility. The amnesia could have been genuine. That is, it could have been induced by some means by Albert Chinn. Don't ask me how, but our experts say it is not impossible either by drugs or some hypnotic treatment. You can do strange things with people's minds—that's a matter of record; brainwashing by a persistent form of suggestion plus the use of drugs. I don't have to tell you that every government in the world practises more and more sophisticated forms of psychological warfare."

"And you think this was done to Sarah—and then when things went wrong they reversed the process so that she could come back to me? Don't tell me you could believe in any Alice in Wonderland nonsense like that?"

He smiled bleakly. "Opinions officially are divided. But if you want my personal opinion, yes, I do. I think that is exactly what happened. There's one factor which makes me quite sure of it."

"What factor?"

"She still has nearly a year's gap she can't account for."

"How the devil do you know that?"

"How do you think a service like ours gets information from banks, accountants, scientists and doctors and so on? Because we have *got* to have it. Because when you are fighting an enemy there is no such thing as a confidence that cannot be breached one way or the other."

"You mean you twisted Sir Hugh Gleeson's arm? My God, what a lot you are!"

"It took a lot of twisting. But we did it—yes, though only after we had convinced him that it was in your wife's interests.

147

That gap is in her favour. I think that Chinn or whoever it was couldn't entirely reverse the amnesia. She was left with this gap. The fact that she has it proves the validity of the original amnesia. In my opinion, Mr. Rolt, your wife wasn't acting the part of Mrs. Starr. She believed she was Mrs. Starr."

"Then in God's name I don't know how Alexina Vallis tolerated that!"

Garwood shrugged his shoulders. "She either did—or she was forced to tolerate it, Mr. Rolt. That should give you some idea of the kind of people we are dealing with and why you are sitting here this morning."

"But why should they have ever wanted Sarah back? She married me and escaped them. Innocent or not—why not let her stay free to have the life she wanted?"

"Because they don't like losing their own. She could have come to you completely innocent, but they could have had plans for her. She's escaped them again . . . but they could still have plans for her." He tapped the tape transcript. "What they have done once, they might do again. I think that gives us good grounds for expecting you will help us if we ever ask you."

I said, "In the tape they talk about their vulnerability and the violence that is being turned against them. Does that come from you?"

"They're vulnerable in the same way that any clandestine organisation is vulnerable if various parties are seeking it. There *are* other parties, Mr. Rolt. International Industrial Systems is not confining its activities just to this country. Other governments are interested in them. And they've stirred up a considerable amount of bad will with other industrial groups throughout the world. We don't use violence unless it is inevitable. Our interpretation of the word inevitable, naturally, isn't the same as other people's."

"But the fact remains that they're going to ground. Which means, if I read the tape right, that there is a possibility they intend to take my wife with them—willingly or unwillingly, knowingly or unknowingly?"

He nodded and for a moment the expression on his face was that of a man infinitely tired and under great strain. He said quietly, "Yes, that's the way we feel it must be interpreted. That's why you are here. You've got more friends than you will probably ever know in this organisation. That's why you're being treated quite differently—and not without opposition, I may say—from the way another man might be. We want this group wrapped up. I think that makes it not unreasonable for us to expect that we can, if necessary, call on your help."

For a moment or two I was silent. There had been times when I had been riled, had flown off the handle, but now there was no desire in me to oppose him. He had been as reasonable and as forthcoming as his brief allowed. If one thing was clear it was that he was on my side, on Sarah's side, that his sympathy and concern were genuine. There was no denying that my mind was in some confusion from all I had heard. My world was upside down. But that I had to co-operate with him was undeniable. I wanted to, anyway, because I was determined that no power on earth was going to take Sarah away from me again.

I said, "You've been very frank with me, Captain Garwood. I appreciate it. But surely there's something positive I can do?"

He gathered up his folder and the tape transcript and slid them into the desk drawer. "Nothing, Mr. Rolt. At the moment nothing."

"But there must be something I can damn well do!"

"There could be in the future, yes. But for the moment you've got enough on your hands. You've got to go back to Rolthead and carry on your life as usual. Just that is going to be a minor form of hell for you, Mr. Rolt."

I said, "I have an instruction to contact Vickers in case of need—is that still good?"

"No," he said sharply. "Get in touch with me. Vickers is only peripherally concerned with this business now." He took up a pencil and wrote on a slip of paper. "That's my telephone number. Take it with you. Memorise it and then destroy the paper. You can always get me there, or someone will know about you, at any time of day or night."

The paper in my hand, I was about to turn to go when, the tone of his voice changing almost to affability, he said, "Perhaps I should be a little more explicit about Vickers. He still works for us—but in a less responsible capacity. Everyone in this organisation is under strain. If you succumb it can do odd things to you sometimes. Naturally, of course, we look after our own. Vickers now has no authority to have any contact with you. If he does you will report the matter to me at once and disregard anything he says to you."

I nodded, resenting being given orders. But as I went down to the street, I was thinking about nervous, eye-flicking Vickers—with sympathy. How could any sensitive man stay sane for long in Garwood's world?

# PART TWO

*Yet the race abides immortal, the star of their
house sets not through many years. . . .
Assigning in victorious march, laws to the un-
willing nations, and assaying on earth the path
to the stars!*

Virgil. *Georgics.*

CHAPTER EIGHT

THERE HAD BEEN a time when nothing could have altered my opinion that the most beautiful period of the year to look forward to at Rolthead was the Spring. I loved the house, its grounds, and the country all around. Although there was little poetry in me, Spring had always stirred me with its tokens of hope and abundant rebirth. There was always the day when one saw clearly the first, faint green misting of the hawthorn hedges as the young bud broke, the awakening to that morning when the aconites were yellow around the boles of the tall Wellingtonias, when the rook colonies gathered and were noisy and busy in their nesting elms, and suddenly the lawns were flooded with a moving sea of daffodil blooms and the fantail cocks on the stable roofs began to drive and cover their hens. The young lambs were loosed from the nursery pens to the lower slopes of the downs and suddenly went mad in wild bucking and leaping games as the lusty life-drive in them stirred and demanded expression. . . . One waited for the first day of the returning chiff-chaff's calls and the arrogant heralding notes of the first cuckoo. . . . Of all the times of the year it was the one I really looked forward to—but not this year.

*Go back to Rolthead and carry on as usual.*

I went back that day from seeing Garwood and there was one thing which gave me a little grace in which to adjust myself to the slow poison which had invaded my mind. Sarah was away staying with some friends in Wales.

I had dinner by myself that night and, long after Mrs. Cordell had gone to bed, I sat in the study thinking things over, going right back to the beginning of my time with Sarah.

153

Her mother had never wanted me to marry her, and she had been quite open about it. Between Sarah and myself there had never been any question of our love. The feeling which had taken me when I saw her on the hillside pathway was one, she had told me later, which she, too, had shared. And the night when, in the villa garden, I had asked her to run away with me and get married, there had been no hesitation about her . . . she had been wild, almost exultant in her response, and I remembered her saying, 'When it's done, you'll see it will change everything. Alexina will come right round. . . .' And so she had, with a good, outward grace, but the acceptance I felt had never been wholehearted. She had planned another and to her more suitable marriage. In her heart I knew that although she had forgiven Sarah, she had never forgiven me. That, I had accepted as natural—but now I had learnt things about her which were unforgivable and monstrous . . . impossible almost to believe. There were moments, as I sat there thinking over all that had passed with Garwood, when I wanted to get up and start right away to make arrangements to go and see Alexina. I wanted to walk into the Villa Mendola, meet her face to face, assault her with my questions, and demand an explanation. It was a tribute less to my own self-control than to an appreciation of Garwood's sincerity and honest concern with my problem that I didn't do anything. If I wanted to protect Sarah and to clear up the whole puzzling mess then common-sense told me that it could not be done without help. I was wandering in a maze, waiting for someone to come and guide me to the freedom of being that Robert Rolt who asked for nothing else but the right to love his wife, to have her love and cherish her, and to work and live again with the peace and harmony which we had known at Rolthead until the day—and I was now convinced of this—that Alexina had decided to take her away from me.

But how do you learn to live with a poison in the mind? How can you dismiss a suspicion about your wife which has been fed to you by another? Was Sarah completely innocent of all involvement in her mother's affairs? I knew damned well that she must be, had to be. But that did not disperse the poison. It worked and moved and harassed me with a life of its own and I had no way of gripping it to throttle and choke the life from it.

I got up and walked through the long hall to Sarah's private room. It was a big room with a pair of large mullioned windows that looked out over the front of the house. In daylight she had a wonderful view of the distant sea through a break in the trees. Originally it had been my mother's music room and her old Steinway was still there. Sarah had insisted on its staying when she had taken over the room. There was a large flat-topped Regency desk in one of the window bays. An old-fashioned Chubb safe stood in a far corner and along one wall were hung her rose paintings. It was at once a comfortable and a working room. During the bad months an open log fire always burned in the big fireplace around which were chairs and a long settee. I sat down in an armchair by the dying fire.

Garwood's voice came through to me against every wish in me to shut my mind to it. I got up and went to the desk. The top was neat and tidy, furnished with a red morocco leather blotter, a crystal ashtray, an alabaster paperweight, the telephone and desk lamp and a neat arrangement of pens and pencils in a shallow silver tray. It had always surprised me that the impulsive woman I had married had this orderly side to her nature. After working at her desk she always left it tidy and ready for the next time. There were two wide drawers at the top of the desk and smaller drawers in each supporting pedestal. I knew why I was standing by the desk. I only had to lower a hand and check which drawers were locked or unlocked. I had come away almost liking Garwood. Now I wondered if part of the reason why I had been called to him lay in his knowledge that at some time I would stand like this by her desk or some bedroom bureau and find that there was an immoral, independent life in my hands, stronger than any virtue arising from my love and respect for Sarah, that would move them to open the drawers, and give me unlicensed liberty to seek and pry and probe and so, by one small initial movement, forfeit a part of my love, respect and faith in Sarah. I was sure that such a hope had been, if not with him, then in the minds of the people behind him.

I turned away angrily and left the room, but there was no denying that the temptation had been with me.

Before I went to bed I crossed into her bedroom, not now pursued by any form of temptation. The room downstairs belonged to one Sarah. But here there was for me the true Sarah. The woman I loved with the same devotion as she loved me, the unrestrained, passionate woman who gave and shared her womanhood with my manhood. The place was full of her, her scents, the sound of her voice and her laughter, and the thousand memories of her body and movements and the changing delights of her face in every mood. Without thought, my voice calm and free of all passion, I said aloud, "Nobody is going to take her away from me." And I made myself a promise that when she came back from her visit she would find the same Robert Rolt she had left for a few days.

\*    \*    \*    \*

There were moments, of course, when it was hard, and times when I was glad that my work at Rolthead took me away, driving on my own visiting our farms. Now and then, in the isolation of a field of young wheat, or in my car, I could let myself go. Restraint I could impose on myself when I had to. But release I needed as well. Anyone seeing and hearing me at these times might with justice have written me off as a dangerous, foul-mouthed lunatic. But these moments of release were essential for me. And time, of course, worked against the uneasiness of my thoughts. Each day brought some respite, however small; habit and the recurring routines of life laid a shielding layer over the sore in the mind.

Whether Sarah noticed any change in my manner I couldn't tell. To me she was just the same as she had always been and

156

I tried to be the same with her. During the day we saw—which was normal—little of one another. The evenings—when we did not go out or entertain guests—we spent together as we had always done. Sometimes I would watch her when she was absorbed in her book or the tapestry work she liked doing, and those were the moments when there was a strong desire in me to break through the barrier between us . . . to move to her and tell her all that had been told me, to bring the whole thing into the open. God knows, I wanted to do it, to sweep away everything but complete honesty between us. But there was a force even stronger than my own intolerance of any sort of deceit between us, and this was that honesty and frankness might precipitate the one thing I was determined to prevent, that I might set in motion some train of circumstances which would take her from me. Sometimes as I watched her, bridling the anguish and impatience in me, she would look up from her book or her work and smile at me, wrinkling her nose and making a mouth, in the familiar signs of her happiness. Those were blessed moments for they signalled more than our comfort and joy in one another, they signalled an expression of her complete innocence. And on the nights when we made love there was with me sometimes a passion to possess and be possessed stronger than any I had known before.

The weeks moved us further into Spring and the days brought their customary anniversaries; the Easter service at Rolthead Church, the day we took our fly rods and first fished the park lake for trout, the morning wakening to the early house-martins' return, flashing up under the eaves to begin the refurbishing of their old nests, the bold blaze of the banks of early rhododendrons flaring against the dark background of spruce and firs, and the first evening when from beyond the lake came the sudden heart-stopping, magical call of the nightingales as Sarah and I lay in bed together.

Nothing had changed, I could tell myself. This was Rolthead as it always had been. This was Sarah as she had always been. I understood then how easy it can become to ignore facts, and deny the existence of doubts, to make the world as you want it to be, and to give life to a false image. The world of Vickers and Garwood, of memorised telephone numbers and distorted tape recordings, was a part of some distant nightmare.

But that world existed in no nightmare. It came again in its own time to Rolthead. It was an early May night and I had worked late in my study. During the evening a strong south-westerly wind had risen. I went to bed and I had been asleep for about an hour when I was awakened by the sound of one of my partly open windows rattling against its catch. I endured the noise for a while, reluctant to get out of bed, but in the end I could bear the irritation no longer.

I went to the window to close it. The wind was stronger now and dark patches of cloud were scudding across a moonlit sky. Directly below my room was a paved courtyard and beyond it a stretch of lawn that ran away to a low fence bordering a small field lane. As I stood there I saw a shape move away from the fence and begin to cross the lawn along a small path. The moon raced clear of the clouds for a moment and the lawn was bathed in pale, white light. The shape stopped moving. It was a man wearing a cloth cap and what looked like a windbreaker. The moonlight persisted and the man moved on. My first instinct was to push open the window and to bellow at him, to ask him what the devil he was playing at. There had been a time earlier in my life when I wouldn't even have bothered to do that. I would have gone for the old twelve-bore, which I used to keep in my wardrobe, and have fired a couple of shots over his head to scare the life out of him for interesting himself in other people's houses at three in the morning.

Now, I watched him because there was an instinct in me which told me that the period of peace and healing was over, that Rolthead was being invaded, that the dark world of Garwood, of Vickers and God-knew what others, had sent out its first patrol.

The man moved down the side of the lawn and then

diagonally across the courtyard under my window and disappeared around the side of the house. I stepped back into the room, pulled on my trousers over my pyjamas, slipped my feet into my shoes and went quietly down through the house. I didn't hurry. The instinct in me told me exactly where he would be going. I had no intention of doing anything that would rouse the household. I was going to deal with him myself and quietly.

From my study I got my father's old Colt .45 revolver. It was unloaded and I left it that way. In the darkness I walked down the long hall and stood outside Sarah's sitting-room. Very slowly I turned the door handle until the catch was free and then eased the door inwards an inch and let the catch slide back noiselessly. No door lock or hinge went unoiled in Rolthead in my father's day nor in mine. I eased the door a little more open and part of the room, lit by the reflected moonlight on the drive outside, came into view.

One of the long mullioned windows was open. The man was standing sideways to me, half-crouched in front of Sarah's desk. The top drawer in the right-hand pedestal of the desk was half open. He had a bunch of keys in his right hand and was trying one of them in the bottom drawer. On the desk itself was a small pile of documents and envelopes which he had taken from the open drawer.

He found a key which fitted the bottom drawer and drew it open. I knew—because I had bought the desk myself for Sarah—that there was a separate key for each drawer. The people in his world would have sent him prepared for that.

As he bent over the drawer I pushed the door open, stepped inside, and closed it behind me. The man jerked upright and turned towards me. I raised the revolver and moved quickly to him.

I said, "If you make any trouble, I'll use this. Understood?"

He looked at me in silence for a moment and then nodded.

I said, "Turn your back to me and then do as I say. Keep your hands above your shoulders where I can see them."

159

He raised his hands and turned. I went up until I could prod him in the back with the barrel of the revolver.

"Go out of the window then to the left along the terrace and down to the lawn."

He stepped through the window on to the terrace and I followed closely behind him. When we reached the lawn I directed him down the edge of the drive and along a path through some rhododendrons until we reached the high red brick outer garden wall. I wanted to be as far away from the house as possible.

When he was close up to the wall, I said, "All right—turn round but keep your hands up."

Although he was a taller man than myself I didn't doubt that I would be able to handle him if he started any trouble. Frankly, I was hoping that he would because this was the first time that I had had a near opportunity of physically expressing the tension and repression in me. To hit someone even remotely concerned with the dark world around Sarah would be a primitive joy and relief.

As he turned, the garden was bathed in moonlight. He swung round slowly, his hands up, and faced me. I recognised him at once and I am sure that he must have recognised me, but he gave no sign that he had done so.

"What were you looking for in the desk?"

For a moment he didn't answer. Then he shrugged his shoulders and said, "Anything that might be going. I'm an opportunist." His voice was easy and clearly shaded with insolence.

His windbreaker zip-fastener was pulled half-way down and it occurred to me that he might have stuffed something into the breast of the garment.

I said, "Open the front of your windbreaker, right down, and then put your hands up."

He dropped one hand and jerked the zip down and clear from its bottom fastening. The windbreaker swung open. Nothing had been hidden there. Beneath the windbreaker he was wearing an open-necked shirt with a thin silk scarf tied around his neck.

He said easily, "I've taken nothing. That's God's truth. I had no time."

I said, "I know you and you know me. I know you're not a sneak-thief. You may be all sorts of other kinds of bastard, but not that. I want to know what you came here for."

With the insolence clearer in his voice, he said, "I'm not in the mood for any chit-chat. You're an honest, law-abiding citizen, Rolt. Then act like one. Take me back to the house and call the police." Then he paused, smiled, and added, "But perhaps you don't want to do that?"

I was angry then, stirred by his self-confidence and also by the truth he had driven home. The last people I wanted were the police.

Furiously, I said, "You're bloody well going to tell me what I want to know even if I have to beat it out of you."

He shrugged his shoulders again and said, "You could do that, I suppose. I'm bigger than you but I don't go for the rough stuff. Still, if that's the mood you're in I'm too much of a gentleman not to oblige——"

He was quick, very quick, and he moved before he had finished speaking. And he took me by surprise. His left hand suddenly came down swiftly and the hard edge of its palm hit my wrist and sent the Colt flying to the ground. As the gun went from me he stepped in close and jabbed his right fist at my face. I flicked my head sideways. His fist went over my shoulder taking him slightly off balance. An angry joy fired me and I went into him hard. His initial attack had been good, but he had nothing to back it up. He flayed wildly at me in a way which told me that he had never been in a ring or worn gloves in his life. I hit him three times, sending him staggering backwards, and finished with an uppercut that sent him up against the brick wall. He rested against it, his face thrown up to the moonbright sky, and his mouth was open retching for air. Slowly, as his breath came back, he lowered his head and suddenly he spat at me.

At that moment I was hit hard from behind. It was a fierce rabbit punch that crashed savagely into the side of my neck. I went sprawling to the ground.

I was kicked viciously in the ribs twice and then heard the sound of running feet. By the time I rose they were gone and I knew that it was useless for me to go after them.

Angry and disgusted with myself for being so easily tricked, I went back to the house. I stepped into Sarah's sitting-room and closed the window behind me. The window-catch, I guessed, had been lifted from outside by a slip of perspex or a thin blade. I took the pile of stuff that lay on the desk and put it back in the one opened drawer and closed it.

The next morning at breakfast I told Sarah about the visit but I considerably amended the facts. I told her the truth up to the point where I had entered the study. I said the man had got the one drawer partly open and was reaching to take the contents out when I had disturbed him. He had run for the window and, although I had chased him through the gardens, I had lost him.

"I came back and fixed the window and closed up your drawer. I think, Sarah, love, you should check and see if anything is missing. If there is I'll get on to the police. Otherwise there's no point in bothering."

She said, "Robert—you shouldn't have gone in on your own like that. Once you'd seen the man you should have telephoned the police. He might have turned on you and——"

"I wish he had. I'd have sorted him out. You just check your things. If there's nothing missing we'll forget it. But I'll have to do something about the window catches. The old man was always talking about putting in a burglar alarm. I think we'll have to do it."

Sarah checked her drawer and came back. "There doesn't seem to be anything missing. It's just the drawer in which I keep some of Alexina's letters to me and odd stuff like bank

statements and catalogues. In fact there's a whole heap of
rubbish in there." She came round and kissed me on the
forehead. "And the next time we have visitors at night—you
call the police and keep clear. It's not worth getting knocked
about or shot for a few bits of silver or whatever. . . ."

When she had gone I sat there over a last cup of coffee. I
had amended my story. It was a convenient word—amended—
but it was not the right one. Falsified was the word. Deceit lies
in withholding as much as in distortion. I was a liar. I was
lying to Sarah. There had been a time when the very thought
would have been unthinkable. I remembered then my father,
quoting Shelley in connection with some diplomatic practices
he had had to accept, saying that there was no man ever
secure 'from the contagion of the world's slow stain'. By God
he was right. There had been a moment before I had put
Sarah's papers back into her desk when I had hesitated and
known again the temptation of glancing through them.

Later that day I telephoned the number Captain Garwood
had given me. It was a hard decision to make. I didn't want him
back in my life. But if Rolthead was to be broken into to be
searched there might follow other events which, for all I knew,
could harm Sarah and that was the last thing I wanted. I spoke
to him from an outside telephone booth on my way over to see
my brother. I told him all that had happened, including the
small deceit I had practised with Sarah. When I had finished
my account I said, "This was nothing to do with your people,
was it?"

"No, of course not. I told you that there were other parties
involved. You are positive you recognised this man?"

"Absolutely. I'd know him anywhere considering that he
damned nearly killed myself and my wife with his speedboat
at Amalfi. He's called John Chambers, an American, and he
rents a small villa part of the year at Positano."

"Why did you never report this speedboat thing?"

"Why the devil should I? I thought it was a stupid bit of
carelessness."

He said, "Do me a favour, Mr. Rolt. In future if anything odd happens—even though it looks accidental—be kind enough to let me know. Was the other man with Chambers last night the one who was water-skiing?"

"I never saw him. But I doubt it. The crack I got on the back of the neck wouldn't have been his style. But I may be wrong."

\*　　\*　　\*　　\*

About a week after the night visit of Chambers I was sitting in my study having a drink before dinner and waiting for Sarah to join me.

When she came in, she said, "Sorry, darling, but Mrs. Cordell kept me talking. That nephew of hers is in trouble again."

As I mixed her drink, I said, "I'm not surprised. He always will be. He likes the good things of life and is too damned work-shy to get them honestly. I'd sort him out if he ever came up in front of me." I was a Justice of the Peace for the county, one of a long line of Rolts who had served. It was not a job I cared for much, but like a lot of other public duties it was a service that no Rolt of Rolthead could refuse.

Sarah laughed. "We're very magisterial tonight, aren't we? Well, here's something else to put a frown on that craggy face of yours. Alexina's coming tomorrow to spend a couple of nights."

"Alexina? I thought she was in Italy?"

"She had to come over on business for a few days. She's down in the West Country now and wants to stay on her way back home." As she took her drink from me she added, laughing, "You're very pleased, aren't you? My dear mother who thought you were a very unsuitable match for me."

"And still does, I fancy."

"Nonsense."

"Well, I can't honestly say it's good news, but it certainly is an excuse for me to have another and stiffer drink."

164

Sarah said, "Anyone who didn't know you would think you were a real old curmudgeon."

My back to her as I helped myself to another drink, I said, "What the devil's she been doing in the West Country?" The last person in the world I wanted to see was Alexina. I had learnt to preserve my natural relationship with Sarah—no matter how my thoughts ran against the grain from time to time. Her mother was another matter. I was absolutely convinced that all our troubles stemmed from her. At one time I had wanted to go and confront her frankly and get the truth from her, but had seen the stupidity of doing so. But here, in Rolthead, the temptation to have a go at her would be very strong indeed.

"She's been down there on business."

Turning back to Sarah with my drink, I said quite spontaneously, "What business?"

"She's been at Caradon Abbey."

"Well, that explains everything, my love. I've never heard of the place."

"Oh, yes, you have, Robert. I told you ages ago. It's owned by International Industrial Systems Limited. They run it as a training and record centre. . . . Oh, and for all sorts of other things."

Quite honestly, I said, "Well, my memory must be going because I can't remember you ever mentioning International Industrial Systems."

"Well, I can't think why you don't remember because I'm sure I told you about it. Alexina and I have a lot of money in it and it's very successful."

"Doing what?"

"Financing research and new industrial methods. If some small company have a good proposition but lack money to get it going . . . Well, we vet it—or rather our experts do—and we then decide to advance funds or not."

"It's a loan company?"

"Partly. But more often we take a share in the venture. It's done a lot of good. Mind you, there have been times when we've backed a loser, but that's only to be expected. Anyway that's where Alexina's been." She raised her glass to me and grinned, "Wasn't it nice of her to think of calling in here on her way back? I told her you'd be delighted."

"Naturally."

She laughed. "Oh, dear—if you could see your face. It would strike terror from the bench!"

I grinned. "That's my natural expression. The face of the male Rolt has never won any prizes."

So Alexina paid us her visit and there were occasions during it when I found it difficult indeed to keep my temper with her because—apart from all I had learned about her from Garwood —she was most trying and critical. When she heard about the break-in from Sarah she made a song and dance about the security of the house. It was ridiculous, she said, with all the valuables in the place, that a burglar-alarm system had not been put in years before and she was glad to hear that I was doing something about it without delay. And then she thought that Sarah looked tired and not herself and tried to persuade her to go back to Italy for a couple of weeks. Fortunately Sarah—who was looking as well as I had ever known her—resisted this.

We had always had small rows, but this time, though her cool, polite complaints and criticisms were only over trivial things, I fancied that there was a different charge running through them. I'm not a man who is particularly sensitive to other people's moods. There is no strong instinct in me to pick up a feeling of what is going through another person's mind— largely, I suppose, because I expect anyone with something on his or her mind to speak out frankly about it. But now, with Alexina, I had the very strong feeling that our relationship had changed. At first I wondered if she had had some intelligence that I had been in contact with Captain Garwood so that I had now become some sort of threat to her and her organisation. From being someone of whom she reservedly disapproved as the husband of her daughter, she now, perhaps, saw me in a quite different rôle. But I could not really accept this because I was sure that Garwood would not have let any knowledge of contact with me leak out. No, her manner held now a suggestion of quiet, firm confidence, the physical imperturbability of someone knowing that all the good cards were with them. It was an odd feeling and worried me. Some of her remarks, too, now and then seemed to have a veiled meaning—or maybe that was my imagination. Once you have been put on your guard against someone it is difficult not to examine and analyse each action and every expression in search of intentions and meanings which probably do not exist.

Before she left, she was alone in the study with me one evening where we were waiting for Sarah to join us for drinks when she said right out of the blue, "Robert—what's happened to you?"

Surprised, I said, "In what way?"

She said, "I find it difficult to talk to you. No matter the most trivial thing I say you seem these days to find something wrong with it. I know that old business of my not wanting you to marry Sarah in the first place had an effect on our relationship for a while, but I thought that was all past and dead."

"So it is, Alexina."

"Is it? I get the impression that it's still very much alive. I'm sure, for instance, that you weren't very happy about my coming here."

"Nonsense. I might have grumbled—but that means nothing. I grumble at all sorts of things as a matter of form, I suppose. You're very welcome here and always will be."

She smiled. "As long as it's not too often."

She lit herself a cigarette. She smoked some French brand and I could smell them in the house for days after she had left. She went on, "I really think I should tell you something about my original opposition to your marriage with Sarah which may surprise you."

"I don't think I want to know. It's all old history. Why go over it?"

167

"Because I want you to think about it. And, perhaps out of vanity, I wouldn't want you to go on through life misunderstanding what kind of woman I really am. My opposition to the marriage was largely a concern for your happiness rather than Sarah's. I knew she would be happy. I knew she was wildly and truly in love with you. But I was thinking of you. I didn't want her to make you unhappy——"

"What an extraordinary thing to say! How the devil could Sarah ever make me unhappy?"

"Didn't she? Haven't you been?"

"That's all passed and——"

I broke off and stared hard at her, and then said, "Did you have any idea that she would have all that loss of memory trouble? Was it something that was in the family?"

To my surprise, she laughed and said, "Robert—you and the family." She waved a hand round. "The Rolts and Rolthead— the family which is your god. No, memory trouble, as you call it, isn't in our family. And I wasn't thinking of that. You should have married someone from your own world. Sarah's was quite different. I never saw her as being able to fit into all this Rolthead life, so naturally I was concerned for your happiness."

I said firmly, "Sarah fits here perfectly. We're both very, very happy—and that's the way it will stay." And then, suddenly, irritated by the suggestion of patronage in her manner, I burst out, "When two people in love marry, it doesn't matter a damn what worlds they come from! They make their own world together. Anyone listening to you would think that Sarah had come down like a goddess out of the clouds from some far-off planet to marry some clod-hopping yokel of a Rolt!"

At this moment I heard Sarah coming to the door. In the few seconds before Sarah came in, Alexina looked up at me and her face, which was always carefully made up, a serene, beautiful, seldom emotionally marked face, suddenly was marred by a passing expression of almost haggard resignation.

Thinking about it afterwards, of her claim that she had been concerned more with my happiness than Sarah's, and knowing all that I did now of her, I could only come to the conclusion that it was some form of belated, but still veiled, apology or excuse for all that had happened. She had known there was going to be trouble because she was going to be the author of it. She had tried to avoid it by opposing our marriage—for my sake?—and had failed. I wondered if now, and Garwood had as good as confirmed it, an effort was going to be made to take Sarah from me again. I remembered Alexina's words on the tape— . . . *as her mother, I object to any drastic interference with her for . . . well, for a considerable time.* And then, later, the man called Lincoln, saying, *But next time the disengagement must appear absolutely natural—and you know what that means.*

Was she saying to me, as plainly as some imposed discretion allowed her, that the second time was coming, was nearer than I thought and I should be prepared for it? The thought filled me with a reckless, primitive rage . . . Love threatened exposes its other side. I knew now, and not without sympathy, the murderous drive which can rule men and women who find all that they cherish threatened.

It became clear to me within a short while of Alexina's visit that I had indeed changed. More and more I now construed Alexina's guarded words as the nearest she dared give to a warning. The trap had sprung and misfired once for Sarah. Was it being set for her again? I lived now with a hard core of contained belligerence inside me and the patience in me was continually battered by my desire to do something, to go out and find the enemy which threatened the happiness and peace which was Sarah's at Rolthead.

It was this desire which led me to Caradon Abbey. My brother Harold and I had for some years past been slowly acquiring farming properties in Devon and having them worked by competent managers. It was mostly Harold who did the groundwork in this scheme.

About two weeks after Alexina had left, Harold went down with a bout of influenza and telephoned me to ask if I would

169

keep an appointment he had made to view a property that was coming up for sale in South Devon. I motored down and stayed overnight in Tavistock on the edge of Dartmoor. In the morning I met the agent and went over the farm. I did not waste much time with it because it soon became clear to me that it was not—despite the glowing account we had received from the land agent—the sort of property in which we were interested. I went back to the hotel for lunch and while having a drink in the bar found myself looking at a wall map of the district. The words 'Caradon Abbey' caught my eye. It was only half an hour's drive from Tavistock.

There was no hesitation in me. I wanted to have a look at the place. I drove over after lunch, taking the road that ran westwards from Tavistock towards the valley of the river Tamar which separates Devon from Cornwall. The entrance to Caradon Abbey was by a wooded drive that led off a long twisting side-road.

The drive climbed through woods to an elevated plateau on one of the highest points overlooking the steep river valley. In a tall greystone wall, which I later learned surrounded the whole place, was a set of double iron gates and a small porter's lodge. The gates were shut, so I drew the car up and blew the horn.

After a few moments a man came out of the lodge and through a narrow iron gate at the side of the main entrance. I was rather surprised at his appearance. He wore a black peaked cap with some insignia in gold braiding on it, a well-cut, smart black suit with brass buttons on the breast and sleeves, and highly polished black shoes.

I gave him my card and said that I would like to go into the Abbey and see the Director. He studied the card and then said, "You've no appointment, sir?"

"No, I haven't." The insignia on his cap and brass buttons I saw now were the letters I.I.S.L.

He said politely, "He doesn't usually see anyone without an appointment, sir. Perhaps you would be kind enough to give me some idea of your business?"

He had a good voice, much too good I thought for a lodge porter—but then I supposed that International Industrial Systems Limited were monied enough to set their own standards.

"I'm not here on business. This is a social visit. Just give him my name—he'll know who I am."

He pursed his lips momentarily at this and then moved back into his lodge. He came out after an interval that had begun to make me impatient. He opened the gates and waved me through.

"Straight up the drive and then the right fork, sir."

The drive was flanked with woodland for about two hundred yards. Then the trees stopped and before me was an open space of lawns and flower beds and the greystone bulk of the Abbey. It was a square block of three storeys, plain and solid with a wide stone terrace running along its front. From a flagstaff on the roof flew a blue flag with the I.I.S.L. emblem in gold on it. Beyond the gravelled area in front of the Abbey the lawns stretched away to woodlands to give a view westwards and southwards down over the Tamar valley. As I drove up to the wide, scalloped sweep of steps that led up to the main entrance I saw that there were no cars parked on the gravel. But on either side of the broad steps two large entrances, marked IN and OUT, had been cut sloping down into the ground under the Abbey to form, I guessed, an underground car park.

As I got out of the car a man came down the steps to greet me. He was a tall, bulky-looking man of middle age with very close-cropped greyish hair, wearing a heavy tweed suit that sat awkwardly on his great body. He moved in a lumbering, almost shambling manner so that I was reminded of a great ape. His hands were enormous and his face was a wide expanse of broad cheeks, wrinkled forehead and a strong prow of a chin beneath a large loose mouth. He looked like an amiable, oversized idiot of enormous strength.

He came up to me, extended two long arms and gripped me by the elbows as though he were going to lift me from the ground, and said, "Mr. Rolt! I'm delighted. Delighted! Many,

many is the time I've told your wife that she really should bring you down to see us and our work here. And now—unheralded—here you are!" He dropped his hands from my elbows, stepped back, and went on, "Oh, my apologies—my name is Khan. A barbaric name, yes? But then I am built somewhat on those lines, too. I know it. I know it, but then we have to do the best we can with what we've got." His voice matched his bulk. It could have been heard a half a mile away in the woods.

I said, "I happened to be in Tavistock on business and having some time to spare I thought I'd pay you a visit."

"Splendid! You would like to spend the night, perhaps?"

"No, thank you. I have to get back."

"Come then—let me show you what I can in the time you have. Mrs. Rolt knows you are visiting us?" He took me briefly by the elbow and set me on my way up the steps.

"No. I just made up my mind on the spur of the moment."

"Sometime then, you must pay us a proper visit. There is much to be seen here. And, too, the country around is so beautiful." He paused at the top of the steps and spread his long arms wide. "The woods, the beautiful river, and away over there the moors of Cornwall. . . ."

He boomed away and within two minutes I had made up my mind that it would take a lot to make me spend a weekend at the Abbey with him around, and thankful, too, that I did not have to work under him. His manner would soon have made me want to bury a hatchet in his skull just to stop the booming flow of words. But, I told myself, there had to be virtues and skills in him which offset his manner otherwise he would never have been employed by I.I.S.L.—not with Alexina owning a slice of the shares. Some part of his other qualities he did indeed show me as he took me round the place, urging me gently by a big hand on my elbow from place to place, and keeping up a steady booming stream of explanatory talk.

The Abbey, he told me, was used for a variety of purposes.

172

Apart from being a conference and training centre, and a record depository for the company, part of it was also used as a recreational establishment for higher-ranking members of the company. There was a swimming pool, tennis courts, stables and a small nine-hole golf course. The Abbey was built in the form of a rectangle with a small inner open court around which ran a pillared and covered walk. In the centre of this courtyard was a weather-worn marble statue of the original founder of the company.

I was shown the conference hall and a set of rooms which were used for training-courses, the dining-room, a typical guest suite for important visitors, and one of the bedrooms which ordinary staff used. I was swept along passages to see the computer room, staffed by one man and five girls, and into the kitchens where everything was gleaming and polished and immaculately clean. At the end of an hour I was exhausted and longed to get away but I was politely manhandled into a large drawing-room that looked out on to a croquet lawn and beyond to a sharp fall of woodlands to a curve in the distant river. As I sat there with Mr. Khan a pair of peacocks strutted across the lawn. There was no doubt that I.I.S.L. did every-thing in style. The furnishings of the Abbey must have cost a small fortune and I think it was then that for the first time since my marriage I realised just how wealthy Sarah and her mother must be between them. At Rolthead the fact never obtruded itself. But here it suddenly came home to me as a manservant in the black uniform and the gold monogrammed buttons of I.I.S.L. brought tea on a silver tray and Mr. Khan boomed the praises of his company and gave me typical ex-amples of the activities of International Industrial Systems Limited. Briefly, before finishing my tea and making my bid to escape, I wondered what he would have said had he known that I knew a great deal more of the company's activities than he could possibly realise. Curiously, however, although I knew that I could come near to disliking the man simply for his manner, there was something about him which attracted my admiration. He was a noisy but efficient dynamo. His big body was packed with energy and enthusiasm and it was obvious that he had a quality which I always respected in others when I met it. He was dedicated and clearly happy to be so. To him I.I.S.L. stood for everything that was to be wished for in a company. To believe in something passionately—even though that object merits no such passion—is at least an exercise in loyalty worth far more than idling in a void of apathy.

Sitting there, too, it was hard to believe all that Garwood had told me about the company. To me it looked exactly like the establishment of any other international company which had decided—and plenty had—to take part of their organisation outside the noise and rough-and-tumble and discomforts of London.

In the end I managed to get away after making an insincere promise that sometime I would come back with Sarah and spend more time at the Abbey.

"It would be a pleasure and an honour, Mr. Rolt. We all owe so much to your wife and her mother. To us they *are* International Industrial Systems."

I drove away through the lodge gates, glad to be on my own. I went down the narrow driveway through the woods and had almost reached the small side road when a hundred yards ahead of me a man came out of the trees and held up his hand for me to stop.

I drew up and leaned out of the window. He was a tall man wearing a Norfolk jacket and breeches with high boots, and carrying a double-barrelled shotgun under his arm and I took him for a keeper. He came over to the car and bent down to talk to me. On his head was a crumpled cloth cap and the lower part of his face was covered with a growth of long black beard.

In a roughish, country voice he said, "Good afternoon, Mr. Rolt. Nice to see you again."

As I looked at him, puzzled, he grinned, his eyelids flickered, and I suddenly recognised him.

"Good God—Vickers, isn't it?"

"That's right. Vickers—the gamekeeper. Or, rather, Johnson, the gamekeeper. The Abbey own about a thousand acres around here. I got the job last year. And if it were only game-keepering I should enjoy myself. If it's not inviting a rough answer—what brings you here?"

I told him about my spur of the moment decision to visit the Abbey and finished, "I understand the beard now. I suppose you're keeping an eye on things down here?"

"There's not much to keep an eye on. I don't get into the Abbey grounds often. Twice I've been in the house. But I've taken Mr. Khan shooting quite a bit. Good shot, too. How is Mrs. Rolt?"

"She's very well, thank you."

"I'm told she got her memory back."

"That's right . . . well, almost all of it."

"You don't sound very happy about it."

Spontaneously, I said, "The whole thing's a bloody mess. Quite frankly I feel out of my depths—and your people don't help much."

He shrugged his shoulders. "They can't help much until they agree among themselves. Frankly they make me sick. That's why I like it down here. I don't have to watch the pantomime they put on. One of these days I may take off and get a real keeper's job. What did you make of Mr. Khan?"

"He'd drive me mad with that booming voice if I had to work for him."

Vickers chuckled. "That's his 'director's' voice. He just booms to impress. He sounds quite different when he's being natural. You should know—you've heard him before."

"I have?"

"Of course. Only briefly, I understand. But you've heard him. His full name is Lin Khan—there's a touch of the tartar about him in more ways than one. He's the Lincoln you heard on Garwood's tape. By the way, I think you ought to let Garwood know you've been here. I shall be reporting it anyway. Nice seeing you." He gave a flick of his hand and stepped away from the car and moved into the trees.

As I drove on a car came in view down the road behind me. Vickers had clearly heard it coming and had decided it would be prudent not to be seen with me.

## CHAPTER NINE

IT WAS LATE in the evening when I got back to Rolthead. Sarah had had dinner. Mrs. Cordell was out for the evening so Sarah made up a tray for me and I had a meal in the study while she sat with me.

When I told her that I had visited Caradon Abbey, she said, "Oh, I'm so pleased you did. I've wanted you to see it. What did you think of it?"

"It's a credit to International Industrial Systems. But I must say that my head's still reeling a bit from facing Mr. Khan——"

"Oh, Lin." She laughed. "He's a bit of a boomer, isn't he? But he's not always like that. Actually he's a very competent and shrewd man and runs the place marvellously well."

"Where on earth did the company find him?"

"Oh, he's been with them for years. I think he was a friend of Alexina's from her old days in the Argentine."

"Is he South American?"

"No, I don't think so. It's an odd sort of name, isn't it? I fancy his father was Russian or some sort of Slav."

"How long have you had that place down there?" It was no good even trying to pretend to myself that this was idle chatter. I wanted to know all I could about Mr. Khan and Caradon Abbey. But I hated myself for wanting to know, hated myself for knowing, too, that I had now been drawn further into the world of Garwood and Vickers and that I was, no matter in how limited a way, co-operating with them.

"Oh, donkey's years." Sarah leaned forward and poured

177

more wine into my glass. "But the company now is beginning to outgrow it. The computer and records sections are over-flowing and Alexina was telling me that very soon we shall have to find a bigger place—and not in England."

"Why not?"

"Because it's an international company. Staff come from all over the world for courses and training and so on. We're beginning to do a lot of business with the new African countries and the East. It hasn't been decided yet where we shall go ... Greece, India, maybe America. I really don't know."

"I should have thought this country was as convenient and well placed as any of those."

Sarah laughed. "Dear Robert—no place like England."

"Well, there isn't. Doesn't sound sensible to me to move. You could save yourself a lot of money by expanding down there. You've got plenty of room. Travel from any part of the world is nothing these days."

"Well, there are other considerations. Business ones."

"Who's the chairman of the company?"

"He's an Italian called Martino. But he's just a figurehead. He doesn't hold much stock. Alexina's the real power but she likes to hide behind Martino."

As she was speaking, I was wondering whether the real power, Alexina, had already made her plans. Caradon Abbey was to be closed up and the organisation moved. When that happened—would that be the moment for an attempt to make Sarah move with them, the moment when she would be taken from me? I was sure it was. But for the life of me, I couldn't understand why it might be so important to have Sarah with them. Why the hell couldn't they just forget about her—clear off and leave us both in peace?

That night we were together and, later, as Sarah slept in my arms, I lay listening to the sounds through the open window. June was running out. Now and again the nightingales gave a brief serenade. A fox called from the downs and one of the dogs in the stables began to howl in reply. All around us was

Rolthead, every inch of which I knew like the back of my hand. I loved the place with a love difficult to explain to other people. I loved Sarah, too—but that was another form of love. I wanted the two to endure, to be with me all my life and, suddenly, in the depths of the cool night, with Sarah in my arms, I was possessed by the slow onslaught of a deep misery . . . a desperation of the spirit. Maybe, I thought, I had been given too much. My lines had been laid in pleasant places. Life could not be all happiness. Perhaps the time for the payment of an excess of love and happiness was coming. It was a long time before I slept.

Garwood telephoned me the next day and asked me to see him in London. I went up the following day. He was in uniform and the gold bands on his sleeve matched the gold of a few tulips which someone had put in a vase on his desk. He knew I had been to the Abbey from Vickers.

He said, "This was genuinely a visit made on the spur of the moment?"

"Yes."

"What was your wife's reaction?"

"She was pleased. She'd wanted me to see the place. She tells me they're moving as soon as they can find a new place."

"Yes, we know that. We know the real reason, too. Things are getting too hot for them here."

"I'm sure my wife doesn't know a damned thing about that."

He smiled. "If you say so. But I'm not concerned with that at the moment. We've tried for years to get someone into that place and never succeeded. They have more security arrangements than you could guess at. And all the personnel are incorruptible—which in this day and age is a miracle. The nearest we've got is to put Vickers on the outside staff. He's allowed into the Abbey once in a blue moon and then not beyond the main hall and Director's office. What did you think of Mr. Khan?"

I told him, and added, "Why did you call him Lincoln in the tape transcript?"

179

"That was just the way the typist interpreted the sound of the name."

"But you knew it was Lin Khan?"

"Oh, yes." He pulled open his drawer and took out some sheets of plain white quarto paper. He pushed them over to me. "You've been in the place. You've been given a conducted tour. It won't have been exhaustive but I'd like to know about everything you saw. Draw, as well as you can remember, a plan of the place floor by floor—one on each sheet of paper. I'd like a list, too, of everyone you saw and where or in what rooms you saw them."

It was a tall order, but I did the best I could. While I worked at it, he produced a decanter from one of the filing cabinets and poured sherry for both of us. When I had finished he took each sheet in turn and questioned me about the floor's layout.

He said, "What was the name on the statue of the company founder in the courtyard?"

"I don't know. I only just glanced at it. The inscription was pretty worn. But the date was 1801. Anyway that would be in the company records."

"Yes. . . . Did Khan show you their picture gallery?"

"No. I didn't know there was one."

"I gather there is—and with some pretty good stuff in it. They have a subsidiary which speculates in fine arts and they've made endowments to quite a few galleries and museums." He paused and refilled my sherry glass. Then he went on, "If we thought it might help . . . would it be difficult for you to visit the place again? Maybe, spend a weekend there?"

I said, "Captain Garwood—let me be frank with you. Right now I have a conviction that when they close that place up and move—that's going to be the moment when they could try to take my wife from me. Anything I can do to stop that I will do, right up to the hilt. I don't want to go back there but I could—if you think it will help. However, if you're interested in the Abbey—and you've got good grounds against

I.I.S.L.—why the devil don't you get a search warrant and go over the place officially? I can't see what good shilly-shallying about can do. If they're up to no good, then bloody well crack down on them. That's the way to do it."

He leaned back and twiddled the stem of his sherry glass and then said quietly, "Believe me, Mr. Rolt, there are moments when I feel the same. I can get as impatient as you. But doing that would only scoop up a netful of small fish. No, we want the big boys and, more than that, we want the big answer to the big question: Why are they doing what they are doing, and for whom?"

\* \* \* \*

It did not seem to me that the big answer, as he called it, was the big problem. Garwood and his people knew that International Industrial Systems was a cover for various kinds of espionage and illicit data collecting. What did it matter to whom they sold their secrets? If I knew that some poacher was taking my pheasants I didn't keep my hands off him just because I wasn't sure to whom he was selling the birds. But there it was. I suppose that with any government agency it was a matter of pride and tidiness not to be content with any half-measures. Personally I felt that the sanest course would have been to pick up a few of the poachers and then make them talk. I'd noticed that over the years in many security cases people had been allowed to run free for great lengths of time in order, presumably, to give someone a chance to produce the big answer. The usual result was that some traitor was given more rein to do more damage than might have been the case if he had been picked up quickly—and still no big answer had been forthcoming. Anyway, I didn't want any big answer. I just wanted I.I.S.L. squashed quickly before they could get to the point of moving and possibly take Sarah with them. And, as always when I thought of I.I.S.L., the name was personalised into the figure of Alexina.

All the way back to Rolthead in the car, I toyed with the

idea that there might be something I could do independently of Garwood and his people. I didn't want the big answer. I just wanted to make sure that Sarah could not be taken from me. If necessary I was quite prepared to let Garwood know that I meant to act independently and let him do what he must. My first loyalty was to Sarah.

I regretted now that I had not taken some opportunity of attacking Alexina about the whole affair. It couldn't do any harm if she learned from me that Garwood was interested in her company. According to him she knew it already, otherwise there would have been no plan to vacate the Abbey. The time for beating about the bush, I decided, was over. The situation demanded plain action and straight speaking. In the long run these paid better dividends than any other methods. Also there was the fact that, although I had learned to live with the knowledge I had and to handle my life with Sarah with apparent naturalness, it was no damned way to live at all. Small deceits and avoidances of completely free correspondence between Sarah and myself were slowly building up a corrosion within me . . . an abscess that would grow and which I wanted to kill.

By the time I reached Rolthead my mind was made up. Without any reference to Garwood—and be damned to anything he might think he could do to me afterwards—I was going to find some excuse to go over to Italy and see Alexina. There had to be a showdown.

(A man can never be more nor less than what is done to him by other people. Your blood-lines determine your character as much as your shape, but the body is a strong vessel and holds fast against all but mutilation. But the mind, a man's character, can be moulded by human contacts and pressures. The Rolts in the distant past had always been rough and violent in the defence of what they knew to be theirs. Only Sarah meant anything to me. For her safety I was equally ready to be as rough and violent as any thirteenth-century Rolt.)

I decided to wait until Sarah went away visiting for a few days or decided to spend some time in London on business. While she was gone I would make a quick visit to Italy. Afterwards I would tell her about it and get everything off my chest, but to begin with I didn't want her to know I was going. The time was come to finish with the ambiguities of people like Garwood. I wanted everything in the open between Sarah and myself because I was sure that there was nothing she could say to me that would alter my love for her. I trusted in our love knowing that it could create and sustain understanding and forgiveness on both sides.

Two days after coming back from seeing Garwood I received a letter which made me defer my plan to go to Italy. The letter was typed on plain paper. No date, address or signature was given.

> *Mr. Rolt: This is a serious and sincere communication. We are completely aware of the domestic problems which afflict you at the moment and sympathise with you. However, as sympathy is of no help to you, we would like to make a proposition which we assure you would lead to the removal of all your troubles. If you are interested please treat this communication as of the highest confidence and within a week insert a personal advertisement in the* Daily Telegraph *which should read*—Tom. See you soon. R. *A further letter will then be sent to you.*

I put the advertisement in the *Daily Telegraph*. There was no hesitation in me. I might, I told myself, be clutching at a straw, but in my new mood I was prepared to try anything. A few days before, I would have told Garwood about the letter but now I only briefly considered it and then rejected the idea. The conviction was steady with me that I had to help myself. Garwood and his organisation were only peripherally concerned with me and my problems. The 'big answer' filled their horizon almost completely.

The morning after the personal column advertisement

appeared I received another letter, with a London postmark, which read—

> *Mr. Rolt: Thank you. You have a fishing day on the Avon Tyrrell water this coming Thursday, Beat 1. Please be there. You will be picked up from the field adjoining the Duck Gaze at 10.00 hours.*

I burnt the letter. Somebody was well informed about my movements and the rotation of the fishing-beats. The Duck Gaze was the name given to a stretch of water near the top of Beat 1.

Curiously there was no excitement in me about all this. The offer of help had come out of the blue and I was ready to accept it. I wasn't, however, fool enough to think that any proposition would be entirely one-sided in my favour. Something would be demanded of me. There was little that I was not prepared to give. The advertisement had appeared on a Monday. The letter came on a Tuesday. I could have wished that my fishing day was a Wednesday. Impatience moved in me constantly now. For too long I had been content with inaction.

On the Wednesday evening Sarah and I drove over to have dinner with my brother and his wife. When the women left us with our port and cigars I was very much tempted to take Harold into my confidence. The wish to do so had been with me often before, chiefly, I knew, because it would be a relief to me to have someone of my own flesh and blood as a confidant. I think I would have done so if there had not been in me, much stronger than a natural wish to tell Harold, an obstinate and powerful conviction that some god or fate had imposed all this trouble on Sarah and myself and that it would be bad luck for me to show the smallest human weakness in dealing with it. It was my burden. I had to shoulder it to the end.

Passing the port to me, he said, "Sarah looks well. Funny, isn't it, how soon things are forgotten?"

"What things?"

"Well, all that business of her loss of memory. Damned odd, wasn't it, at the time? But I hardly ever think about it now. It's just as though it never happened. Does she still see Sir Hugh Gleeson?"

"Now and then. Just friendly visits."

"Everything in the garden lovely?"

"Of course."

He laughed. "Bobby-boy, you've got your murdering face on. Remember the old man? That's what he called it when you used to stand up to him because he wanted you to do something you didn't want to do. You never really learnt to handle him."

"He could be maddening at times."

"Can't we all? Particularly you. I met that Devon agent the other day. He said you gave him a rare bollocking for dragging you down to see that crummy farm near Tavistock."

"He deserved it."

"Maybe. But that's no reason why he should have got it. We all make mistakes. He's been a useful man to us. You seem to have got a bit touchy lately. Nothing worrying you is there?"

"Of course not."

"Mind my own bloody business, eh?"

I held my glass up to the light. "This is some of the old man's port, isn't it?" I was very near then to confiding in him.

It was a warm night, the sky clear and bright with stars. On the way home Sarah made me stop the car on the top of the downs a few miles from home. It was nothing unusual. On a good night she liked to look at the stars and would ask me to stop. We got out of the car and leaned across a gate. A little way down the slope I could hear the sound of sheep grazing the short turf.

Looking up, Sarah said, "Aren't they lovely? Sometimes I feel when I stare up at them that if I'm not careful they'll draw me up to them . . . floating away and up." She looked at me with a quick, teasing smile on her face. "Would you come with me, Robert? To find a new world and a new life better

185

than anything this tired old Earth can offer? A paradise up in the stars?"

I put my arm around her. "You stay here with your feet on the ground. This is where you belong."

She stared northwards and I could see that she was watching the lights of a distant aircraft crawl across the sky. She said musingly, "Don't you believe that there must be life out there in space somewhere . . . intelligent life on some other planet? I know you tease me about it, Robert—but I know there is, there must be life out there . . . a better life, splendid people who long ago solved all the problems we still struggle with. Don't you believe that could be possible?"

I laughed. "I don't know and I don't care. But if you like to think there is and to give your money to crank organisations that concern themselves with the hope . . . well, that's all right by me. So far as I'm concerned there are enough problems in ordinary, everyday life down here to keep me busy."

She turned sharply and studied me in silence for a moment or two, and then said, "Robert—why do you say that? Is something worrying you?"

"Good Lord, no. What makes you think that?"

"I don't know. It's just a feeling I have sometimes. I just wondered if you were disappointed because——"

She broke off as a shooting-star streamed across the sky and burnt out.

I said, "Why should I be disappointed or worried. I've got you and I've got Rolthead."

"But that's not all you want. Robert—I want to ask you something. I don't want to have a long talk about it now, but just to ask you."

"You can ask me anything you like, you know that."

Looking away from me, she said, "We've waited now for quite a while and . . . well, nothing's happened. I wondered if perhaps we shouldn't consider again about adopting a child."

Holding her close to me, I said, "Yes, of course. We'll do that."

186

She twisted in my arms and kissed me and then her head dropped against my shoulder and her arms suddenly strained tightly around me. It was an unforgettable moment, a moment when there was nothing but love between us, the sheer primitive sense of belonging to one another—and the moment when I knew that if the need arose I would kill to keep her with me.

*     *     *     *

I arrived at the river just after nine o'clock and parked my car by the fishing-hut. It was a clear morning with greenshanks and lapwings flying and calling over the wide water meadows. I left all my fishing tackle in the car and walked up the right bank of the Avon to the large meadow that bordered the Duck Gaze. To the far right of the meadow the river took a sharp bend and in the angle was a small growth of tall trees and alder and willow scrub which screened the pasture from the distant road and the few houses on the far side of the river. Some miles upstream was Ringwood and not far downstream the river ran into its tidal waters above Christchurch. There was a constant noise in the sky from planes moving in and out of Hurn Airport. It was this noise which some time later masked the approach of the helicopter.

I was sitting on the stile which led into the copse when the machine dropped out of the cloudless sky and touched down about twenty yards from the trees. It was a small private helicopter, painted blue.

The rotors stopped turning and a man got out of the machine. I walked over to him. He was a young man with a good-natured face. He wore a suit of blue denim, short flying-boots and a blue silk scarf round his neck. He struck me as the type who even when he dressed casually took care about his appearance.

As I came up to him he gave me a friendly nod and said, "Mr. Rolt?" and then grinned and added, "As though it wouldn't be, of course."

187

"Yes, I'm Rolt."

"No objection to flying? No, I shouldn't think so. Don't look the windy type. Hop in." He was clearly someone who asked questions he was well prepared to answer himself.

I got into the machine and sat in the passenger seat alongside him.

He said, "Won't take us long. If you wish you can still get in a little fishing this afternoon." He pulled a black scarf from his pocket and ran on, "Sorry about the cloak-and-dagger stuff, but I'm only the hired man and have to do as I'm told. Do you mind?" He held up the scarf to bind it round my eyes. I let him fix it without comment and he said, "When we land just keep it on. I'll help you out and then some other lackey will take over. All clean fun—or I imagine it is. Anyway, the pay's good."

We went up and away and from that moment there was no more talk from him. I sat there in a shaded world and made no attempt at any deduction of which way we were going. Curiosity was abated in me, curiosity about small things that was. I was content to wait. We flew for about half an hour and then the engine note changed and we came down.

He said, "Hold tight."

I heard him get out and then the door at my side was opened and a hand took my arm and I was helped out of the machine and led a few yards away. I felt gravel under my feet.

He said, "O.K. that's it. I'll see you later."

Another, less firm hand took my arm and a new voice said, "Just come with me, Mr. Rolt. There are some steps, eight of them, and then it's straightforward."

I let myself be led forward, found the steps and went up them. A door closed behind me and I felt carpet under my feet. I was led, I imagined, through a corridor or hallway and then was stopped. I heard a door open and the new man with me said, "Take four steps forward."

I went ahead on my own. Behind me I heard the door close gently.

A voice said, "Thank you for your co-operation, Mr. Rolt. Please take the blindfold off."

I took the scarf from my eyes. I was in a large, semi-circular conservatory. A wide arc of tall windows was lined with beds for flowers and plants. I could see little of the outside world, just part of a terrace and a piece of lawn, because outer canvas awnings had been pulled down. Some of the plants from the beds had grown up supports and wreathed themselves across the roof space. The house wall which held the door through which I had entered was blank except for two narrow niches either side of the doorway which held less than life-sized classical figures. In the centre of the floor was a small pool, the water plated with lily pads and starred with five or six red and white blooms. Beyond the pool was a glass-topped wrought-iron table with three wrought-iron, cushioned chairs arranged around it. At the side of the pool, and only a few feet from me, stood a tall, slim man who, at a guess, I put to be nearer seventy than sixty. He wore an immaculate dark blue suit which showed a lot of crisp white shirt cuff and his tie was a brightly flowered concoction. He was almost bald except for a sparse show of iron-grey hair above his ears. His face was a wrinkled, sun-tanned parchment, a long, narrow face with a small hawk-beak of a nose and bushy-browed eyes. He gave me a pleasant smile and waved a hand towards one of the chairs by the glass-topped table. The gesture told me a lot about him. He wore his authority as he wore his clothes— draped about him fresh each morning. To command, I guessed, was as natural to him as breathing.

I sat down on a chair and he went to the head of the table, stood with his hands poised on its corners, and said, with a nod at a tray that rested before him, "Would you care for a drink, Mr. Rolt?"

"No thank you."

He walked round the table and sat down opposite me in front of a briefcase that lay on the glass.

He said, and his accent was faintly American, "You will

189

understand that for reasons which, if not apparent now, will be later, I can't extend to you the courtesy of giving you my real name. But that is a small matter. I suggest you refer to me as Mr. Smith. The important thing is that I genuinely wish to help you and—since I'm a businessman—I hope that you will be able to help me. We have, if not common, then certainly allied problems."

There is usually a very early moment when I meet someone new when I decide—rightly or wrongly—whether I like or trust them. With this man I felt that probably no such moment was ever going to come. He was too remote and too self-controlled to know quickly. My only concern with him was that he might be able to help me. What he might want in return would have to be examined when he made it clear.

I said stiffly, "Unless you subsequently make it important to me, I'm not interested in your name. You indicated that you might be able to help me. That's why I'm here, Mr. Smith."

He nodded. "I can help you. But before we get to that point there are some preliminaries to clear away. If I should say anything that offends you—I'm told you have a quick temper—please forgive me." He smiled, and then went on, "First let me put some cards on the table. I know in considerable detail your personal situation at this moment. To crystallise it—that you fear your wife may be taken from you."

"That's true."

"I know a certain amount about your wife and a great deal more about her mother, Alexina Vallis. And I know even more about International Industrial Systems. I also know of your connection with Captain Garwood."

"How can you know about Captain Garwood?"

"Not because of any breach of confidence on his part. But governments are not the only people who run intelligence agencies. We have our own, too."

"We? Or am I not supposed to ask questions?"

"You can ask as many as you like. I would expect it. When I can answer I will. Yes, I said 'We'. That is myself, my interests, and the other interests I represent—which are threatened by certain activities of International Industrial Systems. One word describes our interests. It is oil. The oil interests of this world may often seem, and indeed sometimes are, fragmented and at war with one another for markets, concessions and franchises. But like any quarrelling family, if a threat comes from an outsider then the family is at once united to meet it. The oil interests of this world have always maintained an organisation to watch for and eliminate such threats."

"I see. And what particular threat is being offered at the moment?"

"The biggest and the one which has always haunted all oil producers: the possibility of the discovery of another and infinitely cheaper form of power. Let me explain. There are billions and billions of dollars, pounds, all the world's currencies, wrapped up in oil. Not just in the primary processes of finding it, extracting, refining, and selling it, but also in millions of subsidiary enterprises. Things like the automobile and aviation industries, and a vast number of industries that take petroleum by-products. Not only is private enterprise concerned in this. Governments have their stake in it, too. Quite frankly, a cheaper and new form of universal power would play havoc with the world's economies—and every government in the world knows this. The threat to us is also a threat to them. Why else do you think the government agency Captain Garwood represents—and almost every other government agency in the world—is so interested in International Industrial Systems? Not only because of their subversive intelligence gathering activities. No—oil is the main thing on their minds."

"I should have thought, Mr. Smith, it was something they would have welcomed—another form of power. I understand that the world's oil supplies are running out?"

"That's nonsense. Each year new fields are found. The North Sea. Alaska. And scores of other places, many still to be found. There is enough oil potential in this world to last for at least the next five hundred years or more. If you were the head of a State, would you tolerate the introduction of a cheap, new power form to create immediate industrial, political and social problems when the whole thing could be deferred for hundreds of years and could be met eventually by a carefully controlled long-term plan of changeover? No, Mr. Rolt, heads of State don't think—and, by Hector, don't want to think—so far ahead. They have their immediate problems and, God knows, they're complicated enough."

"And is that what I.I.S.L. have done—found another power source?"

"It is what they are well on the way to doing. I'm sorry if this seems to have little to do with your problem, Mr. Rolt. But, believe me, it has. You are caught up in it as much as I am and the interests I serve." He smiled. "Be patient with me. We will come to brass tacks very soon. But I trust you take my point about the concern of the oil industry?"

"Yes. But is the threat such a near one?"

"The threat is close enough for us to want to take action now. For many, many years I.I.S.L. have been financing numbers of small groups, sometimes just individuals—some of them, I may say, as crack-brained as they come—who are dedicated to the discovery of a new power. Let me say in fairness to them that there is good logic behind the search. The internal combustion engine and rocket-propelled vehicles are clumsy, wasteful and dirty. Any oil-man worth his salt will admit that. And any oil-man or responsible statesman would also say that the ordering of such a changeover of power systems is something human society just couldn't handle at this moment. A thousand years hence . . . well, men may then be saner and less self-interested. At the moment we have the world we know and we have to live in it. A new power source would raise hell."

"But what is this source?"

"Various fields are being studied. As you're not a technical man I will only go into them briefly. There's anti-matter.

Anti-electrons, anti-protons and anti-neutrons have all been traced and it is now possible to produce anti-matter in a laboratory. This is common knowledge. When particles and anti-particles flow into one another they generate a thousand million times more energy than the most advanced rocket fuel. The problem at the moment, fortunately—and no state or ordinary industrial laboratory is going to attempt it—is to produce and harness this energy in a commercially viable form. Even our friends the Russians have held back on it."

"Common danger, Mr. Smith, produces strange bedmates?"

"You're damned right it does, Mr. Rolt. But I.I.S.L. aren't jumping into that bed. They're big and bold and have unlimited funds. In addition to anti-matter they have people experimenting with projects like anti-gravitation. Gravitation is a comparatively weak force. Overcome it and you're free to move upwards and onwards. The atmosphere and the universe around us teem with energy, literally. Every second of every day this earth is being bombarded by positive electrons and giving off negative ones. Power is in the air we breathe, waiting there for us to reach out and take it. The whole of space and matter is a vast power-pack waiting to be tapped— and this is no science-fiction dream. It's a fact." He grinned. "If I weren't an oil-man and didn't dread the havoc that could be caused then, frankly, I wouldn't be talking with you now. I would be talking with Alexina Vallis and wanting an in with I.I.S.L. no matter what it cost me. Oil is primitive but we're stuck with it. I.I.S.L. won't accept that. They work in secret, disguise their projects, and they've got our industry and every major government greatly concerned."

I said, "Captain Garwood never mentioned any of this to me, Mr. Smith."

"Of course he didn't. He says what he's instructed to say— a lot of flim-flam about clandestine activities and espionage. Crap! Mr. Holt. I.I.S.L. have an intelligence service like any other big industrial outfit. No more, no less. Sure, they break a few regulations, but what company doesn't? Mind you, there are certain unique features about I.I.S.L.—which I'll come to later—that make them very different from other industrial empires. No, Mr. Rolt—your Captain Garwood is a nice guy, but when he talks to you the words are put in his mouth by some very mixed-up and worried people behind him. Why do you think he was so interested in your visit to Caradon Abbey? Specifically?"

"I don't know."

"I'll tell you, Mr. Rolt. Caradon Abbey at the moment is the main world I.I.S.L. centre for the storing, analysis, and recording of secret computer data on various new power forms. That computer room you walked through, Mr. Rolt, is a treasure cave vastly richer than any Inca or Spanish Emperor could ever have dreamed of. It's Aladdin's cave to the 'nth' degree and, although they guard it well, they know the forces lining up against them—so they plan to move. And I don't damn well blame them."

He leaned back and drew a deep breath, straightening his long, lean form. He reached out and said pleasantly, "I don't think a glass of whisky would come amiss at this point. Yes?"

I nodded. I realised then that I had been sitting in my chair completely forgetful of the urgent personal reasons behind my visit here. For a while he had taken me into his world and cloaked me with his own habit of thought and a sense of his own loyalties and apprehensions. Personally, I could wish that the internal combustion engine had never been invented. Progress I was convinced had taken the wrong turning a long way back. Arcadia should have been man's destination. But now all the signposts pointed to chaos.

Mr. Smith dropped three ice cubes into a large glass of neat whisky and handed it to me. He fixed the same kind of drink for himself. He raised it to me and then drank. As he did so I saw his eyes close and over his face was something like the same mask of absolute tiredness that I had once seen on Garwood's face.

I drank, too, and then said, "So, it seems that Captain Garwood was less than frank with me."

"He couldn't be any other way, Mr. Rolt. I'm the one who is being indiscreet but only because I need your help and I can pay for it."

"How did you know I'd been to Caradon Abbey?"

"There's no mystery. This I.I.S.L. business has naturally led to a lot of divided opinions in government security agencies. Frankly, there's one lunatic element that would opt for going ahead with the development of a new power and face the chaos as it came. Captain Garwood's security council fortunately has a majority in it that sees things my way. From time to time information is passed to me." He grinned, the wrinkles on his old face tightly webbing the brown parchment skin. "You look shocked. Don't be. It happens the world over, and Garwood is well aware of it. I know you went to Caradon Abbey. I know you can go there any time you like to spend a weekend. And that's what I would like you to do for me sometime in the near future."

"Just spend a weekend there?"

"Maybe a little more than that. But before I outline the little more, I'd like to make an apology to you on the part of some not particularly bright members of my organisation. I wouldn't want to prejudice our present, I hope, good relationship."

"Go ahead."

"These dim-witted associates of mine once gave orders for an attempt on the life of your wife at Amalfi. There is always some fool who thinks there is a short cut."

I took this calmly. Perhaps I had known it without putting it openly to myself ever since I had entered the room. I said, "Murder can be one of your weapons? You approve of that?"

"Only in the last resort. Furthermore, to clear the board between us, two of our men broke into your house recently. I make no apology for this. The action was necessary in your wife's interests as I will explain later." He paused, tugged at

195

one of his shaggy eyebrows and said, "So far you are taking all this very calmly, Mr. Rolt. I was told that you could be quite spirited in your reactions at times."

I said, "Yes, I can be, but I'm not prepared at the moment to waste any time on anger. I want help from you—and you want something from me. What is it you want?"

"Simply that you should spend a weekend at Caradon Abbey in the near future."

I shook the melting ice cubes around in my glass. I had a respect, even a kind of admiration for this man, but I was not fool enough to think that he sat there as any form of philanthropic paterfamilias. He was an oil-man, old and seasoned in stratagems, and his true concern had to be the security of the great complex of the world's oil industry. I had, too, a strong conviction that the moment he went into details of this weekend, the rest of our interview would be absorbed by it. He clearly had time on his hands and there were questions I wanted to ask him.

I said, "Before you go into details of this weekend, there are some questions I would like to ask you."

"Ask."

"Do you know the real identity of Albert Chinn?"

"No. I think he is a myth."

"And the ultimate authority behind I.I.S.L.? Clearly—I imagine you have picked this up from Garwood's associates—Alexina Vallis and Lin Khan are far from being the top people. Who runs the whole shooting-match?"

"I can go beyond the two people you mention to some extent. But, frankly, we do not know who is at the top. I.I.S.L. has only stepped into its present rôle since the end of the Second World War. Before that it operated under another name and was founded at the beginning of the nineteenth century as an ordinary trading company. I wish I could answer your question about the ultimate authority. So do a great many other people of all nationalities. I could speculate but it's not a form of exercise I have much time for. Give me

196

some facts to go on and I will find the answers. There are no facts about the true leadership—only guesses and a few Alice in Wonderland theories."

I said, "Does Captain Garwood know you are seeing me?"

"He may. I learned long ago never to underrate men like Captain Garwood." He finished his whisky and then turned and jerked what was left of his ice cubes into the pool behind him, saying, "There are a couple of goldfish there who don't seem to mind a little whisky flavour to their water now and then. Now, any more questions—or do we come to the really hard-core stuff?"

"Tell me what it is you want from me."

"Let me say first, that what we want we will pay for. You help us and in return I'll explain to you all that happened to your wife—and absolutely guarantee her future with you."

"Go ahead."

"I want you to make arrangements soon to spend a weekend at Caradon Abbey. Not with your wife. By yourself. I want you to drive down on a Saturday and when you park your car in the underground garage I want you to put it as near as you can to the far right-hand corner. A tolerance of ten or twenty yards will make no difference." He gave me a slow, wintry smile. "How good is your sense of topography?"

I said, "I haven't seen the underground garage, but such a position would probably mean that the car was almost under the wing of the building which has the computer room. And the computer room is slightly below ground level."

"Correct. We just want you to park your car and then proceed normally to enjoy your weekend. The guest apartments are in another wing of the house. Before you drive down we should have to have your car for a couple of days to prepare it. Outwardly it will be the same car. In actual fact, it will have been turned into a mobile bomb of very high power . . . an explosive and incendiary weapon. The car will be fitted with a timing device to explode it at two-thirty in the morning. The first—and most important—objective is to blow up the computer room, and the second is to set the Abbey on fire and hope for the maximum amount of destruction in the record and administrative offices that occupy the same wing." He paused for a moment, gave a dry grunt to clear his throat, and went on, "So far as we can co-ordinate the dates, arrangements will be made for the same kind of operation in two other I.I.S.L. subsidiary centres. One in America and the other in Italy. All this, of course, won't stop I.I.S.L. for good, but the damage, destruction and confusion will put them out of effective operation for quite a few years. During that time we shan't be idle, though that phase does not concern you. At the moment our objective is to hit the enemy hard and cripple him. No sane person can make a valid case for violence, Mr. Rolt. But sometimes it is the only way if you find you are living in a jungle—which we all are."

He reached for the whisky and refilled our glasses. For a moment there was only the sound of ice cubes clinking against glass. He was an old man, spruce and self-contained. I had no doubt that he was as wealthy as he could ever wish to be. His years were running out fast, but there was no desire in him for peace or retirement, no ache to free himself from the pressure of affairs. He was a creature from a world other than mine—or rather than mine had used to be. I sipped my whisky. Before I had come to him I had guessed that I could expect some form of proposition like this.

I said, "Do you know whether the computer room is manned all night?"

"No. But it is highly unlikely."

"Assume it is."

"Then whoever is there will be killed. Your car will be no toy bomb."

"Do you know how many people are usually in the Abbey at a weekend?"

"The Director, Lin Khan, and his secretary. A few domestic staff—most of them, though, sleep in a staff house well away from the Abbey. There could be other guests, but they will be in the guest wing with you. Every wing is fully fitted with fire-escape equipment. There's a night porter on the door in the main wing. The computer and secretarial staff all live out in surrounding villages." He sipped his whisky, his grey-green eyes steady on me. "Putting it at its highest—probably two or three people could be killed."

"By my car—clearly."

"It will be totally destroyed with any others, obliterated beyond any possible hope of a technical investigation producing any proof that it was the source of the explosion."

I said coldly, "No technical proof would be needed. I.I.S.L. would know that I was responsible."

"Does that matter, Mr. Rolt? They will know that behind you we stand. If they turn to the police or urge any ministerial investigation—and they know this—they will get no satisfaction."

"Garwood knows about this?"

"No. But a certain section of his agency does. And the Government itself, while it would not yet instigate an act like this, will breathe a sigh of relief and co-operate in suppressing any over-eager investigation. I'm quite sincere about that. They've done it many times before."

"If it puts I.I.S.L. back ten years—all because of me—then out of sheer vindictiveness they might be more determined than ever to interfere with Sarah."

He smiled. "It's a good point. But the answer is no—they won't touch her for a very simple reason. *For the first time* they will realise just what your backing is—us, and by implication a great weight of government interest in many countries. Don't think we haven't lines of communication with them. I know Alexina Vallis well. I know Lin Khan and others—and they know what I represent. The word would go from us to them that if they touch your wife—then one of them will be killed."

"As simple as that?"

"We all want to live, Mr. Rolt. Alexina Vallis does. So do

Lin Khan and others. We should take violent action. That is all the security you could possibly ask for, complete security for yourself and your wife. So, what do you say? Will you go to Caradon Abbey for us?"

I stood up, glass in hand, and walked away from him. I stood by the lily pool and watched two golden orfe circle under the water like pale submarines. Outside the sun was lacquering the tight-mown grass with silvery highlights. A missel-thrush stood, legs astraddle, head cocked earthwards listening for the stir of a worm. The season was rich with growth, the July sun pouring its life power into plant and bird and beast and man. And I stood in a shaded conservatory which I knew now housed the slow rot of death and corruption. Maybe there would be one or perhaps two people on night duty in the computer room. They would die. Be blown to oblivion in the closing of an eyelid. Maybe the guests in the Abbey were well provided with fire escapes . . . but people panicked, fire fed a hundred fears and some stupid woman or drink-heavy sleeping man would die—charred and mummified by flame. Did that matter so long as I kept Sarah to myself . . . that our happiness endured? If anyone died then the blame went truly from me, back to Alexina Vallis and all the others with her. I would have walked into this with the innocence of a man turning a corner and finding himself in the midst of a murderous affray and out of sheer instinct raising a stick and killing to protect himself. . . .

I turned back to Mr. Smith. He was sitting with his elbows on the table, shoulders hunched forward, his lean hands cupped around the ice-cold whisky glass. I thought of all the Rolts, all those years back, who had killed and pillaged to protect their own and—there was no escaping it—to take from others. I had their blood—but I had more, surely. I had an understanding which their violent times had denied them. No, it could not be done. Whatever had to be done I would do my way—not his way, not the way of his world and Garwood's and of cynical statesmen and power-greedy industrialists. Love for

Sarah—and there was no power in my life greater than that—could not make me accept murder.

I stood opposite him and he looked up at me and slowly rubbed one hand about his strong chin and said, "Well, Mr. Rolt?"

I shook my head. "I can't do it—not if there's the remotest chance of anyone being killed."

He nodded, slowly took a deep breath, and said, "It is no more than I expected. If you had said you were willing I would have made a rare error of judgment."

"I think I'd better go back and find my own way to a solution. Thank you for the offer."

He said evenly, "If you do that, Mr. Rolt—you will never see your son, never take an heir back to Rolthead."

## CHAPTER TEN

FOR A MOMENT or two I stupidly wondered whether I had misunderstood or misheard him.

I said, "I have no son. My wife and I haven't been blessed that way. In fact, we are going to adopt a child."

He shook his head and said, "You're wrong, Mr. Rolt. You have a son. He is just over two years old. Please sit down again."

I said, "By Christ—I hope you're not fooling about with me!"

"Please sit down, Mr. Rolt."

I sat down. He pulled his briefcase towards him, opened it, and passed a coloured photograph across the table to me. It was of a very small boy. He was sitting at the top of a flight of terrace steps. Behind him was part of the façade of a house with an open doorway overhung by thin pennants of bougainvillaea. I recognised it at once. The boy was fair-haired, his face was square and well shaped but a little obscured with shadow. He sat in a musing position, his elbows resting on his knees, his chin resting on the knuckles of his chubby fists. He wore a blue shirt and white shorts and his legs were bare and browned with the sun.

He said, "That is your son."

He reached out and took the photograph back from me. One of the fish splashed suddenly in the pool. Over his shoulder I saw a swirl of water break the mirror of the surface and then watched the pool slowly reburnish itself. A turbulence of spirit was born in me and I held it firmly in check.

I said, "The boy has my wife's hair, something of my stockiness in his body and I could persuade myself that there is a look of myself in his face. I know the steps, and I know the house behind them. I know, too, that you want something from me. I should tell you that if this is a trick it is an extraordinarily dangerous one."

"This is no trick. I'm not such a fool, Mr. Rolt." He took a paper from the briefcase and slid it across to me. "Ethics do not come into our battle with I.I.S.L., Mr. Rolt. Your wife has a physician in London. He also happens to be a gynaecologist. What you hold is a confidential report—extracted from him for a consideration. Your wife has never seen it. It's dated just after your wife returned to live with you at Rolthead. The physician states positively that in the course of a general examination of your wife he observed signs that she had had a child not more than two years prior to the date of the examination."

I read the report only half comprehending it. It talked of pelvic and vaginal changes and almost imperceptible skin and muscle-tone recoveries and it finished with the phrase—*Mrs. Rolt is in extraordinarily good general health and the few outward signs of a past pregnancy would not only be unapparent to any layman but also easily overlooked by a general practitioner unless he were specifically searching for such evidence.* Suddenly the phrase and the fact that the man was talking about Sarah loosened emotion in me.

I said, "What kind of physician is this? The bloody man ought to be kicked out of his profession!"

He shrugged his shoulders. "When we want something there are always ways of getting it. We want I.I.S.L. and you want your wife. For everything there is a price—but the option remains with the individual to decide whether he's prepared to pay it. I am just explaining a situation which we have researched in detail."

"How the devil could my wife have had a child and not tell me about it? It's impossible!"

Mr. Smith leaned back in his chair and drummed his fingers on the glass table-top, his grey-green eyes steady on me. Then with a sudden harshness in his voice, he said, "Mr. Rolt, I think it's time things were straightened out for you——"

"And, by God, I think so, too!"

He nodded, and said, "Damn' right. So let's try from the beginning. Why do you think Alexina Vallis was opposed to your marriage? For personal reasons—because she didn't like the look of your face?"

"God knows."

He grinned. "I guess He does. And so do I. For dynastic reasons, Mr. Rolt. The great I.I.S.L. dynasty which has been in the hands of a few families since it was started. The business, right from the beginning, was their god, and their loyalty to it over-rode everything. And, by Hector, they always made sure that anyone coming into it by marriage was the type who would fill their bill. Your first loyalty had to be to the firm and its families. It wasn't your face that didn't fit, Mr. Rolt. It was that you already had an unshakable loyalty—first, foremost, and always—to Rolthead."

"But that's ridiculous since——"

"Is it?" he interrupted. "How would your father have reacted if you'd refused to give up the Foreign Office in order to take over Rolthead after him?"

"There'd have been hell to pay."

"Sure. And there was hell to pay when your wife—knowing quite well what was expected of her, and already engaged to a suitable man—kicked over the traces and married you. Alexina Vallis, no matter how she pretended, never forgave that and never stopped hoping that a chance would come to get Sarah back. And she got her chance. Your wife had only been back at Rolthead a few days after a visit to Alexina in Italy when she disappeared. Right?"

"Yes, that's so. She went out for a quick visit. She had some urgent business to settle with her mother."

"Any idea what business?"

205

"No."

He fingered the whisky glass before him.

"You've got a good wife. Mr. Rolt. She defied the whole I.I.S.L. set-up because she loved you—and she genuinely thought her mother had forgiven her. The one thing you both wanted was a child. Your wife thought she was pregnant but she didn't want to raise your hopes until she was certain. So she went home to Alexina and told her, and Alexina arranged for her to have a pregnancy test out there. That test was positive. We know because a year ago we got a copy of it. But Alexina told your wife that it was negative—that's simple deduction, otherwise your wife would have come back and told you the good news."

"The woman's a damned monster!"

"A clever and dedicated one also. Dedicated to this family I.I.S.L. group. You've got to understand, Mr. Rolt, that I.I.S.L. with them isn't just a business, it's a religion, a cult, the whole of their world—and they don't give up their own easily. It's happened damn' few times in nearly two hundred years. Alexina was determined that you should never have the child to bring it up for Rolthead, and she saw also the chance to take Sarah from you—no matter what changes would have to be made in her future life. A few days after Sarah's return to you she was abducted and taken to Italy. With I.I.S.L.'s resources it wasn't difficult."

He held up the whisky bottle and looked questioningly at me. I shook my head. He helped himself and said wearily, "I guess you're finding some of this hard to take, believe even?"

"I'm listening," I said coldly.

"Human nature is full of surprises, though one would have thought by now that there's nothing mankind can do by way of evil that would surprise anyone—but, by Hector, that just isn't true."

"Just go on telling me what happened. I'm in no mood for anything but the truth."

"Alexina and her associates took your wife. They wanted

her and they wanted the child. But they knew Sarah's strength of character, knew the power of her love for you—so they determined two things. One, that she should never know she'd had a child; and, two, that she should have a new personality and a new life which they would see would be dedicated to I.I.S.L."

"How in God's name could they do that?"

He sighed. "I could tell you of things which I.I.S.L. have researched and perfected that would make your hair stand on end. Mr. Rolt—the human brain is one of the last fortresses standing out against modern science. Somewhere inside the brain is the smallest and most comprehensive computer in the world, and in that computer man has his memory bank—still an enigma; but less of an enigma to I.I.S.L. than others. I.I.S.L., through their own and subsidised laboratories, and by way of group and individual research grants, are years ahead of anyone else—and so far they have made public only a fraction of what they have achieved. I'm not saying they don't intend to eventually, but for the moment it is not their policy to do so. However, not even I.I.S.L. can guard all their secrets. We know that they have developed a drug which has the power of inhibiting memory, a drug, Mr. Rolt, that puts the memory bank in the brain out of action. It wipes out all past memories and it turns a human being into a cabbage. The power of memory no longer exists. You can't remember what happens from hour to hour. The body goes on working healthily—but you live in nothing but the present, no past, no future—the only thing that exists is the living moment of the present."

"That's impossible!"

"Not at all, Mr. Rolt. It's only a logical, pharmaceutical extension of the anaesthetic, of alcoholic inhibition, of the sleeping-pill, of dozens of drugs that are used in cases of nervous breakdown today. And I.I.S.L. have this drug—and we, by our own means, have acquired samples of it—and tested them. They treated your wife with this drug. She became a cabbage—and she had a child, your son, which very soon after birth was taken from her—and she remembered nothing of it!"

He paused and studied me. Maybe he was expecting some further outburst. But I was beyond that. All my thoughts were of Sarah . . . all those years ago.

"Go on," I said and my voice seemed no part of me, "What happened them?"

"They withdrew the periodic drug treatment. The brain recovered its power to remember—and your wife found herself in the San Sebastian villa. She was no longer a cabbage. From that moment she could remember each hour, each day as it passed—but she had no memory of the past. They could have given that back to her—they have an antidote to the drug which eventually but slowly restores complete recall of all the past in the memory bank—but this didn't suit Alexina Vallis. She turned her own daughter into Mrs. Starr." He pulled a cigar-case from his pocket and selected one which he began to prepare. "There was little difficulty—because there had been a Mrs. Starr, an I.I.S.L. family member now dead. Your wife just took her place——"

"But Garwood's people told me all that Mrs. Starr story was faked!"

"Mr. Rolt—there's only one man being honest with you. That's me now. Garwood and the others were out of their depths—and confused men hug the truth to themselves. They won't let go of it until they know absolutely that it will be to their advantage. They just steered you into the Mrs. Starr set-up and sat back to see what would happen—and what they could make of it. What happened was that your wife, thinking herself Mrs. Starr—but doubting it after your visit—went to Alexina, who told her the whole truth; about the baby, about you . . . everything. And she presented Sarah with an ultimatum. She could have her full memory back, stay with I.I.S.L. as Mrs. Starr—she was to go to America and work for them there and take the boy with her—or she could give up the baby, put it out of her life altogether and go back to you, taking with her the drug antidote which would eventually restore her entire memory. You've got a good wife, Mr. Rolt. She chose you." He drew on his cigar and let a cloud of blue smoke idle from his lips. "But I guess for her own sanity and peace of mind, when her memory came back she decided to pretend there was a ten-month gap still blank. She had made a promise to tell you nothing. She had to pretend there was a ten-month period *of nothing* so that she wouldn't have to speak a lie. Mr. Rolt, if there's one person who's been through hell, by Hector, it is your wife. She's not clear yet—but you can clear her and have your son back with you at Rolthead. But until he is there—all this rests just between us. You've got to live alone with what you know until your boy is back—and you know the terms for that."

I stood up, turned my back on him, and went to the window. Vividly in my mind was the sunny Italian morning when I had seen Sarah go to the little farm on the hill. I saw the peasant woman standing at the top of the steps—and behind her in the house, I knew now, had been Sarah. The thought then of her agonies of revelation, of shock, of opposing loves and cruel decision flamed through my mind in a spasm of physical pain. I prayed that one day, soon, I might come face to face with Alexina.

Behind me Mr. Smith said quietly, "You'll forgive me for this—but the intention was all for your good; my men have been to your house and Alexina's villa and checked their correspondence from time to time. There's never been any mention of the child. Your wife has kept her bargain. The boy is out of her life, because she wants you in it."

I swung round and burst out, "All this is the truth? The whole, bloody horrible truth—you swear it?"

He nodded. "It's the truth, Mr. Rolt. Alexina Vallis took your wife and then lost her to you again—but she came back without your son. The child, at least, she would have to do with what she would, whatever the I.I.S.L. hierarchy decided.

But things have changed, Mr. Rolt. A week ago, without her knowledge, we took your son from her. At the moment we have him safe and sound. There's no reason at all which I can see why within a very short time he shouldn't be at Rolthead with you. But, of course, there is a price to be paid."

A price to be paid. And I knew without hesitation that I would have to pay it ... wanted to pay it because I acknowledged that although the power of my love for Sarah had not been enough to make me heedless of the chances that someone might be killed in the computer-room explosion, there was now another and stronger power in my life which reduced all other considerations—all emotions of decency, humanity and a respect for other people's lives—to nothing. I wanted my son. I wanted the Rolt line to go on. I wanted an heir of my own flesh and blood at Rolthead. The desire was stronger than anything else I could have known in life. And this man had created it in me—and done much more than that. Within a few minutes he had made of me a man like those other men whom I despised. I was no better now than the physician who had betrayed his patient's trust. No better now than John Chambers who for money had tried to murder Sarah and who played the thief and photographed other people's private letters. I was no better than this man sitting across from me who could coldly use death and destruction to defend the financial solidarity of the oil industry. I was no better than Alexina Vallis whom I had called a monster. Without shock or any wrestling with conscience I was become not the Robert Rolt I thought I was, took pride in being, condemning or pitying all others whose standards were not mine, but another man as primitive and murderous as an early Rolt. Centuries of civilisation fell away from me in that place, like a cloak torn from my shoulders by a sudden wind, leaving me naked, knowing myself—hating myself, but determined to live with my humiliation. My son belonged to me and to Rolthead and I was going to take him back there. There was a price to be paid and I was ready to pay it.

I said, "I know you well enough now to understand what would happen if I refused. I should never see the boy. You would make sure of that, though one day I would have killed you because of it. But you are in no danger from me. I'll go to Caradon Abbey and do what you want."

He nodded briefly, keeping his head down almost as though there was a moment of rare penitence passing through him to ease his self-disgust, and then he said, "I am sorry, Mr. Rolt— but there is always some moment in life when the mirror of reality is held up to us and we see ourselves reflected truly. I have learnt that the memory of that moment fades a little with each year. We are in this life to learn to live with ourselves as we are—and, when we have time, to pray that a day will come when man will move on from being what he is to what he knows he can be." He stood up and handed me the coloured photograph.

I took it and put it in my pocket.

He came round behind me and fastened the black scarf over my eyes and said, "Someone, very soon, will be in touch with you."

I heard a bell ring distantly and almost at once the sound of a door opening. A hand took my arm and I was led away from the place. I was flown back to the field by the Duck Gaze and this time there were only the briefest words between myself and the pilot. The cheerfulness had gone from him. Maybe he sensed that he was not taking back the same man he had ferried that morning.

*　　*　　*　　*

As I lay in bed that night, I thought about my father. He had never considered that Rolthead would ever be his. But fate had put it into his hands. I had always loved and wanted Rolthead but had known that it could never be mine—and then fate, at the death of my eldest brother, had put it into my hands. Fate had dowered me with it, and with deep sorrow, too, because I had loved my brother. Time had muted and

211

finally appeased the sorrow. Now sorrow was back because I was in mourning for myself. To be able to hand Rolthead on to my son I was ready to kill. The process of learning to live with that would, I knew, last me the rest of my days but there was no concept in me of ever turning away from my decision. I knew, too, that until I could bring our son back I had to learn to practise small evasions and lies with Sarah. Once the boy was in the house with us I could face her with the whole truth and know her truths if there were more to be learned. Lying there in the night, knowing she slept peacefully and innocently in her room, my father's memory was a ghost by my bed and I could hear him, quoting his favourite Robert Burns, the lines coming from some recess of the spirit unbidden by me——

> I waive the quantum o' the sin,
> The hazard of concealing;
> But och! it hardens a' within,
> And petrifies the feeling!

It could do that to me, I knew, unless this business was cleared up quickly. There was no time too soon for honesty and open, true understanding to come back to Sarah and myself. But until it did I was a stranger in my own house, until then I was neither true husband nor true lover. And lying there, remembering the physician's report, I felt sick and disgusted as though I, after loving Sarah, had looked on her sleeping body and searched it for the signs left by our son's secret coming. It was then that I knew real hate, hatred for Alexina who had done this to Sarah and myself. If I had known that she could have been in the computer room I would have gone gladly to Caradon Abbey.

The next day I had two telephone calls. The first was from Captain Garwood. I was instructed to see him the next day in London. I made difficulties but he insisted and I said I would come. I knew what he wanted. The second call came after lunch.

A man's voice which was strange to me said, "Mr. Rolt?"

"Yes."

"You know the beach road below Rolthead village?"

"Yes, of course."

"If it's convenient I would like you to be there at four o'clock. By the wood where the road turns on to the beach. Please drive your Bentley. Not the Rover. All right?"

"Yes."

I was there at four o'clock in the old Bentley which had once belonged to my father. The beach was about two miles from Rolthead House. The road ran down the side of an oak wood and then out to a narrow track along the length of a steep bank of shingle so high that it hid all sight of the sea beyond. There was a shabby Mini-Austin parked on the corner of the wood. I drew in behind it and a man got out of the Mini and came back to me. He was a short, rather bow-legged man, elderly, with a grey-skinned face, unhealthy looking, but with a small, wry grimace continually on his face as though he were enduring some secret and endless disappointment. He wore a greasy cloth cap and brown, oil-stained dungarees.

He stood back from the Bentley for a moment, looking her over as though she were a horse and he studying her points. Then he nodded and came to the driving door and just touched the peak of his cap to me.

"Mr. Rolt?"

"Yes."

He stepped back a little and eyed the car again. He said, "Pity to bust her up. Still, there it is. They'll fix you up with something just as good. Same year, same model if you insist."

"Just tell me what you want. I'm a busy man."

"Fair enough. Just want to look at her. More bulk than your Rover. We can pack her full of stuff. Nobody'd know. How's the clock? Reliable?"

"Yes."

"I'll check it over. I'll fit a switch under the driving seat. When you park all you'll have to do is throw the switch and the clock will do the rest at half-past two. We'll need it for three days. You can say it's at the garage for a checkover. When we know the timing I'll pick it up at your house."

"At my house?"

"Why not? That's what your garage would do. Okay. That's all." He stepped back, eyed the car once more and said, "Pity. They made cars in those days. Still . . ." He tipped his cap and moved back to his own car. I watched him drive away. He went past me without a glance and disappeared around the corner of the wood.

I sat there. This was the beginning. The first step. I should have felt self-disgust probably, but I didn't. I felt impatient and restless. I wanted the whole thing over and done with. I wanted to come to the point when I could get down to the grinding business of beginning to live with myself again.

I got out of the car and walked up the steep shingle bank. There was no wind and the Channel was as still and smooth as a pond except for a tiny, lacy ribbon of foam and ripple pulsing at the shingle limit. As a boy I had come down here to swim and fish and net prawns, and I loved the place. I had brought Sarah here, too, and she loved it, loved the long length of coastline and the bulwark of the great shingle bank where in storm the waves would drive high and sometimes breach part of the top to flood the road and the low meadows behind. Sarah was a nerveless, daring swimmer and would often go too far out for my liking. . . . Here, soon, when what must be done was done, I would bring my son. He would go through anemone, crab and shrimp discoveries, grow strong and hard and brown, and swim. . . . Impatience kicked in me like a pained nerve.

I drove back and had tea with Sarah in her room. She had been gardening and had filled a bowl on my mother's old piano with a great cluster of polyanthus roses, deep crimson with flaring yellow centres. One of a past litter of dead Frannie's puppies which had now become the house dog lay at her feet. We talked and laughed together over some ridiculous and scandalous story of something that had happened in the village, and her beauty and the joy so clearly in her made me long to have nothing but honesty between us. To prevent any shade of betraying mood from me I pretended to myself that in fact that moment had come and passed and we were free to be ourselves and I liked to think, no, was sure, that there was nothing but that. I willed it to be so, and it was so, that indeed the image of true reality in the mirror was already dimming.

*　　*　　*　　*

There was another man with Captain Garwood. He sat to one side of the desk in a comfortable leather armchair which had not been in the room before. He was a large, fleshy-faced man, dew-lapped from good living, his eyes half-lidded as though he would veil them from any probing light which might give a hint of what he was feeling. His white hair was a little long and deliberately arranged to add to his still, brooding, patriarchal manner. He was not introduced to me but I could place his type for I had met many of his kind in cabinet and committee rooms in my time at the Foreign Office. Behind all governments there were men of this kind.

Captain Garwood came straight to the point.

He said, "Mr. Rolt, when you were last here and gave me details of Caradon Abbey you said that if we wished you'd be prepared to make some excuse and go back and see what else you could find out about the place for us."

"That's true. But I still think you could get a better result by having a search warrant sworn out."

The man in the armchair gave a grunt which could have been a laugh.

Garwood said, "I explained the uselessness of that. I ask you the question now about your willingness to go back not because we are going to ask you to go back, but because it occurs to us that you might take it into your mind to do it without consulting us. Has that occurred to you?"

215

"Yes, it has. Once or twice. But not seriously. What could I do on my own account?"

The armchair old man said, "Nothing—except stir up a lot of trouble for everyone." He pulled a thick leather cigar-case from his inside pocket, selected a cigar, and began to light it. The measure of his importance was marked by the fact that Garwood remained silent, knowing that he had not finished. When the cigar was drawing, the man went on, "You had some Foreign Office experience, I'm told. You've learned one lesson from them. Their needs are often clumsy but their use of language is very precise."

"If you say so, sir."

Garwood said, "I intend to be nothing but frank with you, Mr. Rolt. On your own account you could do nothing. But on someone else's account and with their help you might. We would regard such a project with the utmost disfavour. We know your concern about all that has happened to your wife. Believe me it's one of our chief considerations, too. You must have faith in us and trust us to handle it in our way."

"Come to the point, Garwood," said the man in the armchair. "Mr. Rolt is, I am sure, waiting for you to come out from behind your verbiage. You're talking about his wife, his . . . their happiness. Plain words, sir; plain words."

I said, "Thank you, sir. I imagine that Captain Garwood wants to ask me whether I have already agreed to go back to Caradon Abbey for anyone else. Am I right, Captain Garwood?"

"Yes. I want your word, Mr. Rolt, that you have made no such compact, nor will make any with any outside persons or agencies."

I said, "I have made no such arrangement. Nor will I do so."

It was a lie deliberately and easily told. Neither this man nor Vickers had had any scruples over lying to me.

Captain Garwood eyed me in silence for a moment or two and then said crisply, "You are absolutely certain, Mr. Rolt?"

The man in the armchair said quietly, "Captain Garwood,

your zeal runs away with you. Mr. Rolt is a man of honour. Your last question was unnecessary. It should never have been put."

For a moment I saw the familiar mask of tiredness pass briefly across Garwood's face. He said, "I apologise and withdraw the question."

I said, "Thank you, Captain Garwood." I had lied and I had tossed away my honour. But I had only one loyalty and it imposed its own code on me. I could hate myself but I was inflexible. The Robert Rolt I had once known had put on a new habit. With time I knew that I would wear it with less discomfort each day in the new world which had suddenly narrowed its horizons around me.

Some part of the new manners of this world which I would have to learn was revealed to me by the man in the armchair. When I left Captain Garwood, the old man came with me. We went down in the lift together and on the wide steps running down to the pavement he touched my arm, keeping me with him as I would have moved away, and said, "I knew your father very well, my boy. A charming man. I suppose only a few people besides myself knew that he could be also a violent and flexible man. The world demands it from some of us. Truth and falsehood sit at opposite ends of the spectrum. In between are all the colours and shades of human expediency. Personally I'm glad the damned place is going to be blown up. Don't worry—there are a great many influential people in Whitehall who would be happy to dance around the bonfire, including me—though my dancing days, thank God, are over." Seeing the look of surprise on my face, he chuckled and went on, "Don't worry. Garwood was only doing his job. He wanted a formal denial by you of any interest in Caradon Abbey— and you gave it to him."

Impulsively, I said, "You people amaze me. Anyone would think it was all some sort of game."

He pursed his heavy lips suddenly and then said harshly, "There are moments when I could agree—a game, a fiction

217

designed to cover up truths nobody wants to challenge, let alone acknowledge. When Pandora's box was opened by her husband some say that Hope was the last thing that flew out—and some, that Hope still remains in the box. If it does, if it's still to come, Mr. Rolt, then man needs it now more desperately than at any time in his history, because hope means to cherish a desire for good and a belief in the prospect of its fulfilment." He grinned suddenly. "Your friend, Sir Hugh Gleeson, would say that Caradon Abbey was Pandora's box—with the gift of Hope still in it."

I said, "I'm sorry but all this is way above my head."

He looked straight at me, no humour on his large face now, and said, "That's exactly where it is. Thousands of light years above and beyond us—or so some of my friends think."

He turned and moved off without any farewell.

* * * *

I drove back to Rolthead wondering if Garwood knew how the old man disagreed with him. I presumed he must. Garwood was no fool. Within his agency there were factions whose policies differed behind their diplomatic front. There was a jockeying for power and prestige, a manoeuvring of people and prejudices as though they were pawns and major pieces and the whole thing a game, isolated and unrelated to life. A slight shift of agency policy could have had Garwood ordering me to go to the Abbey. Truth and honour could have been lifted from the board while all backs were turned and then the game taken up again without anyone remarking the loss. I preferred —not facilely and comfortingly because I had joined him—the direct, and unequivocally violent approach of the immaculately dressed Mr. Smith in his green conservatory. To keep and hold what was mine I had joined him. I had become a violent man . . . like my father, though I could never know how or when and where the change had taken him . . . but I knew now something of how he had felt when he had talked about 'the world's slow stain'. . . .

218

A week later the arrangements for my visit to the Abbey were settled. I had arranged a completely genuine appointment to visit the Tavistock agent about some woodlands we wanted to buy on the Devon side of the lower Tamar. I was to motor down on a Saturday early, meet the agent and inspect the woodlands, and then spend the night at the Abbey and motor back on the Sunday. With foresight I chose a weekend when I knew that Sarah would be away, since there was the possibility that she might want to come with me. By myself I could face what I had to do, but it would have been impossible if she had been with me. It was hard enough casually telling her about my intended visit and suggesting that she might telephone Lin Khan and arrange for me to stay at the Abbey.

"Of course," she said. "Lin will be delighted. Whenever you or Harold have to go down on business you should stay there. Oh, dear—it's a pity I can't come, too. But I really can't put off my engagement. . . ."

I knew she couldn't put it off. She was a governor—and a heavy contributor—to a charitably run home and school for disabled children in Warwickshire. The Saturday in question was the day of the annual meeting of the governors and also a fête day with a garden party and sports for the staff and children.

So my weekend visit was arranged. It might have been coincidence or it might have been the result of his own intelligence working in channels unknown to me, but the next day I received a call from Mr. Smith.

He said, making it neither a question nor a statement of fact, "Your weekend is fixed."

"Yes."

"You know Flaxman's Copse, of course?"

"Yes."

"I'll expect you there—if convenient—at four o'clock tomorrow."

"I'll be there."

Flaxman's Copse was a clump of beeches on the downland

less than four miles from Rolthead. It was Crown land and open to the public. A well-made road ran to the copse at the crest of the hill and there was a small car-parking space for sightseers who came to enjoy the view and walk the downs.

It was a warm, cloudless day, July almost over. There were only four cars in the parking-lot. His was a red Rolls-Royce parked well away from the others. I drew in alongside him. He was sitting in the back with all the windows open. On a little table let down from the seat in front of him was a Thermos flask, a glass of milk and a packet of plain biscuits.

He said, "I've sent the chauffeur for a walk. Get in."

I sat beside him and he went on, nodding at the milk, "Stomach ulcers. The accolade for tireless endeavour in the struggle to keep one's head well above water. Every four hours, milk and biscuits. So it's arranged?"

"The weekend after next. I'm going down to look at some woodlands."

"A good investment. What you take out you can always put back. That's good, honest husbandry. Alfie—that's the man you met—will come for your car on Tuesday morning. He knows more about cars and explosives than is believable. Makes a lot of money, but is a sad man because he always wanted to be a jockey and never managed it."

Although he spoke in a matter-of-fact way, pausing now and then to sip his milk, I could tell that he was in a buoyant mood, though he had it well under control. His battle lines were arranged and he was already tasting a limited victory.

I said, "I want some information and some assurances."

"Naturally."

"You hold the boy at this moment?"

"Yes."

"Then Alexina Vallis must know he's gone."

"No. I.I.S.L. are arranging to move their centres and disperse. So is Alexina Vallis. She's negotiating for the sale of her villa and many of her Italian interests. The boy was placed in the care of a highly recommended establishment in

Switzerland a month ago, I imagine to stay there until Alexina had settled her own arrangements for the future. She doesn't visit him, but she gets weekly reports from Switzerland. She still gets them—but the boy isn't there. Alexina Vallis will only know he has gone when you have him. At that stage there will be nothing she can do. It has, of course, cost us a considerable amount, but money is irrelevant when you have a lot of it."

"Where is he now?"

"I am not able to tell you that. But he is safe, well, and happy—though, I gather, something of a handful."

"How do I know you will hand him over to me when I have done this job?"

He smiled. "You have my word. I don't intend to break it because I don't want to spend any part of my life plagued by the thought that you are after me with murder in your eyes, Mr. Rolt."

"How and where will you hand him over?"

"When you have done your business at the Abbey, you will act as you would if it had had nothing to do with you. Eventually you will hire yourself a car from Tavistock and go home— on the way all you have to do is to make a detour and call on Sir Hugh Gleeson. The boy will be with him."

"Sir Hugh Gleeson! Where does he come into this?"

"He doesn't. He's an old friend of mine and I've often consulted him about problems which are nothing to do with the oil industry. He knows nothing about what you're going to do— but he's a shrewd and gifted man. You won't be breaking any confidence if you want to tell him all about it—afterwards. I leave that to your discretion. The main point is that you can pick up your boy on the way home. After that I have no interest in you or you in me. We go our own ways and face our own problems. As for the replacement of your car——"

"I don't care a damn about my car! I just want that boy waiting for me."

"He will be, Mr. Rolt. You have my word."

I walked back to my car. The sun was silvering the smooth,

elephant-grey trunks of the beeches. The sky was full of singing larks and away beyond the chequered fields and woodlands was the sea half hidden in a heat haze. It was a view I had known from a boy, a view across the sweeping miles of the county of my birth, a familiar and loved world. Behind me, munching biscuits, was a man who inhabited another world and who had pulled me into it to discover a self which I greeted with bitter recognition.

Alfie picked up the Bentley on the Tuesday morning. He had another man with him in the Mini-van who drove the van off as soon as Alfie stepped out. It was a different Alfie from the one I had met originally in that he wore now a smart tweed hacking jacket with a yellow waistcoat and khaki drill trousers. On his head was a clean cap of the same tweed as his jacket.

Walking to the garage, he said, "Thought I'd better smarten up a bit, sir. Never know, driving your Bentley looking like a grease monkey, some nosey bobby might stop me."

In the garage he ran his hand over the rear mudguard as though he were sliding it across the rump of a horse and said, "Beautiful. She's been well kept. Pity, too—still, there it is. I'll have her back Thursday. Don't worry if you're not here, sir. I'll just leave her in the garage, locked up, and hand the keys into the house." He paused for a moment before getting into the driving seat. "When you take her out she'll be all bomb. H.E. and incendiary. But nothing will happen, even if you run into a bus. Nothing can happen until you've flicked the switch on Saturday. Wouldn't be a bad idea, sir, if you filled the tank up somewhere just before you get to wherever you're going. Every little helps."

He backed out of the garage and then halted as Sarah came hacking up the drive on Minto. When she had gone by towards the stables, Alfie said, his face the picture of gloom, "Nice animal. . . . Well, we all have a cross to bear. . . ."

He turned and drove away down the drive. For a few moments I wondered where in his life he had been forced to look into the mirror of reality. . . .

I walked round to the stables where Sarah was handing Minto over to the groom.

"What's wrong with the Bentley, darling?" she asked.

"Nothing, I hope. I'm just having her checked over before I go down to Devon. I thought I'd take her to impress your Mr. Khan."

She laughed and we walked back to the house together.

I was out on the Thursday when Alfie brought the Bentley back. He had left the keys with Mrs. Cordell I went into the garage and unlocked the car. I could see nothing different with her except for the switch which had been fixed under the driving seat in a safe and unobtrusive position. I felt the leather of the front passenger seat and of those at the back. They were much harder than they had been. I took the car out and drove it for a couple of miles. It seemed no heavier than before and handled just as it always had done, but it was no longer the Bentley my father had driven and then passed on to me. It was a murderous weapon which I was going to use without conscience.

That evening we had people for dinner and bridge. There were my brother and his wife, Dr. Blundell and his unmarried sister, and my agent and his wife. It was an evening like a hundred others I had passed at Rolthead. There were moments during it when I forgot completely what lay ahead of me so that I wondered if the time would come when in the years ahead those moments, like beads being slowly fed on a thread, would finally lie close-touching, hiding the dark strand, obliterating it from all thought. I could not believe it.

Sarah and I made love that night and it was as it always had been—the uneasy mind banished by the force of the body's passion and power—which did not surprise me for I had begun to learn that the body and its acts adapt themselves to deceit and submerge self-disgust with ever-increasing ease. Later, when Sarah slept, I went back to my own room and I lay for a long time awake, thinking of the Abbey. I could only hope that there would be no one on duty in the computer room at night. If there were and I could know it, I knew that I would still throw the switch and accept that there was no prayer I could ever offer for them which would not be an obscenity.

On the Friday, Sarah went off after lunch, driving to Warwickshire. She was going to stay the night in the home because the governors' meeting was in the morning fairly early so that it would not clash with the day's programme.

On the Saturday I was up and away by six in the morning and as I drove there was only one thought in my mind. When I returned I would bring my son with me, bring him back to Sarah and Rolthead and with him bring truth into all our lives. I could only pray that the final truth between Sarah and myself would not kill our love.

## CHAPTER ELEVEN

I was down in good time to meet the agent. We looked over the woodlands and then, to make amends for my curtness with him before, I took him to lunch at Tavistock. At some time during lunch I mentioned that I was staying the night at Caradon Abbey.

He said, "I hear they're moving. You're not thinking of buying the place, are you? They've got a lot of good land and some salmon-fishing rights on the Tamar. Odd lot, I'm told."

I said, smiling, "My wife's one of the directors of I.I.S.L."

"Oh, God," he said, pulling a face. "I've said the wrong thing again."

"Don't worry. I'm inclined to agree with you. Why do people down here think they're odd?"

"Hard to say. They don't employ a lot of local labour. But quite a few of their people live out in hotels and rented places around here. They give a lot of money to local charities and good causes. Always very friendly but it's not often that anyone gets asked there. Full of security devices and Lord-knows-what I'm told. You know what local people are like . . . itching with curiosity. What they don't know they make up, and once country people start on that kind of thing they go the limit. Mysterious lights flashing in the sky at night, banshee noises, local lovers scared out of their wits in the woods by apparitions. . . ." He laughed. "Most of it was because at one time they had a night helicopter service coming in from London or somewhere for their top brass. Give a Devonshire- or Cornish-man a chance to imagine fairies, ghouls or what-have-you and he's away. Ghostly riders on white horses, witches flying on broomsticks—I've heard some rich stories. But if they're pulling out, the whole property's worth a packet."

After lunch we drove to another parcel of woodland which —although it had not been on our list—he wanted me to see. We parted about four o'clock. In many ways I had been glad to have his company until then because it stopped me from thinking too much about the night which lay ahead. There was no question of my changing my mind but it had been a relief to have the prospect pushed into the background for a while.

I took a drive around and then filled the Bentley's tank up and went to the Abbey. There was no fuss at the gate. I gave my name and was waved in and as I turned into the gravel space before the Abbey Lin Khan was standing on the broad steps waiting for me. With him was an Abbey servant in the I.I.S.L. uniform who took my case.

After an enthusiastic greeting Lin Khan said, "What a splendid motor-car."

"It belonged to my father. I like to give it an airing now and again."

He said, "Unless you plan to use it again today, perhaps you'd like to run it into the garage?"

I thanked him and drove the Bentley down the entrance ramp of the underground garage. As I passed through the floor-level opening all the lights in the place came on automatically. For some reason I thought of the local people's talk about flashing lights. More than likely when a helicopter landed on the wide gravel space in front of the Abbey the whole area would be floodlit.

There were three other cars in the garage, all of them parked with their noses against the back wall which I knew ran parallel with one side of the inner courtyard of the Abbey. I swung the Bentley away to the right and parked it with its bonnet a yard from the wall which followed the line of the computer room above. The car clock and my own watch showed the same time. I reached under the seat and pushed Alfie's switch over. I got out of the car and locked it. I turned my back on it and walked away. I would never see it again. My father who had originally bought it—a lover of good lines and good breeding; and a man, I knew now, who had once accepted and weathered the imposition of violence in his official affairs—had loved it and it had come to me with his love in trust. My love for it had died the day I had seen Alfie drive it away from Rolthead. I hated it and I hated myself. But tomorrow there would be no car to hate—only myself, and this had to be accepted and weathered, worn down and slowly effaced by time from my conscience. There was no turning back or desire to turn back in me.

Lin Khan, less ebullient than he had originally been, took me up to my room which was on the third floor in the south-west wing. It had everything; a marble-panelled bathroom, a small sitting-room, comfortable and deeply carpeted, and a bedroom which was elegant but masculine, and with low french windows that opened on to a small, private balcony.

Lin Khan showed me round the suite and then left me with the arrangement that we should meet before dinner in the main lounge.

From the balcony of the bedroom there was a view down the drive towards the lodge gates. I could trace the line of the high stone wall away to the left from the lodge until it disappeared into part of the surrounding woods. At one point a wide ride had been cut through the trees to give a vista from the Abbey down to the river valley. I could just see part of the higher houses of the village of Calstock on the far valley side and the tall, arched run of the viaduct across the river which had once taken a branch railway line to the village, a line now long disused. Seeing the disused railway viaduct, I thought of the oil-man, Mr. Smith, and his deadly concern for the crude and dirty power of petroleum. If I.I.S.L. were going to come up with a newer, cheaper and cleaner power form nothing could hold it back indefinitely. It would come even if I.I.S.L. were destroyed. My oil-man with his four-hour milk-and-biscuit diet knew that, but was still impelled to organise a thousand-year-long holding action because he accepted the parochial limits of man's mind. Better the devil you know . . . I turned back into the room and knew that I was far more than a conscript into the ranks of his army. Nobody had pressganged me. I was a volunteer because I, too, wanted to hold time back. I wanted to keep Rolthead and its widespread acres and traditions as they were, the feudal instinct was part of myself and my tradition. Broad acres, a fine house, an ancient name— and a son to inherit them. For these I would murder. For these —the thought carried no mitigation of the deed—men had always been ready to murder.

I helped myself to a large whisky and took it with me while I bathed and changed. I was on the point of going down to join Lin Khan before dinner when there was a knock on my door. I opened it. Standing outside was Alexina.

For a moment I was lost. Under my confusion I felt anger begin to surge in me. Had she been a man I knew there would have been no power which could have stayed my hand from striking, my face from showing my contempt and anger. She was the author of a host of miseries and deceits practised on Sarah and myself. Then, since deceit had started with her, I forced myself to its use and turned the stiff look of near anger on my face to a slow smile.

She gave a small laugh at my confusion and came into the room. She was wearing a long evening dress with a silk shawl spread over her bare shoulders.

"Robert . . ."

I kissed her on the cheek.

"Alexina. What a pleasant surprise."

"Really? It doesn't sound like it. . . ." She laughed, and asked teasingly, "Would you have come if you'd known I was going to be here?" It was a typical Alexina remark, but her tone and manner were light, and unusually friendly.

I said, "I'm happy to see you. Did Sarah know you would be here?"

"No. I had to come to London on business unexpectedly. Lin told me on the telephone that you were coming so I decided to join you. I have to leave early tomorrow morning. How's Sarah?"

"She's fine."

"Good." She turned from me and went to the window. "It's lovely here, isn't it?"

"Very. Can I get you a drink?"

"No thank you. I'll wait until we go down." She turned back from the window. "It's a pity we have to leave here. . . . It's a pity, too, about so many other things. You and I got off on the wrong foot. I think that was mostly my fault. Well, when all this move is over perhaps we can do something about it. . . ."

I was surprised at her words, at the tone in her voice. She sounded genuinely full of sadness. It was the first time in her life that she had ever shown any such emotion with me. Looking at her now, too, I realised how very much mother and daughter were alike . . . tall, beautiful, and with the same violet-dark eyes.

I said, "Why leave, then? You've got plenty of room here to expand."

"It's not just more room we need." She smiled. "You won't like to hear me say it—but this country is no longer the world centre it used to be and there are all sorts of technical considerations. England and Rolthead are to you the centre of life. Your roots go down. I.I.S.L. doesn't have roots. It's more like a travelling circus. We must go where the customers are. We always have since the original foundation of the company."

"The old boy in the courtyard?"

"He wasn't the true original. There were others before him. Has Lin taken you over the picture gallery?"

"No."

"Come. We'll have a look at it on the way down. We don't show it to everyone—only very special guests." She touched my arm briefly, a gesture almost coquettish. I followed her knowing that I was being shown a side of her which she had always kept hidden from me. Usually aloof, self-controlled, almost icy at times, she offered now a glimpse of ordinary, warm-hearted womanliness. For a moment I wondered if some sense of destiny, a prescience of things to come had vaguely possessed her and that she now wanted me to emend the reading of her personality and character which I had made. This woman had once taken my wife from me, had abducted my son—and now, when we both stood on the lip of crisis, maybe she sensed it, and was genuinely, although far too late, holding out her hand to me in a belated gesture of near friendship and human concern.

She led me through the long corridors of the first floor to the rear section of the Abbey and into a high, vaulted gallery which was hung with oil paintings. Although the light was still good, the gallery held shadows. She threw some switches at the doorway and lights came on over the paintings. Some of the wall spaces were empty and in the centre of the gallery was a pile of flat packing-frames.

Alexina said, "Some of the paintings are already packed. They'll all be gone by the end of the next week."

She took me to a picture just inside the main door. It showed a middle-aged man in dark knee-breeches and a long-tailed brown coat open over a white waistcoat. He sat sideways at a small table, one hand resting on it and holding a wine glass. He had a round, plump face and was smiling as though the artist had just amused him with some joke. Underneath, a gilt plaque was inscribed—'Obiah Santora, Great Park in the County of Worcester, 1798'.

Alexina said, "He was one of the early founders. There were four families. He brought them and all their interests together into a trading company which has eventually become Intertional Industrial Systems. He never had any children, but he had a much younger sister—Evangeline—who married into one of the other founding families. He left all his fortune to her."

As she moved to the next picture I knew that it could not be —nor any other picture in the gallery—that of Miss Evangeline Santora of Great Park because Sir Hugh Gleeson owned it and Albert Chinn had wanted to buy it. I wondered if Sir Hugh had ever known or guessed why Chinn had wanted it.

Alexina took me round the gallery explaining the various paintings, running through family histories and tracing the slow growth of the comprehensive business structure that had become I.I.S.L. Now and again—and without any surprise— I noticed a painting of a girl or a woman showing the left-hand Saturn finger quite clearly. I made no comment on it, nor did Alexina. None of the men carried the slight abnormality.

Alexina took me right round the gallery and finished halfway down the left-hand side of the room. From this point the wall ran on, blank of pictures, but marked with faded rectangles of wall paper where paintings had been hung.

I said, "You've not mentioned your family, Alexina. No pictures?"

She gestured at the faded spaces on the walls. "I'm sorry. They've been packed already. We came late into the empire— a distant side branch of the Santora family through Obiah's uncle and his children. The earliest painting was of my . . . my grandfather. He was called Ferenc Volgesi and was half Hungarian." She smiled. "Over the years all the families' blood lines got mixed." She nodded at the packed crates. "It's a pity they're packed. I'd have liked to show you my mother. One day I will. Looking at her—she was painted when she was about thirty—you would take her for Sarah or—" the touch of coquetry came plainly to me—"if posed in a soft and kind light, perhaps me." She was silent for a moment and then she put out a hand and touched my sleeve and went on, "We all make errors of judgment, Robert. Understanding between some people is a matter of years not minutes. I'm sorry we never got off to a smooth start. I'd have liked it but it wasn't ordained that way——"

As a purely conventional expression—nothing could alter my feelings for her now—I said, "I didn't help. Maybe I shouldn't have rushed those first fences. I just saw Sarah and loved and wanted her—and she was the same. Love is often a selfish affair. I'd like to see the painting of your mother sometime . . . very much."

"You will. I'll see you do when——" she waved a hand to the packing frames and cases—"when all this business is over. Oh, dear, what an upset and trouble it all is." Suddenly she looked and sounded old and very tired.

*　　*　　*　　*

We had dinner in a large alcove at the top of the dining hall. In the main room there were only three tables occupied by about ten or eleven people in all and most of them I learned were staying the night at the Abbey. Dinner alone with Lin Khan was a prospect I had already faced. It would have been polite and almost formal and I should never have felt out of my depth. But with Alexina present the occasion became a mixture of long periods when I felt lost, completely out of touch with them as they inevitably slipped into some discussion of their own business affairs—almost deliberately it seemed to me to a point nicely calculated—and then came back to me; Alexina with almost apologetic friendliness drawing me into the talk with chatter about Rolthead and Sarah and my own farming and estate interests. One moment I felt comfortably part of the company and the next I was an observer. Lin Khan, I noticed was much more restrained with Alexina, holding down his natural ebullience. It was clear to me—no matter how they had sounded on Garwood's tape—that Lin Khan was of far lower status than Alexina. It was a demonstration that excited my curiosity about the 'authority' which they had spoken of as controlling them all. I could not imagine a person, and far less a

232

committee or board of governors, controlling Alexina easily. Clearer still was that Alexina's new manner to me, shown in my room and in the picture gallery, was not for public display. Within the natural limits of a guest-and-host relationship, she had reverted to her usual social attitude to me. I was thankful for this. It was far too late for me to think of beginning to like her. We were enemies and I was going to destroy much of her work here. I was content with that.

Nobody can control the conditions or the temperature of human passion to the point of a precisely timed procession of cause, effect and event. Conscience is as slippery as an eel. It needs a practised hand to contain it. Mr. Smith could have known this, just as he could have known that Alexina would be at the Abbey. The first three hours after midnight are those in which a troubled, guilty mind can twist and turn on itself and resolution weaken, no matter how strongly bolstered by emotion. A man full of intent to destroy can always change his mind. This he might have postulated on my part. That he could have been devious to that extent I would have been willing to accept. Or it just could have been that Alfie, grieving over a past that had held no starting-tapes, no animal surge over the high fences, had for once let a faded dream confuse his normal efficiency. The time mechanism in the Bentley went off at one o'clock. If it were deliberate it was unnecessary. No sudden flash of warmth or sympathy between Alexina and myself, no consideration for whoever might be at the Abbey and be destroyed or injured would have made me go down and reverse the switch under the Bentley seat. I was a Rolt. My wife had been cruelly treated. I had had a son held from me and two years of his life's happiness denied me. There was no instinct in me to turn away from the promise I had given in that green-shaded conservatory.

I was lying fully dressed on my bed when the explosion came. To begin with there was no great noise. The bed under me shook as though from an earthquake shock and there was a curious moment of giddiness in me as the building stirred sharply, like some animal muscle-jerked in mid-dream; then from the window came the high sharp sound of the glass panes vibrating and whining under pressure like a sprung bowstring. As I rolled to my feet I heard the sound of breaking glass from behind the drawn curtains and then the long, deafening howl of the pent-up explosion in the underground garage breaking free with a blinding light that flamed around the curtains' edges and lit the room briefly. A second and smaller explosion quickly followed the first. There was the smash of more glass and the rumble of cascading masonry and then the growing crackle of fire and flames. Poised on the moment's edge before action, standing there in the room I knew the swift weakness of regret, of wishing that I had never come—and then forgot it as I rushed for the door.

*　　*　　*　　*

Most of the front of the Abbey had collapsed into a shambles of rubble that spread its detritus deep across the terrace and down the wide steps, spilling on to the gravel where loose masonry blocks cast sharp, dancing shadows in the light from the flaming façade.

With the other guests and some of the servants, I stood well back from the fire and destruction on the far side of the gravel space. Some of the people were dressed. Others wore coats or dressing-gowns. Far away to the north I caught the first sound of siren and bell above the roar and crack of fire eating into the building. There was nothing that could be done until the fire engines arrived. In the untouched part of the Abbey I knew the automatic sprinklers would be working.

We stood in a group like herded sheep, all eyes impelled to watch the growing fire, until Alexina came around the far corner of the Abbey. She hurried up to us. She was fully dressed and carried a clipboard in her hand.

She stood in front of us, looked us over calmly in the way of

234

one who had known emergency before, who had trained and been trained to meet disaster, and said, "As I call your names would you please answer and then make your way round to the Staff House at the back of the Abbey. There is no need for rush or panic, but please keep well away from the main building. . . ."

She consulted the sheet of paper on her clipboard and said, "Mr. and Mrs. Stanton . . ."

A young couple I had seen dining together moved up to her. She ticked their names on the sheet and they moved away.

I stood there listening to the names being called.

". . . Mr. John Preston . . . Miss Danvers . . . Signor Mangato. . . ."

One by one their names were checked and they went away and, watching her, I knew that even if my name were not at the bottom of the list I would not be called until last. She stood there in the summer night, a light coat hanging over her shoulders, underneath it the dress she had worn for dinner, and the flames lit her face and the draughts and sudden wind currents from the growing fire lifted her loose hair. I had no pity for her because she had never had any for me. Given her way, then Sarah would still have been a Mrs. Angela Starr, a woman without a past. I knew that she needed no telling now why I had come to the Abbey.

When only I remained she called, no change in her voice, "Mr. Robert Rolt. . . ."

I stayed where I was and she slowly came over to me. She held the clipboard against her breast, raised her free hand and brushed loose hair back from the side of her face, and then she said, "You could never understand. You could never have been told. Sometimes lately, out of love for Sarah, I have wondered whether I was wrong—that she knew better than I did. But what you have done tonight leaves me in no doubt." Her lips tightened with contempt. "There are still far too many of your kind."

235

I said, "I did what I had to, and you know why. Has everyone been accounted for?"

"Would it matter to you if they hadn't?"

"No. The guilt would have rested with both of us. You tried to take my wife from me—to deny me what was mine. You shouldn't have chosen a Rolt to do that to."

"Nobody has been killed. A lot of work has been destroyed." She nodded away down the drive towards the lodge gates. "Now—go away from here."

She turned and began to walk across the gravel after the other people.

I went down the long drive to the lodge gates. As I reached them a fire-engine came up the wooded hill. I stood aside for it and then walked on, turning to the left from the roadway and along the outer side of the wall which would take me to the long ride cut down through the woods to the valley top and so to the old viaduct. I could walk across it to the village on the other side of the Tamar. Somehow, at some time, I would get myself a car and drive to Sir Hugh Gleeson. There was an impatience in me, but it was not a physical one, not something that laggard time could swell. I was going to claim my own and that thought alone held a joyful, pure impatience.

I went down through the cleared ride and at its end turned along a well-worn path through hill scrub and young chestnut and oak growths. Finally I came out on to a small road. Opposite me was a gate that was half opened and beyond it the run of the old railway track. I moved along it, passing through an old cutting, the sides thick with broom and willow-herb, and so came out on to the viaduct which spanned the deep valley through which the river ran.

There was no moon but the night was bright with stars. Calstock on the far side was a straggle of houses lining the hill and spreading around an open quay. The river here, though miles from the sea, was tidal still and now the tide was at half-ebb. From the reed-fringed banks long sweeps of smooth black mud showed, running down to the narrowed river. I went out on to the viaduct which spanned the valley to the disused station on the far side, the river lying nearly two hundred feet below. The parapet of the viaduct was high, and here and there broken with a recess in which formerly the rail-gangers could stand back for the passage of a train. I walked clear of the centre of the track, keeping to the small path that ran close to the parapet wall. When I was about a third of the way over a man stepped out of a parapet recess just ahead of me. It was Lin Khan. He wore a white open-necked shirt and dark trousers. The shirt was crumpled and smeared with dirt and dark ash streaks. He stood a yard from me, tall, dwarfing me, his big face night-shadowed, creased and heavy and savage.

I knew at once that he shared no part of the mood with which Alexina had dismissed me. He had seen me go and had slipped ahead to be waiting for me and I knew exactly what was in his mind before he put it into words, into his first words.

He said, "Mr. Rolt—I am going to kill you."

He stepped forward quickly. Before I could protect myself, he struck me with a clenched fist on the side of the neck. I went down and backwards to the ground. As he stood over me, I made no move to get up. I wanted time to recover from the blow which had half-choked and half-stunned me.

He said, "I shall suffer for it in no way that you can under-stand, but I am going to kill you." His right foot came out and thudded into my side. Through a haze of pain and growing anger, I heard him say, "You brought violence here to repay trust and goodwill. You came like a man and acted like an animal. Very well, let us both be animals. . . ."

He kicked at me again, but I was ready for him and I rolled away quickly and got to my feet, my back against the stone parapet.

I said with bitter anger, "What kind of bloody man are you to talk of trust and goodwill? You know what you and your kind have done to me and mine."

As I spoke I went for him and I rammed my right fist into his stomach. His feet slipped on the loose stone ballast of the track and he went over. I flung myself on him and got my hands about his thick throat. After that there were no words between us. We fought like animals, twisting and turning, and rolling and gouging; using feet and fists and butting heads. Blood became a quick, bitter taste in my mouth, and the combinations of our bodies and our movements a dark, grotesque frenzy. And I knew I could never kill him, never hold or wear him down, because for all my power and all the savagery which it gave me an indecent delight to loose against him, I knew that he would master me . . . he was a Tartar, a giant, and there was an anger and a bestiality loose in him which overmatched and would overpower mine.

In the end limp and sobbing from my body's spent force, I was held by him, by one great hand that circled my throat and pinned me against the parapet wall. He had but to loose me to have me drop to my knees. And he did loose me, and I fell and lay on the ground. For a moment he stood over me, his great shoulders heaving, and then he began to bend down, to take and lift me as easily as I could lift a corn sack, to lift me high and roll me over the top of the parapet and let me drop.

Though my body was battered, bruised and bloody, and every spark of high Rolt physical pride was crushed from me, my mind was clear and curiously detached. He was a monster but a thinking one. If he had waylaid me in the middle of the viaduct I would have gone spinning downwards to the river waters and chance might have taken a hand and saved me. I might have survived the fall and the river. But we were only a third of the way out on the viaduct and below us lay the smooth, deep, soft mud banks and my body would hit mud, and the mud like a loose, lascivious mouth would take me, close over me and suck me down forever.

He put one hand behind my left knee and the other under my right armpit and the pressure of his fingers bit into me like clamps as he raised me. Then he jerked me to lie across his chest as he steadied himself for the final lift and drive of arms and shoulder muscles to pitch me over.

Then, as he stood poised and I could feel the rise and fall of his breath pump through his lungs for the coming effort, a voice said sharply from behind us, "No, Mr. Khan."

Lin Khan swung round, taking me with him, holding me across him like a shield. A tall, dark-bearded figure stood on the track centre behind us and the summer starlight shone on a raised automatic.

Dimly I knew that it was Vickers. But I was too far beaten to know any sense of relief. I was held there like a loose-stringed puppet and heard Vickers go on——

"Put him down, Mr. Khan, and go away. That is what Madame Alexina would want."

Hoarsely, his words fighting the strain of his breathing, Lin Khan said, "He goes over!"

He half-turned back to the parapet, but Vickers' voice stopped him, beating hard and full of contempt into the night. "Do it then! Put him over and in the moments before I kill you, in the moments while he falls and you die, you will know what you have done. Some part of hope will die and you will have killed it."

I had no idea what Vickers was talking about, could hardly register it, but I could feel the change take Lin Khan, the slow physical expression of some spiritual collapse or reversal inside him. Slowly he eased me round and put me against the wall, my back to them, my hands holding the parapet top for support, my body heaving from the brute entry of air into my lungs which my body and blood clamoured for.

I heard Lin Khan say, "You're not Johnson."

"Not any more."

"Who are you?"

"I serve many men, but my mind belongs to myself. Now go."

Almost in a whisper I heard Lin Khan say, "I thank you. What is torn down can be rebuilt. . . ."

I heard the sound of Lin Khan's steps crunch away over the loose ballast. A hand touched my shoulder and Vickers said quietly, "When you feel like it we'll go. I've got a small cottage in Calstock. Ten minutes at the most—when you feel up to it."

After a moment or two I turned and faced him. He held out a flask which I took and brandy went like a flame, raw and searing, down my throat.

I said, "You followed me down?"

"All the way. You did well against him but you never had a chance, Mr. Rolt."

Anger leapt in me. "You could have stepped in earlier, couldn't you?"

"Yes."

"Then why the hell didn't you? The bastard could have slung me over."

Vickers shrugged and rubbed a hand on his beard and said calmly, "I took a chance with you, with him, and with myself . . . no, *for* myself. In fairness to you, since it was your life I gambled with, I'll tell you about it. The reaction of a Rolt will be interesting." He nodded at the flask. "Have another go at that, Mr. Rolt, and then let's be on our way."

\*     \*     \*     \*

Vickers' cottage was on the valley side a little way down the river from the village. It was untidy but comfortable. I had a wash and freshened myself up in the bathroom. Apart from a swelling on the left side of my jaw my face was unmarked, but my body had been battered and kicked and I was sore and stiff all over. Although I had been soundly beaten there was no humiliation in me. Powerful though I was, it would have taken a far, far stronger man than I to have handled Lin Khan.

It was half-past two and most of the summer night lay ahead of us. Through the uncurtained window of the cottage sitting-

240

room I could see, high up and far across the river, the fire glare in the sky above Caradon Abbey.

At first Vickers was solicitous of my welfare, showing me where to wash and providing me with coffee and brandy and, while I drank the first cup, sitting opposite me with his own, eyeing me so that through my diminishing distress and physical aches I sensed that there was still some major point of decision in him to be settled. When he refilled my cup it was clear that he had composed whatever doubts might have concerned him since our walk back from the viaduct.

Lying back in his chair, bearded, long legs sprawling, stripped down to his shirt, collar open, he said, "This is going to take a long time. But there is no point in your leaving here until morning. You can have my car."

I said, "If you're going to interrogate me—don't. I don't care a damn for Garwood and your Whitehall people. I've got nothing to say."

He smiled. "The need for interrogation is long past. I've decided to clear some things up for you. And I'm not going to do it officially. What you do about it is your business. When you leave here I shall go too. But in a different direction and with the hope—a little more than a faint one—that I shall find some background, some place into which I can slide and remain unfound. When I first called on you at Rolthead I was tired and unhappy because of what I had become. Now—" he shrugged—"the process of self-discovery is complete. I don't want to go on being what I have been. I want no more part of the work I've been employed to do." He reached for the brandy bottle and poured a large helping of spirits into his half-empty coffee cup. "Do I go on, Mr. Rolt—or would you rather stay wrapped up in the cocoon they've spun around you?"

"They?"

"My bosses, still your bosses, the world's bosses. The men who say Yes or No whether we like it or not."

I said, "At the moment I have my own problems. I'd be a

fool not to understand something of yours. But, frankly, and selfishly, I don't want to hear about them unless it will help me."

He grinned and said, "Honest Robert Rolt."

I was too tired to be angry. I said, "If what you're going to say needs to be coherent you should lay off the brandy."

"I will when the moment comes. Since my frankness just then displeased you, let me say something that should make you happy. Tonight you killed Albert Chinn."

I sat forward quickly. "Then I'm bloody glad I did!"

He shook his head. "There was no blood, Mr. Rolt. You do not have to adjust your conscience to murder. You killed a joke."

"What the hell are you talking about?" For a moment I wondered if he had been at the brandy bottle long before he had arrived on the viaduct.

"About a joke. A family joke. All families have their special jokes. And I.I.S.L. is a family. For some reason unknown to me the name Albert Chinn means something to them. They've given it to various men from time to time, men who were simply extensions of the real Albert Chinn, the brains and the power behind the various shadowy manifestations of himself that he sends out from Caradon Abbey. Or did send out. You killed him tonight, Mr. Rolt—when you blew up the computer room. Their computer—more advanced than any other in the world—was Albert Chinn. That's what the I.I.S.L. family called the computer between themselves." He sipped his brandy. "No blood on your hands, Mr. Rolt. But ten, maybe more, years of work destroyed, progress halted for I.I.S.L. Your oil-man will be happy. So eventually will Garwood— and a lot of other people in Whitehall and around the world— though Garwood will be hopping mad that you danced to the strings someone else pulled. But you need have no worry. Only a few official people will be unhappy—but there's nothing they can do because they are powerless and, like myself, regarded as lunatics."

242

I said, "Tell me what you want to." I reached out for the brandy bottle and put it out of reach on a table behind me.

He smiled and said, "You needn't worry, Mr. Rolt. I'm not drunk, nor am I going to be. Mad you may call me before you leave—but certainly not drunk."

## CHAPTER TWELVE

HE MADE HIS own personal statement first. Of its sincerity there was no question. Knowing something of the modes of his work, conscious of the distortions of principle once forced on my father, now on me, by the combinations of official policies and expediencies, I could sympathise with him because the pressures on him over many years and many assignments must have been very great and cumulatively destroying—and impossible to disguise from his employers entirely.

When he had first come to me that sunny morning to bring me hope for the recovery of Sarah, he had already been marked as possibly unreliable and shortly afterwards had been given the gamekeeper assignment at Caradon Abbey where he could still carry out some useful functions but be sufficiently removed from the heart of policy-making and the arcane store of information and secrets of his and allied agencies.

He said, "I had a question mark against my name. In my service there is—if it is not policy—no retirement, no opting out, no handing in of one's notice. By this time tomorrow the question mark by my name will be gone. Only a simple operation will remain for my employers—to erase my name from their records, and the man behind it from existence. Naturally I want to live so I shall go to Alexina Vallis and ask for sanctuary and such safety as she can give me——"

"In return for what?"

"Nothing. There is nothing I can tell them that they don't already know. I shall ask for their charity because I have had a change of heart. If I don't get it I shall fend for myself for as

245

long as I can. I shall not have become a traitor—simply a refugee from a state of mind and a human condition which my employers, the majority of them, represent."

"And you think you'll get her charity?"

"I might. It's not unknown in the I.I.S.L. organisation. There are things about them which are even more remarkable. In their whole history they have never used physical violence——"

"Don't be damned silly! They abducted my wife and monkeyed about with her mind. They've kept my son from me——" I broke off sharply.

He said, "It's all right. I know about that. And we'll come to it in a moment. But the truth remains that they have never used violence, physical violence against any person. No murder, no torture . . . none of those things which are commonplace in every government agency in this world. You had proof of it tonight. Lin Khan, because you had destroyed their precious computer, lost control of himself. He would have thrown you over the viaduct after beating you up—but he turned against it the moment I gave him the smallest pause to stop and remember the I.I.S.L. code. I told you once to keep a weather eye open for violence against yourself. That was not a warning against I.I.S.L. It was against us and against the people your oil-man represents—and you did have a taste of it." He smiled and said, "Human beings have little consistency. The oil people once tried to kill your wife and you. In return you planted a bomb for them at Caradon Abbey."

"There were sound reasons for that!"

"There always are, Mr. Rolt. Such sound reasons. Good family ones, good national ones . . . always good, good."

I stirred angrily. "Let's keep to facts. You haven't got me here just to tell me you've had a change of heart and are going to defect to I.I.S.L.—if they'll have you. That's your affair—not mine."

"It's your affair as well." He stood up, walked to the back of the room and opened a cupboard. He came back with two

246

glasses and a fresh bottle of brandy. He put one glass close to the half-full bottle on the table near me and then sat down and poured himself a drink from the new bottle, saying, "Don't worry. I've a hard head. Now . . . let's consider how it is your affair, Mr. Rolt. You married a beautiful woman. You lost her for a period and then she was returned to you. But the fact that she had had a son by you was withheld from you."

I said, "I'm listening to you. But if you go one inch over the mark I won't be responsible for what I might do."

He sat forward sharply and said with a sudden, curt vigour in his voice, "You listen to me, Mr. Bloody Rolt. You listen, because I could be doing you the biggest favour of your life. I like you and I want to help you and I want you to understand all that has happened—and if I go over the mark you'll just sit there and take it like a bloody man and not some apoplectic country squire who hasn't yet dragged himself into the twentieth century!"

For a split second I was almost out of my chair. No bastard, mixed-up intelligence man was going to talk to me like that— and then, God knows why, a sense of his sincerity hit me like a blow in the face. I leant back in my chair and screwed round for my glass and brandy bottle and said, "I'm not overfond of the twentieth century but I'll try and catch up with you. All right—go ahead. Take your liberties and overstep the mark. You're entitled to it. You brought Sarah back to me."

"Thank you, Mr. Rolt. Now let's consider the question of your wife and the things that have happened to her."

As he began to speak, I poured brandy into my glass. Watching him, I remembered the man who had stepped out of a car at Rolthead and had come into the study with his selection of films. Then he had been hesitant, embarrassed, and clumsy. For me, one look at his nervous, flickering eyes then made him a man I would have turned down at any interview for almost any job I could think of. . . . That man had had to be acting or there was now a remarkable change in him physically and personally. His eyes were steady, and there was

247

an air of authority about him. His lean body was hard and all muscle. Even when he lounged back in his chair the strength showed and the lean, suntanned, bearded face was that of a woodsman pioneer. In that moment I hoped that when morning came and he moved away into the rough country of his future he would find somewhere in it whatever it was that his spirit now goaded him to seek.

He said, "Before your oil-man got you to come down here, I presume he must have given you his explanation of all that happened to your wife . . . why she was taken from you and so on?"

"Yes, he did."

"And what was it?"

Very briefly I outlined to him all that Mr. Smith had told me, and finished, "Are you going to tell me that that's all nonsense?"

"No, I'm not. I think it's probably all true, except for one important point."

"Which is?"

"The question of loyalty, Mr. Rolt—this enormous bond of loyalty which embraces all the I.I.S.L. families. Your Mr. Smith says it's so strong that Alexina could do all she did to Sarah. So strong, you think, that Alexina could abduct her child—take it out of her life for ever—and Sarah could agree, choosing between her love for you and her natural love for your son? And not only that, Mr. Rolt—so strong that Sarah pretended to you that she still had a memory-gap covering the pregnancy and birth of the boy so that she could find some mental shield to ward off the distress of knowing that she *had to deceive* the man she loved, keep from him forever the knowledge of the one thing in the world he longed for—you think all that could spring from a loyalty to I.I.S.L.?"

"Well, yes I did."

He shook his head. "It's a human weakness, Mr. Rolt, not to analyse logically situations or problems which may cause a change in our beliefs. You accepted it because you wanted to come down here, do what Mr. Smith wanted, and get your son back. Your wife did all these things, there's no doubt about it; and you accepted the motive Mr. Smith gave you—loyalty to a big industrial concern and the small group of families that control it? You're more intelligent than that—but at the time you were blind to everything except the obsession to get your boy back. I don't blame you. But now you've done what you came for, do you still believe that a family-cum-commercial loyalty could possibly have been strong enough to make your wife do all this?"

For a moment I said nothing. Through the window I could see that the flame-light in the sky over the Abbey had paled to a dim glow. There was a feeling in me then that maybe the wild, dark grotesqueries of this night had not yet passed.

I said frankly, "Looking at it coldly now . . . well, it seems a bit far-stretched. But what other reason could there possibly be?"

He sipped at his brandy.

"Some other loyalty, some other love, Mr. Rolt. Your wife made a sacrifice that included you and your son. What could make a woman do that? Plenty of things. Men and women have gone to the stake for their religious faiths. Human love is strong, but there are other far stronger loves. For an idea, a vision, a principle, children have been sacrificed before, love denied and human happiness jeopardised——"

I cut in, "You're evading the point."

"For the moment yes, because even now I am wondering if you can take what I think is the truth."

"Get on with it—but I hope to God it's leading to some sort of daylight."

He smiled. "Daylight is not a fixed thing. Each day's light is different from all others. And each love, too, is different from any other—and so is each truth."

I said sharply, "You've slowly come to your own truth, Vickers. That's why you're talking to me. Now—don't fence with me any longer. Even though it may not be acceptable to me, I'll know the truth when I hear it."

249

He sat forward in his chair and topped up his brandy glass. He said, "If I'm taking a long route to what I believe, it's because I know what kind of man you are, Mr. Rolt. Frankly, I don't think you will believe it—but I've nothing else to offer——"

"For God's sake, man!"

"All right, here it is. Some of it is fact—some theory. Let's consider first of all this group of families represented by I.I.S.L. They do two things. They collect information openly and clandestinely. Some of this they pass on, but most of it they keep within their organisation for development by themselves and their subsidiaries. While they are very much interested— and successful—in making money through normal industrial and financial practices, they are also extraordinarily altruistic. They endow and control all sorts of research work, and they subsidise all sorts of specialists, scientists, doctors and researchers in many fields. While some of their activities would with proof be open to prosecution in most countries of the world they have never so far as our records show used any form of violence. As a matter of fact their image is presented as considerably blacker than it actually is. Now why do they do all this? Just to make money? Because they hold to an unpopular truth that all human knowledge should be held in common—that State and scientific secrets only lead to trouble among the different peoples of this world? Well, possibly. But for my money the real reason is that they have a secret family belief, an absolute conviction that almost amounts to a religion dominating everything they do. Whether it is true or not, I don't know. Some facts we possess support it. But absolute certainty is out of our reach. But there is no doubt how they feel. They are looking for something which will ultimately benefit this muddled-up world of ours and at the same time demonstrate the truth of their belief. Everything they do is in preparation for the day when they can set out for the promised land . . . the land in which they will no longer be alien people. Quite simply —they want to go home. The waters of the Red Sea parted for

250

the Israelites. The I.I.S.L. family are waiting for the moment when time and distance can be rolled aside . . ."

I said, "What the hell are you talking about?"

He shrugged his shoulders and said, "I can assure you that it is me talking and not the brandy. I and quite a few other very responsible government people know that the I.I.S.L. family believe that they did not originate on this earth of ours. They are convinced—for all I know, have proof—that the original family members were stranded here on earth in the late seventeenth or early eighteenth century. This they believe absolutely. And their belief—like that of any fanatical religious sect—governs everything they do."

He paused, his eyes fixed on me.

In that moment I was sorry for him. Whatever pressures had been on him for so long had done their work. He was another victim of the system he served.

I said quietly, "Look, old man, you can't expect me to believe that. I mean, it's complete nonsense."

Calmly he said, "If you think I'm mad, say so."

"Well—it is a bit off beam, isn't it?"

"Maybe, but not unbelievable. Am I the mad one—or is it you and millions more like you who want to keep their minds and their eyes shut to the fact that you live in the twentieth century . . . that men *have* walked on the moon, that Mars and Venus *are* being photographed and probed by our space vehicles, that any astro-physicist, astronomer, or mathematician will readily concede that the likelihood of life here on earth being unique in all the galaxies and infinite space of the Universe *is* a nonsense? Where there is intelligent life there is a drive to know and to explore. Don't you think this earth could have been visited in the past by strangers from other worlds? Do you believe in the Bible, Mr. Rolt?"

"Well, of course I do."

"Do you remember this? 'And it came to pass that when men began to multiply on the face of the earth, and daughters were born unto them, that the sons of God saw the daughters

251

of men that they were fair; and they took them wives of all which they chose. . . . There were giants on the earth in those days; and also after that, when the sons of God came in unto the daughters of men, and they bare children to them, the same became mighty men which were of old, men of renown.' "

"But that's Genesis, that's——"

"You don't believe the Old Testament? Only the New? The immaculate conception, Christ walking on the waters, all the other miracles . . . you accept all that?"

"Of course I do."

"But you can't believe what the Old Testament says about visitors from space? A curious dichotomy, but it was what I expected to find and——"

"Look, Vickers . . ." I stood up. "I'm sorry, but frankly I think you're round the bend."

He looked at his watch and said, "There's no point in your leaving yet. You might just as well let me tell you what there is round that bend. Don't be one of those men who close their minds and their eyes at the first sign of something out of their experience. Think of the first man who saw the first rainbow. . . . He probably turned his back and said, 'I don't believe it'."

I sat down and lit a cigarette. He was talking rationally and there was no doubt despite the brandy that he was sober. Mad he might be but he was certainly not drunk.

I said, humouring him, "Let's forget about the Bible. I'll listen. More than that I can't promise."

"Well here it is—straight and hard, no frills. There is a body of official opinion, larger and more respected than you can know, which believes that the original I.I.S.L. family were four or five men and women from another Earth-type planet. Explorers, willing to take risks, human in form but with more highly developed intelligences and powers than the people of this planet. Something went wrong. Their spaceship crashed—or broke down beyond repair. They were stranded here and the world they had left wrote them off, didn't know they'd reached the Earth. But they were here and they wanted to go back.

They did what all good intruders do when stranded in hostile territory. They destroyed all trace of their ship, of their coming, and they integrated themselves among the natives whom they resembled. *And they saw that the daughters of men were fair and they took them for wives.* They had to because they were determined to survive. They might not get back themselves but one day the sons of their sons and the daughters of their daughters would go. But they knew that their blood-lines were going to be diluted with each generation so they picked their mates carefully and from that time on nobody married into the family unless he or she was considered absolutely suitable—unless he or she were the type who could eventually be let into their secret and give complete loyalty to their dream of one day returning. Their loyalty to that overrides everything. Not even your wife—no matter how much she loved you—could ultimately ignore it. Your Mr. Smith knows all this—whether he believes it or not, I don't know—but he certainly wasn't going to tell you about it." He smiled. "Alexina didn't want you, Mr. Rolt. You weren't I.I.S.L. material. But your wife wanted you, loved you almost beyond her I.I.S.L. loyalty. That's why you have your present trouble."

I was silent for a while. There was no belief in me, but that could not still the onset of obvious questions which came to mind and, with them, past memories. I had always thought that Sarah's interest in astronomy and the possibility of life on other planets was uncharacteristic—frankly a bizarre excess for such a practical person. If I could have accepted Vickers' theory—then her *folie* became understandable. But I couldn't accept it, nor understand how others—excluding Vickers— could either.

I said, "Are you telling me that people like Garwood and Smith, the oil magnate, and certain people in Whitehall have given even a moment's serious consideration to this theory?"

"Yes, I am. And that simple answer makes me a traitor of sorts."

"Why did they never put the possibility to me?"

He shook his head slowly, smiling.

"Ask yourself that question. You now think I'm mad. You would have thought them mad—and then they could never have manipulated you. The Albert Chinn computer at Caradon would still be intact. Get this into your mind, Mr. Rolt: every major government secret agency in the world is aware that this theory—and the whole concept of intelligent life-forms from outer space existing and, perhaps, being on the brink of making contact with us—could be a true one. There's enough *prima facie* evidence to give it high priority. Do you expect them to broadcast it over radio and television now? No—wait until the moment is inevitable, is their credo. So, you and the rest of the honest, unimaginative, gullible world go on the waiting-list. Do you know anything about hae-mophilia, Mr. Rolt?"

"Very little."

"Only men can suffer from it and it can only be passed down the male line. It always jumps a generation. Father can't hand it on to son. There's something like that in the I.I.S.L. families, only in reverse. A slight deformity of the middle finger on the left hand of the women. Your wife has it, but not her mother. I've seen it in other women of the family. . . ."

And so had I in the portrait gallery at Caradon Abbey.

"Do you know what your wife's blood-group is, Mr. Rolt?"

"No."

"It's an extremely rare one—and it's common to most members of the family. You don't, of course, believe in U.F.O.s, flying-saucer sightings, and observations of strange things seen in our skies . . . all that nonsense?"

"No, of course not!"

"Well, your wife does, doesn't she? She shares the almost religious belief of the I.I.S.L. families. And thousands of ordinary people all over the world believe in these things and hundreds claim to have seen the evidence with their own eyes. And now official eyes have been forced open. There's considerable concern in all the major governments about such things. I can tell you that there is a great body of open and suppressed evidence which points to periodic surveillance or interest of some life forms from outer space in this world. Every government in the world is gravely concerned about it and is secretly doing its own research and investigation. When I talked about the lunatic section in our Whitehall agency I was talking about the men who aren't shutting their ears and their eyes. Lunatic, they're called—but they are taken seriously. A lot of whitewash is thrown about but it wears thin. The public must not be alarmed. The Americans have had their debunking Condon report. If you were to ring the Ministry of Defence at this moment and say you'd seen a strange, glowing disc-like object streaking up the Tamar and then hovering absolutely stationary with no noise, you'd get a soft answer. The Royal Air Force has a staff who do little else but eye-wash the public. But right at the very end of the corridors of power in London, Washington, Moscow—every big capital in the world—there sit men who know. Men who are also out of their depth. This isn't theory now, Mr. Rolt. *This is a fact.* And it's one the public should know. Those same men don't regard this I.I.S.L. explanation I'm giving you as a mad theory. They have an open mind about it mostly. But opinions are divided. Some believe it absolutely. Others don't. But the simple fact is that there is *no other way* of logically explaining the actions of the I.I.S.L. family group. They have this fanatical, overriding belief, Mr. Rolt. No matter how much she might like to ignore it, your wife has it and has had to act by it often against her will. You and she, Mr. Rolt, have been its victims. I.I.S.L. want a new power to lift them off the earth. The oil-men want I.I.S.L. destroyed because they don't want the development of a new power which would kill their own industry. But among the men who sit in the world's rooms of power there is another reason why they don't want the I.I.S.L. family to produce a power form that could take them back to their own planet, be it in our solar system, or far more likely in some other. They don't want that because it would be

255

the beginning of viable communications between inhabited planets and that could lead, so their human minds argue, to anything . . . to invasion of this earth or simply to a change of the whole ethos of this planet. They're frightened, vicious and confused men, Mr. Rolt."

While he had been talking I had watched him. He was an intelligent, capable man. He had worked for long years in an organisation that demanded he should be such. Now and again he showed emotion in his speech, but there was no wildness about him, no fanatical stir or extravagance of mood. I sat there, uncommitted and unbelieving, but I was impressed and surprised to find myself so. Although he was on the verge of creating enormous personal problems for himself, I could not overlook the fact that he had made time to try and help me with mine . . . though, God knows, I couldn't see where this farrago offered any help. But, I decided, the least courtesy I could pay him was to match his own sincerity—no matter how warped or misconceived it was—with my own.

I said, "You must see that I'm the kind of man who would turn his back on the first rainbow. I can't help that. One needs practice in handling miracles or the unknown. But some of the things you've said strike home. It's true that in a sense I'm nearer the thirteenth century than the twentieth but that's because I believe that the world would have been happier without most of its discoveries . . . or, at least, would have been happier if they could have been spread over a hundred rather than a score of centuries. Granted your theory, I can see why Alexina Vallis would never want me as a son-in-law and would be anxious to keep my child. But I think it's just on this point that your whole theory falls down. If these few adventurers from somewhere out there—" I nodded to the wide stretch of sky, now dawn-streaked, over the river valley—" if such people came here at the end of the seventeenth century and married and had children, and from then on those children went on marrying and increasing, the I.I.S.L. family by now would be a very, very large one. Far too large that by any stretch of

256

imagination they could have kept their secret or held their freemasonry and family loyalty intact. More and more the human strain would have become dominant in them. They would have had their share of human weaknesses and perfidies and greeds which would have destroyed the original family obsession of one day finding the propulsive power that would take them back. No, sorry, Vickers, but on that alone I wash my hands of the theory."

He shook his head at me. "It's a good point. The fact that you make it confirms my liking and respect for you. You can think straight, but not for you *per ardua ad astra*. No dreams. Work the broad Rolt acres and pay the Church its tithes. But you should look to your Church. In their teachings you can find the answer to your objection." He reached to the side of the fireplace and pulled a Bible from one of the flanking shelves, leafed through it to find his place, and then read, " 'And all the days that Adam lived were nine hundred and thirty years . . . And all the days of Methuselah were nine hundred sixty and nine years . . .' Men lived long in those days, Mr. Rolt. Noah was five hundred years old when he begat Shem, Ham and Japheth. The good book says so. Man's life has shortened— maybe because we have betrayed some spiritual contract unknown to ourselves. But these adventurers had a different life-span—they came from a less abused world. And their children when they married here inherited this characteristic. You've seen Sir Hugh Gleeson's painting of Miss Evangeline Santora?"

"Yes."

"A nice-looking woman. Painted in 1820. She died a few years ago at the age of a hundred and seventy."

"What damned nonsense!"

"Is it? Long life isn't unusual in some parts. There's a tribe in Asia whose men live usually to a hundred and twenty years old and more. I personally checked the Evangeline Santora records. It wasn't easy because the I.I.S.L. family group cover their tracks well. All their members develop more or less

257

normally until they are around the sixties and then the process slows down, the physical process of ageing that is. Also, for some biological reason, the women don't conceive easily—and when they do, usually late in life—and seldom have more than one child. That's why they place so much importance on children—why Alexina could give up Sarah to you in return for your son."

"Vickers—you can't be serious about all this?"

"Indeed I am, Mr. Rolt. Why should I choose this moment to pitch you some fairy story? I wouldn't be surprised if Alexina Vallis wasn't at least eighty years old. No, no——" He raised a hand to stop any interruption from me. "Do you remember the tape Garwood played you? I was instrumental in getting it. He didn't play it all to you. They cut and distorted it. But I know it all by heart. Remember these bits?" He closed his eyes and recited, " 'We're a long time here. No matter our first loyalty, it's always been policy to concede these periods of withdrawal from the overall design.' " He opened his eyes and smiled wryly. "We're a long time here . . . That was Alexina Vallis speaking. And again she says, 'Dear Lin Khan . . . even with all the time we have on our hands don't you sometimes wonder about it all? Don't you ever get tired? Don't you ever wonder whether the whole thing hasn't been framed wrongly?' And, now Mr. Rolt, I'm not going to argue with you about it any more. I've told you what I believe to be true. My belief is supported by many facts—more even than I would want for your own safety to tell you."

I said, "Assuming all this is true—why have you told me?"

"Because you'd have seen for yourself eventually that ordinary, deep loyalty to I.I.S.L. wasn't enough to explain things. Now you know exactly what your wife has sacrificed for you, and the power of her love for you. You may decide not to tell her you know the truth; but without knowing it how could you possibly realise just how much you mean to her? You've a problem, too, on your hands—only truth can help you with it. You're going back to Rolthead, to your wife—and you're taking your son with you. You've got to face that moment with your wife——"

"I knew that when I agreed to plant a bomb in the Abbey."

He stood up. "No, you didn't. You thought only of getting your son back. But now you've got your wife to face. You've got to go to her, Mr. Rolt, and find and face the truth for yourself and then learn to live with whatever it brings or takes away from your life." He pulled his hand out of his pocket and tossed a key-ring to me. "Those are for my car. It's outside. I don't want it again." He looked around the room, then shrugged his shoulders and went on, "There's nothing I want here. . . ."

He picked up his jacket from the back of his chair and walked out of the room. I heard his steps around the house and then saw his tall form move past the windows as he crossed the garden.

I sat frozen in my chair, hearing his last words, seeing him against the new day's light as he passed the window, and hearing now the first few notes of morning birdsong throb achingly over the river and the valley side. I knew then that although the night had been one long assault after another against my body, spirit and mind the final confrontation was still to come.

I poured myself half a glass of brandy and drank it without let. As I put the glass down I heard myself in the tones of some stranger say, "For God's sake, how can any man be expected to believe such bloody nonsense!"

## CHAPTER THIRTEEN

Driving back, I thought a great deal about Vickers. There was no doubt in my mind that he was the victim of the conflicting strains which his service had imposed on him. Give a man too much to carry and he can make it so far, but eventually he cracks. Vickers, I was sure, had cracked. There was nothing I could do but thrust the whole of his nonsensical theory away from me—but it was impossible to forget it. It kept coming back and demanding my attention . . . particularly his remark about the first man and the first rainbow.

I was a Rolt—a bread-and-butter man. I saw the world and the people around me as they were, but that didn't mean that I was bigoted enough to think that the world had nothing new to offer; although often the new things were received initially with derision and disbelief. Although I had both feet firmly on the ground I couldn't ignore that we lived in an age of remarkable discoveries and achievements. Like anyone else I now accepted as commonplace things whose reception in the past had seemed unthinkable . . . mad, impossible, wishful fancies; the reality of meteorites, the continental drift theory, the existence of germs, the city of Troy and Pleistocene man, and the advent of radio, television, heavier-than-air flying machines, the split atom, nuclear power, and of men walking on the moon —a living miracle watched by millions on their television screens so often that it had become a banality. Was it so incredible that ages ago adventurers from space, like our own moon men, had been stranded here and cherished the idea of a return home one day, a dream that passed down through their children? My whole instinct was to reject it. I did reject it.

Vickers was round the bend. But the idea was lodged in my mind. Much as I disbelieved it I knew that it could not be denied house room.

On the far side of Exeter I stopped and telephoned Sir Hugh Gleeson from a roadside callbox. He showed no surprise at being called.

I said, "I'm on my way back from Caradon Abbey."

"Yes, I know. Vickers called me a little while ago to say goodbye."

"You know all that happened?"

"Yes, Robert." His voice was flat, emotionless.

"You have something for me, I think."

"I have—and it's pretty lively, too." Just for a moment a hint of humour touched his voice.

"I've decided to go straight back to Rolthead. I'll come to you tomorrow."

"I think that's wise. Do you know what you're going to say to Sarah?"

"No. I just want the truth—whatever it is—to be out in the open."

"Truth is something which should be handled carefully. Some people can be as irresponsible with it as a small boy in a barn with a box of matches. I sometimes think that few human beings are capable of handling truth."

Impatiently I said, "I'm in no mood for riddles, Sir Hugh."

He laughed dryly. "You never were, Robert. Your feet are solidly on the rich soil of Rolthead. Your eyes function on an horizontal plane. If you want to see the stars, the truth, Robert, you have to lift your head. That's no riddle. It's a statement of physical and optical truth."

I said, "You and Vickers would get on well."

"Did get on well, Robert."

"You know what he told me? All that nonsense?"

"Yes. All that nonsense. That's what they said back in 1616 when William Harvey described the way blood circulated in the body."

"You believe what he told me?"

"If you mean have I evidence which can't be ignored, real proofs—then no. But a man can have a belief without proof. Belief is only a dream. Reality is the sum of dreams come true. Go back to Rolthead, Robert, but remember this—be gentle. People who walk in their sleep, dreaming an ancestral dream, must be wakened tenderly."

He put the receiver down. I stepped out of the callbox and ran the few yards to the car. I was in no mood for dreams and woolly talk. I wanted everything penny plain. That was the only way to live sanely.

The day had changed while I had been driving. A fierce summer gale had come up from the south-west. A driving wind was sweeping low, dark clouds and sudden, blinding rain squalls before it. I drove fast, not thinking, wrapped in an icy cocoon. The weather grew worse, the wind stripping the green leaves from the battered trees, the road and the ditches running with storm water.

Two hours later I arrived at Rolthead. Sarah was back. Her car was parked on the forecourt by the main steps. I parked behind it and ran up the steps. Mrs. Cordell was in the hall.

She greeted me and said, "Madame's had lunch. She's in her room taking coffee."

I went to the old music-room. Sarah was sitting at her desk, writing a letter, a coffee tray at her side.

"Robert!"

She stood up and then paused, held by her surprise and pleasure. In those few seconds before either of us moved I knew an anguish and love sharper and more vivid than any I had known before. This woman was my wife, Sarah. She was my love and my life. She stood there with the gale's wind and rain beating at the tall mullioned windows behind her, fair-haired and lovely, the loved one I had brought in pride to Rolthead, a woman whose wildness in passion I knew and a woman whose turmoil and agony of spirit I had now to understand with a deep and final truth if there were to be

263

any honest future for us. A flare of lightning seared the world outside and lit the room with a cold blue flame. A fast-following roll of thunder shook the skies above Rolthead.

She came to me, into my arms, and we kissed one another and we were lost to everything for a few moments. Then I half-released her, my hands on her arms, holding her from me.

She said, "Oh, darling, it's nice to see you. Have you had lunch? Would you like some coffee. I'll——"

"I don't want anything." I dropped my hands from her. The cocoon around me was gone, ripped aside. I was awake from a nightmare and in control of myself. I was master of myself and I was here at Rolthead which was our place. That mastery and ownership I was determined to have free of all deceit and ignorance. I wanted the truth and I was prepared to live with it because I loved her. But I wanted the truth not as other people had given it to me, not as other people wanted it to be. I wanted her truth and I knew there was only one way to it. No matter what the truth was, I loved her and would accept it.

I moved away from her to the window.

Sarah said, "Did you have a nice time at Caradon?" Then in the light that came from the storm-dark day through the window she saw my face and cried out, "Robert—what's happened to your face?"

"My face is nothing. Sit down, Sarah." I nodded to her chair.

"Robert—what on earth's the matter with you?"

"Please Sarah, sit down and listen to me!"

Slowly she sat down in the chair and her face changed. I felt then that this was a day marked from all others. I said, "I've lived too long in a disordered world. Disordered and disorderly. A world full of half-truths and half-lies. I want no more of it. I love you and I want you—not part of you, not some of you for some of the time. This is Rolthead. We came to it with love, and I want you here for as long as we

264

live as man and wife and with only trust and truth between us."

Quietly she said, "Robert—what's happened to you? What is this all about?"

"You don't know?"

"I only know that I love you and you love me. True, there have been things happen to us which you couldn't describe as ordinary. But that's all in the past."

"To be forgotten, Sarah? Accepted? Never questioned?"

"That's what we've done, isn't it?"

"It's what we've tried to do. But we haven't been allowed to bury the past. Other people have kept digging it up. And other people haven't just been content with that—they've manipulated our lives each and every day. Now I want an end to that. I want the truth and only you can give it to me. No matter what the truth is, I want it."

She stood by her desk and looked at me in silence for a while and there was no doubt in my mind that she was at some crisis point. Then her eyes closed, her face became an expressionless mask, her body still.

I said, "There's nothing you can say to me which will alter my love for you."

Her eyes opened and she said tonelessly, "Why talk about truth, Robert? Isn't our love enough? That's all I've ever wanted——"

"It's not enough. I want the truth. I want to know what kind of hell you've been through so that it can't happen again. You've got to tell me. Sarah—what happened during those ten months you say you can't remember? You do remember them, don't you?"

Slowly she nodded. "Yes, Robert, I do remember them."

"Then let's finish with it very simply. We all make mistakes. God knows, I have. What bargain did you make, Sarah, that was worth denying me the son you had had by me?"

At that moment the telephone on her desk rang. She reached out a hand for it, half-turning from me, hiding the anguish on her face. I said and did nothing. The question had been put.

My love for her could allow her all the grace in the world to come to the point of truth.

Into the receiver she said, "Yes, it's me . . . Yes, he is. . . ."

I watched her. She just held the receiver and listened. Then suddenly I saw her body stiffen as though she had been given some physical blow. She cried out, "Oh, no, Alexina! Oh, no!" Then she put the receiver back and turned swiftly to me.

Her face was tight with shock and despair. There was an immediate fury in me that at this moment Alexina should have come between us again. Then Sarah burst out, "Why did you have to do that? Oh, Robert, how could you! How could you!"

I said bitterly, "Like you I made a bargain—but one which I can't regret. I didn't kill anyone, but I could have and I don't care. But you made a bargain, too, Sarah—just as dark as mine. For God's sake, let us come clear of it all now and finish with it!"

She shook her head. "Oh, Robert . . . how can you know what you've done. This terrible, terrible thing. . . ." She looked at me and, as she went on, there were sudden tears in her eyes. "A little while ago I was waiting for you to come, waiting here, longing for you, knowing that I could——"

She broke off and moved slowly past me, putting out no hand to touch me, no smallest gesture to close the gap between us, and I knew with a sudden surety that burnt white-hot in me that I had come too late to ask her for the one thing I needed from her. The Rolt anger blazed uncontrolled in me.

"You had my son! And you would have kept him from me for ever! Why? Why? Tell me! Make me understand!"

From the door she turned and looked at me, and her face held nothing. For a moment she was a carven figure and I stood there, offering her no movement, no words, only my anger and my frustration.

She turned away and went out of the room. I looked down at her desk, at the end of her coffee cigarette that still smouldered in the ashtray, and at a single white rose that stood in a small vase by the telephone. Suddenly the anger in me turned and tortured me with its own truth. . . . She was my Sarah, my love, and in the moment of her trial and agony I had found no more to offer her than the blunt-edged, brutal onslaught of a savage delighting in the wounds he gave because they were the balm he needed for his own.

I moved then. As I did so, I heard the sound of a car starting on the drive outside. I ran out into the rain and the wind and saw her car slew round the circle of wet gravel, spray and grit spurting away from the fierce bite of spinning back wheels. I shouted to her but the storm smothered my voice with its own roar.

I jumped into Vickers' car and went after her. By the time I got the car started and turned she was gone from the drive-way. As I went through the lodge gates I saw her car ahead through the rain. A cloud of spray was flung up behind her and she was driving now as she sometimes rode, fast with no thought of danger. A mile down the hill the road came to a T-junction. I was a few hundred yards behind her when she reached it. She swung the car to the right. I eased up and took the corner slowly. To the right the road ran down through oak woods to come to a dead end on the pebble and shingle ridge that faced the sea.

When I reached the far end of the wood I saw her car drawn up where once had stood Alfie's car. I drew in behind it and jumped out. She was just breasting the top of the high shingle rise.

I shouted, "Sarah! Sarah! Wait!"

The gale took my words and drowned them in its own noise. I began to plunge desperately up the steep, sliding face of the bank with no thought in my mind except that I had to catch her and hold her. I had to have my hands on her, grip her and stay her, and then somehow I knew the world and the life we had shared would be made whole again. Just the hard contact of flesh against flesh, of body against body would be all that was needed.

When I reached the top of the rise Sarah was a hundred yards away, running just below the crest of the bank with the rain and wind of the gale at her back, tearing at her hair and her clothes so that she seemed to have wings frantically beating to take her away from me. I raced along the loose, sliding pebbles of the bank after her. To my right the long roll and crash of storm waves came sweeping in from the sea with all the force of the gale behind them. Spume and froth were whipped from the crests and slashed across the bank in ragged bursts like sleet and hail. Once or twice a larger breaker with all the force of a long sea-run behind it came seething and boiling higher than any others, swirling around my feet. The distant sky over the sea was stabbed with a vicious spear of lightning. In its light I saw the massive roller which had just reached me run diagonally down the line of the bank, its power and bulk growing almost as though it were a living thing, enraged by the solid bulwark of the land that opposed it.

Lightning seared over the sea again. I saw Sarah stumble as the great breaker broke about her feet, swirled around her and then, power frustrated, drew back, sucking loose pebbles and stones with it. As it went it took the ground from under Sarah's feet and she fell and lay still.

I shouted her name again and struggled forward as fast as I could. I was ten yards from her when another breaker came thundering in, foam and scud flying from its curling crest. It lifted her like sea-wrack and spun her forward. Then as it fell back down the steep bank, she went with it, her body rolling and slewing sideways. She disappeared in the bursting crest of another wave which, as it drew back, sucked her away and out of sight in its undertow.

I ran down to the point where she had disappeared and went in after her. A few yards from me I saw her face, white against the dark, marbled side of a gathering wave. She stretched out a hand towards me and called my name as I plunged towards her. It is a moment etched always in my memory, her hand reaching out for me, her face half-wreathed in her loose fair hair—and then the sea drawing her back from me, her face drowning and her arm and hand lifted in a bid for help or the agony of a farewell. I knew nothing then except the frenzy in me which drove me again and again to reach her against the malignity of the roaring seas and the storm. And the sea, having taken what it wanted, spurned and mocked me, sweeping and throwing me back on to the steep bank time and time again until the moment came when I lay spent on the shingle. The rain hissed down on me and, above, the dark, purple, cloud-massed sky raged with thunder and loosed its lightning over the storm-whipped world.

\*   \*   \*   \*

I brought the boy to Rolthead and I called him Henry after my father and he was baptised in Rolthead Church. He is my son. He has my face and figure and the hair and eyes of his mother. Sir Hugh Gleeson would have told me what he was called and other details about him, but I refused to have them, to know anything about them. At his age a day was long and full of new wonders and small fears and there was little past for memory yet to feed on. He is a Rolt and Rolthead is his place.

Apart from Sir Hugh Gleeson, and I still see him from time to time, I have had no contact with any others. No Garwood, no oil-man, no Alexina . . . nobody from that world which invaded mine and left it changed but far from destroyed. Vickers is dead for I saw his obituary notice in *The Times* a year after I lost Sarah. All I know of the manner of his death was that the notice said 'quietly in his sleep' and the name of a nursing-home was given for wreaths. I did not send a wreath because I knew he would not have wanted one from me. From the moment I left his cottage I would, if I could have done, have put the memory of that long night from me. But memory is not to be killed. There is no belief or disbelief—nor any true understanding—in me because my mind is not fashioned to contain them. Rolthead is world enough for me.

If in the future, when I am gone, someone tries to take it from my son then he must fight his own battle and there is little I can do to prepare him because it will be a world vastly different from mine. There will be new miracles become commonplace. But there will be little change in man because man is unique—he is the one truly corrupt animal the world has produced. The gods who used once to walk among men have abandoned them.

Late that fateful Sunday when I came back from searching the storm-swept run of shingle bank I went into the old music-room. On Sarah's desk was the letter which she had been writing when I had returned.

It read:


*Darling Robert,*

*I am going to give you this letter when you return and ask you to go away and read it. There is something you have to know, something you may find impossible to believe. When you have read all this and come back to me I shall know at once from your face whether there is forgiveness, understanding, and, I pray to God, love still there. I have a confession to make . . .*


The letter had never been finished. Lying alongside it in a small cardboard box were the original engagement and wedding rings which I had given her. I sat there for a long time, holding the rings in my hand, grieving for her and knowing that I had failed her.

Since then I have altered my life but little, though something in me has changed for ever. I live quietly and I husband Rolthead. My son will learn to do all the things my father taught me, to fish, to hunt, to shoot, to ride to hounds and to swim from the long shingle bank where Sarah was drowned and her body never recovered. There is a plaque in Rolthead Church which commemorates her. My son and I see it when we sit in our pew. One day he will read all this, maybe with a better understanding than I could ever have had. But long before then I hope he will have come to a true understanding of love which is that it excels all things, includes all things, and forgives all things. It is beyond all cherishing because it is the last dim spark of divinity in man.

# ABOUT VICTOR CANNING

Victor Canning began his career in a government office in Plymouth, England, writing adventure stories for boys as a sideline. By the time he was twenty-five he had had his first outstanding success with MR. FINCHLEY DIS-COVERS HIS ENGLAND and gave up his government career entirely. Since then he has written more than a score of books under his own name and under the pseudonym of Alan Gould—most of them in the category of international intrigue and suspense. Most recent among these are QUEEN'S PAWN (1970), THE GREAT AFFAIR (1971), FIRECREST (1972), THE RAINBIRD PATTERN (1973), and the present THE FINGER OF SATURN, novels which have earned him such accolades as that of V. S. Pritchett: "Victor Canning is a master of his craft." One notable departure from this genre is his Smiler M. series of three related novels, which began with THE RUNAWAYS (1972), continued with FLIGHT OF THE GREY GOOSE (1973) and will be concluded with the publication of THE PAINTED TENT (summer, 1974). A golfer and an avid fisherman, Canning now lives in his native Devonshire.